SUNNY SANDS

A CRIME NOVEL

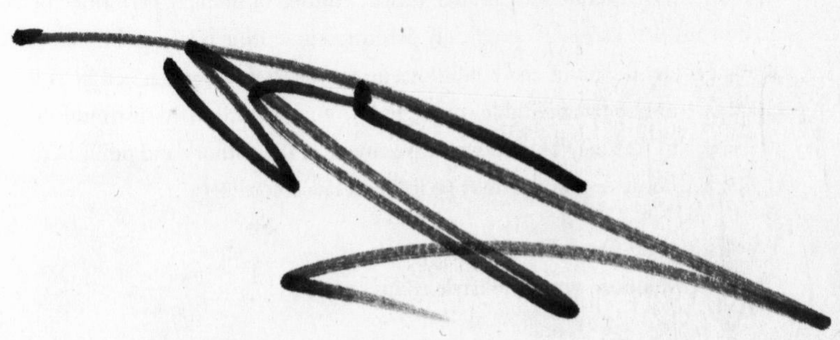

Sunny Sands a crime novel

Published by The Conrad Press in the United Kingdom 2018

Tel: +44(0)1227 472 874
www.theconradpress.com
info@theconradpress.com

ISBN 978-1-911546-26-9

Typesetting and Cover Design by:
Charlotte Mouncey, www.bookstyle.co.uk

The Conrad Press logo was designed by Maria Priestley.

Printed and bound in Great Britain by Clays Ltd, Elcograf S.p.A.

SUNNY SANDS

A CRIME NOVEL

TREVOR TWOHIG

For the Family T,
who believed in me

1

I stood on Folkestone beach, watching the sun sparkle on the breaking waves.

It was a sweltering Sunday, the third of July. The seafront was busy with families revelling in the English summer sun.

'Come on Dad, I'm bored! Let's swim!' shouted my five-year-old daughter, Maddie.

A few moments ago, I'd gently kicked our football towards her, but she'd ignored it. My hopes of getting Maddie to enjoy ball sports continued to be thwarted.

With fatherly pride, I watched her race towards the ocean's edge, her little legs spraying sand haphazardly, ruining the golden carpet beneath her feet.

Every two weeks I was allowed to see her for a weekend, in compliance with the court order – it wasn't enough. The gap was too long from one visit to the next.

We both ran into the water. It wasn't as warm as I would have liked, but it wasn't cold either. Indeed, the feeling of the water stopped me thinking about how much I missed her when she wasn't around.

I walked into the water up to my knees. Maddie jumped, giggled and, to my surprise, made it up to her tummy before screaming gleefully and scampering back through the froth.

As we walked back to our belongings, I suddenly noticed a crowd of people about fifty yards from us, where the rocks from the harbour's edge jutted out. Maddie saw where I was looking and sensed my anxiety.

'Daddy, what's going on over there?'

'I'm not sure, honey. Help me pack away our things and I'll find out.'

She put away the toys and towels while I grabbed my mobile and badge, stuffing them into my trunks. I quickly put my t-shirt on and helped Maddie with her summer dress and sandals before walking her up the promenade steps and sitting her on a wooden bench.

'I need to go and look at this, Maddie. Will you wait here for me like a good girl?'

Maddie sighed, she didn't like being left on her own at all and I couldn't blame her. Folkestone was still a strange, new place to her. I didn't like leaving her, not for a moment, but the crowd concerned me and, whatever was there, I didn't want Maddie to see it.

I still wasn't over the separation from my ex, Jo. The twenty-third of November last year was indelibly printed on my thoughts, the day I left our home in Faversham and moved to Folkestone.

Every day of those seven months, I missed Maddie sleepily entering our bedroom early in the morning and tugging me to come downstairs to play with her. I missed our weekend drives down the country lanes near Faversham, usually to get fresh eggs so we could make breakfast for the family, but those days were gone now.

'Dad, did you bring the iPad?'

'No, but take my phone, I won't be long.' Maddie grabbed it and almost at once became transfixed by the lure of pixelated graphics and cartoon animals that awaited her.

I hurried down to the beach and towards the crowd. One of the coastguards I knew, Bill Davis, nodded to me as I approached.

'Clear the way! Police coming through,' he said in an authoritative tone. The crowd began to part.

Police coming through. I was one of those who went towards danger and chaos when everyone else was moving away from it.

2

The first thing I saw was white human flesh lying on the yellow sand. The body was hidden behind brown, craggy rocks, but the pale, youthful flesh of the leg and abdomen was unmistakable.

As I moved around the rocks, I saw this was the body of a woman. I grabbed her arm and felt for a pulse. I leaned in to listen for breath, but there was no breath at all.

I glanced back at the crowd, 'Step back and give her some privacy. Can I have a couple of towels please?'

'Is she... is she dead?' a middle-aged lady near me asked.

I glanced at the lady who'd asked the question. 'I'm afraid I think she probably is.'

There was a collective gasp from the remnants of the crowd at the tragedy and finality of my words, as I covered the body with a couple of multi-coloured beach towels.

I went to my pocket for my phone, then remembered it was with Maddie.

'Bill, pass me your phone.' I opened it up and tapped in the number of my DCI at Folkestone Station, Dave Marsh.

'Hello?'

'Dave, it's Charlie.'

'How're you doing?'

'Not good, bad news. I just found a girl washed up on Sunny Sands. She's dead, boss.'

I heard Dave tell one of the coppers at the station to call an ambulance. He also radioed for two squad cars to my location.

'How long do you think she's been dead?' he asked.

'At least a few hours.'

'Jesus. Right. Clear the beach as quickly as you can - cordon it off. Is the coastguard there?'

'Yeah, Bill's here,' I replied, thinking ahead. These people would've trodden any evidence into the surface of the sand. I needed to move fast. 'I'm here with Maddie. I left her on the promenade and need to get back to her.'

'Good. Get him to stay with the body. You go and look after your daughter, Charlie. Leave the rest to me and Bill.'

'Thanks, boss.'

I passed Bill's phone back to him and asked him to wait with the body until the ambulance arrived.

I hurried back to Maddie, still happily playing her game, legs swinging languidly from the bench. She looked up at me, her face in the shadow I cast over her before sitting down. She smiled her cheeky grin and I put my arm around her.

'What was it, Daddy?' she asked.

'A girl's had an accident,' I said, quietly, not having any intention of giving Maddie any more details of the tragic scene I'd just witnessed. The more we were apart, the more I tried to cling to the role of her father and protector.

'Oh no, is she OK?' she asked, genuinely concerned.

'I hope she will be.' OK, now I was lying, but Maddie was only five.

'The ambulance will be here soon. Anyway, what are you playing?'

It was best to deflect her thoughts. I didn't want her childhood memories of Sunny Sands to be tainted by what was found today. On average, there were around five murders in Folkestone every year. Two or three of those were usually of the homeless, or drug-related; this was not a common event.

I checked my watch – eleven thirty-six am.

'When are we going home, Dad?'

‘In a moment.’ I knew my colleagues would be here soon. Once they’d arrived, I could go. They could take over from Bill.

‘Darling, I thought you might want to stop in town and get an ice cream first?’

‘Oooh, yes please, Daddy!’

‘OK. We just have to wait here a minute, until my police friends arrive, and then we can go.’

Maddie started counting to sixty. I loved how her world was so simple and beautiful, I wanted to preserve that innocence, so she could be spared knowing the horrible truth: the tragedies and failures of the adult one. I put another layer of sun cream on her face and shoulders.

Five minutes later, Detective Constables Jimmy Wade and Karl Bullen arrived. They drove slowly past me down the promenade, blue-lighting but with no siren, and pulled up in front of the bench where Maddie and I were sitting. They jumped out.

‘Hi Karl, the girl’s down there.’ I pointed to Bill waiting patiently below on the beach. ‘Get down there and clear the last of the stragglers as quick as you can. Jimmy, cordon off the beach at both entrances, make sure no-one else comes anywhere near, it’s potentially a crime scene.’

Despite Sunny Sands being a small, secluded beach, it was accessible by a ramp at the Market end near the town, and by foot from the promenade.

‘Where’s the DCI?’

‘On his way, Charlie,’ Karl replied.

‘OK. After clearing the beach, direct the ambulance when it arrives. It’ll come via Fisherman’s Street and down the ramp there.’ I pointed to the area and Karl rushed off in that direction.

Maddie watched this strange world of orders and directives intently, as the DCs went to do what they had to do. I asked her for my phone, and she passed it back to me. We walked towards town, seeing who could spot the most seagulls that were now descending in great force upon the empty beach in hope of a stray chip or an abandoned ice cream cone.

Dave arrived within five minutes, driving his silver BMW a little too quickly on the narrow promenade. Luckily, it was clear now and he pulled up behind the squad cars.

Dave burst out of the driver's seat of his vehicle, I noticed his customary furrowed brow first and felt slightly more relaxed. He was always in control, a permanent frown on his face, looking for danger, intensely managing the most difficult of situations.

He looked like something from the 1960s, he had a short-sleeved white shirt on, unbuttoned at the collar. His hair was teddy-boy style, slicked back and to the side. He wore his side-burns long, past his ears and his trousers were probably a little too tight for his age. He was an individual though, and that's what I loved about him.

As he approached me on foot, along the promenade, a wave of sickness returned. My heart was racing like a speedboat and I couldn't focus. I was worried I was going into shock, bodies don't just wash up on Folkestone beach. I wanted to be back with my colleagues, searching for clues. I needed to get home as quickly as I could to start making some calls. Also, I didn't want to let Maddie down and give her mother another excuse to cut me out further.

We walked along Fisherman's Street just as the ambulance came hurtling past. I wanted to follow it and help, but also, I knew my time with Maddie was limited. My ex would be picking her up in a few hours and she would be going home.

We were holding hands. Maddie leaned into me when something startled her, like the ambulance or a truck, but then she smiled and skipped when she saw the candyfloss seller. She waved at some girls of her own age, who were dancing to the music pumping out of the pubs in the Harbour.

In her child-like innocence she'd already forgotten the heated rows, the arguments and the icy atmosphere in what was once a warm home. She couldn't remember, or I hoped she couldn't, how two people, who were once in love, violently drifted apart.

I hoped Maddie had forgotten the time, at the end of my marriage to Jo, when she woke from her slumber, stomped downstairs with clenched fists and tear soaked eyes, shouting at us to be quiet.

I wished I could forget all of it too, but I couldn't. All I could do was try not to make the same mistakes again.

We stopped at the Bertrand Ale House for lunch. Maddie asked for the fish cakes; I ordered the halloumi skewers. We waited, sipping on our fizzy drinks and I pulled a pack of *Top Trumps* cards from my bag.

'Daddy?' Maddie asked furtively, the way children ask when they know they shouldn't.

'Yes darling?'

'Why don't you love Mummy anymore?' she looked at me with confused eyes.

'Maddie, you know being apart is for the best, we've talked about this. Mummy and I both love *you*,' I reassured her.

'But Daddy, I miss living with you!' She grew more tearful.

'Yes and I miss you, but do you remember the arguments and fights? It wasn't nice was it?'

She pondered this, 'I s'pose not…'

'Look, now there are no fights and there's no shouting and I get to beat you at Top Trumps every other weekend!' I said, taking her last card, much to her disappointment.

'Oh, Daddy!' she shouted, pretending to hit me.

We finished lunch and stopped at Bella Torino's for an ice cream to eat on the train back. I was not a big ice cream fan, but Maddie was and had three different flavour scoops in her tub.

Returning Maddie to her mother was the lowest point of my weekend. The pick-up point was still Faversham. I didn't like to drive there, because it strained and pulled at our connection, whereas the train ride was half an hour and I could give Maddie my full attention. Not to mention, Maddie enjoyed the train.

'When am I going to see you next?' she asked, halfway through our journey. She was slurping strawberry ice cream, dripping it on her dress. I grabbed a tissue from my bag.

'Soon. Two weeks. But I'll call, and we can Skype every couple of days, like normal.'

'OK Daddy. I'll miss you,' she said, beginning to well up.

'You'll be fine, it'll be good seeing Mummy in a minute, won't it? And you've got gymnastics after school tomorrow.'

She looked pensive, then nodded and smiled; then it was me who became overwhelmed by sadness, an occupational hazard of being a separated parent.

Jo was waiting at the station. She smiled at Maddie, who ran into her arms.

'Hello darling, lovely to see you!' Jo smiled, picking her up. I looked with jealousy at a full-time bond and relationship I'd lost. I was now Maddie's part-time Dad.

'I missed you, Mummy!' Maddie said, becoming more childish and girly with every word.

'You're only wearing a dress? It's a bit cold for that now. Have you had sun cream on?' Jo asked Maddie, despite it being aimed at me. It was four in the afternoon and it was still about twenty-three degrees, but Jo loved to have her little digs at my parenting skills. Since this was loosely aimed at me, I thought I would respond.

'It's a hot summer's day and we've been on a warm train. Yes - she has had sun cream on all day,' I said.

'We'd better get in the car *quickly*,' Jo said, ignoring me entirely. 'Say goodbye to your Dad.'

'Bye Dad, I love you.' Maddie waved at me as the black Vauxhall Meriva, my old Meriva, drove swiftly away.

3

I felt empty and bleak immediately after Maddie left the station. I had a Sunday evening alone to look forward to, waiting for Dave's phone call, and then I'd start work again tomorrow.

The Total Garage at the end of the road had become a salvation for me since the separation. It was a small bottle of vodka this time.

I took the train back to Folkestone West and walked back to my flat on Brimstone Avenue. From my jacket pocket, I took out my notebook and made some initial notes about what I saw on the beach today.

Immediately, the abnormality of the scene struck me. Bodies were not often found on the beach in Folkestone. Had the girl washed up? Perhaps she was planted there? I made a note to talk to Bill – the coastguard – and find out exactly how and when the girl was found.

I went to the bathroom and relieved myself. I turned to wash my hands and looked at myself in the mirror. I wasn't unattractive, in fact some might say I still had some of my looks from youth. I was thity-six years old and my dark brown hair was greying at the sides. My parting had fallen somewhat, so I scooped it back into place.

I was tall, about 185 cm, but I had lost my muscular frame somewhat as I got older. I kept up a few bicep curl reps in the spare room when I had the motivation, but the middle age spread, although small, was well… spreading.

I had deep green eyes, which one of my ex-girlfriends decreed as 'dirty dishwater eyes.' That didn't do wonders for my confidence for a while.

I was lucky though, although my weathered face didn't quite have the youthful exuberance it once did, I think most women would say that I still retained a rogue-ish charm.

My mobile phone rang, piercing the silence.

'Charlie, Dave here. Are you good to talk?'

'Yeah, sure.' I pulled my pen and pad closer to me.

'We've checked missing persons and I think we've found a match… Green, that's it… Amy Green.' The name was familiar, but I couldn't think why.

'I'm going to need you to go to the parent's home – Twyford Gardens – and get them to ID the body,' Dave said.

'OK. Anything else we know about the girl?' I wrote the name and address on my pad.

'Just turned eighteen. Went to the HG Wells Grammar School on Blooming Lane,' he continued.

'Eighteen?' I dropped the pen I was holding and watched it slowly roll across the wooden floor.

'Well technically, she's on the school's books until she receives her results – twenty-third of August. There's not much else until the autopsy results come back.'

'What do you think killed her, boss?'

Dave was, I knew, too professional to guess, but I cared about Dave's opinion and I was curious.

'Who knows, but we need to treat it as suspicious. Charlie, I want you to lead the case. It's going to get ugly - needs sensitive handling. I also think, y'know, it could help… at the moment.'

'Oh, I need help now?'

'You know what I mean. How are things with Jo?'

'Not worth discussing, boss. You know how it is. I'm the worst bloke in the world. It's either one-word text messages or pages of abuse.' I sighed.

'Hm, I can imagine what the one word usually is. How's Maddie? She OK after the beach?'

'She's great - thinks it was an accident.'

'And the break up – how's she taking it?'

'She's confused, doesn't understand what's going on. I'm just trying to keep things as normal as possible for her.'

As much as I appreciated Dave's support, having to think and dissect the situation caused me twinges of pain.

'Good, Charlie. I know it's tough at the moment, but it will get better. Anyway, this case will be good for you, keep you on the straight and narrow – off the booze,' Dave asserted, as I took a quiet sip of my vodka.

'Thanks boss.'

'Get 'round to the parents' house first thing tomorrow, Charlie – they're expecting you.'

'OK boss, see you.'

I took another slug of my drink and sank further into the chair.

Who was this girl really? Had she fallen into the water and drowned, undressed by the pulse of the tide? Or had something more sinister happened to her?

Either way, I was determined to find out.

The following morning, I stood on the doorstep of the Green's household.

They lived in Twyford Gardens, an affluent cul-de-sac in the west end of Folkestone. This quiet part of town seemed eerie today, as if the streets and houses knew some awful event had occurred and were silently licking their wounds in protest.

Normally on a summer's evening, you could hear children play on the Leas, or even the calming breath of the sea, but not today. Today, the trees waved languidly in the breeze.

The Green family front door was large and blue with a heavy gold knocker in the centre of it. I picked up the weighty metal object and pounded the door, a little too hard for comfort.

Mr Green, Amy's father, opened the door and greeted me. He wore a pair of beige fitted chinos and a pastel blue linen shirt. His demeanour was understandably subdued and he had a browbeaten air about him.

He shuffled his black hair into a parting nervously before beckoning me inside.

I followed through a whitewashed hall, with dark wood laminate flooring and into the first room on the right. Mrs Green jumped up at my entrance, bleary eyed and red nosed.

'Hello, officer,' she said. 'I'm Jennifer Green and this is my husband Alex.'

'Good morning, Jennifer and Alex. I'm Detective Sergeant Charlie Stone,' I replied. Jennifer Green wore a black pencil skirt and a red blouse. Despite her tearfulness, she looked efficient and in control. Her eyes never met mine.

She sat softly in her chair, as if she didn't want to make an imprint on the seat. Her greying bob covered a large part of her forehead and her blue eyes skittered around the room, unable to focus.

'Can I get you something, officer? A drink?' Alex Green asked softly.

My mouth was dry and I had the sour aftertaste of a hangover lingering.

'Yes, that would be lovely,' I said, I didn't even care what he brought back, as he scuttled away to the kitchen.

'After that, I think it's best we go to the hospital,' I continued, sitting down as gently as I could.

'Oh, erm, OK,' Jennifer Green said, fumbling for a tissue, dropping it and cursing.

'I'm sorry, Detective, you don't need to hear that,' she muttered nervously to herself. 'Now, where's that bag of mine? I'm always losing it.' She searched frantically around their large sitting room. 'Alex, Alex! Do you know where my bag is? I just...' but she didn't have the energy to finish the sentence. She burst into tears and collapsed into the large green armchair, covering her nose and mouth with the soggy tissue.

'I have it here,' Alex returned with the bag, saw his wife in tatters and looked at me apologetically. He took a step toward her, then checked back to me, his face red and full of indecision. I nodded, which released him to go to her.

'Darling, it's OK,' he said.

I shifted from leg to leg before turning away, caught between doing my job as professionally as possible, yet also being a fellow parent and showing understanding.

I hoped it was not their daughter. I hoped the girl on the beach was someone unknown, who had fallen through the system, no parents, no family, but, deep down, I knew it was her. No-one else on the missing persons list matched her description.

'I'm sorry, Jennifer, I think it's best we go now,' I said again. The middle-aged pair rose to their feet as if in unison, Jennifer with her face still buried in a tissue.

4

The body was resting at the Victoria Hospital in central Folkestone. It was nearly nine o'clock in the morning and it was sunny. The old hospital cast an eerie shadow over Radnor Park.

I felt nauseated at how London continued to be nurtured by foreign investment, while Kent's coastal towns felt the rough edge of underfunding and neglect.

Lack of money kept this institution firmly in the dark ages; it was cold and depressing. I shivered and felt the usual heaviness at seeing the peeling walls and curling brown laminate floor. We made our way through to Pathology, the smell of detergent and the thick warmth of NHS hospitals filled the air. A light flickered as we came to the room Amy was in.

Before entering, I stopped and turned to the beleaguered couple behind me.

'Are you OK?' I looked at both parents. Jennifer still couldn't look up, but Mr Green took a deep breath and put his arm around her.

'Is she in there?' Jennifer sniffled.

'Yes, are you ready? I returned as softly as I could.

She nodded at the floor. 'Then I need to see her. I need to know. I want to see my little girl.' She dabbed her eyes again.

'OK, Jennifer.' I slowly turned the old, rickety handle.

We were greeted by closed, blue gingham curtains. The pathologist poked his head around and acknowledged me with a nod. He looked at the parents and made some apologies, as if he were speaking from a script. I slowly pulled back the blue curtain and the three of us entered.

The body was covered in a white, linen sheet. The pathologist took a deep breath and pulled the cover from her face and down to the tops of her shoulders. Jennifer broke down in tears and buried her face in her husband's chest.

Alex ran his free hand through his hair and turned away, grabbing his wife, as they both fell back against the wall. Alex's legs seem to give way and they both collapsed to the floor in a violent exhalation of grief. I ran around the bed to help them. I was compelled to hug them, but remembered my professional duty and stopped myself as they sank deeper into the wall.

The journey home was spent in silence, but it wasn't long until we pulled up outside the Greens' house.

They climbed out and I shook Alex's hand. I scratched my head, not knowing why I did it, but I didn't know how else to express my sympathy.

I told them I would return to see them in the morning to ask some questions. They nodded at me before turning towards the dark house that was recently a happy home.

I went straight into my living-room, booted up the laptop and searched for Amy Green on the PNC. She was a straight-A student, studying English, Business, Geography and French; she had a part-time job at the garden centre on Edgar Road; her father, Alex, was a banker in London and her mum, Jennifer, worked part-time at the local doctor's surgery.

I opened Facebook. My profile, which I barely used, flashed up.

A friend of mine had bought a new puppy, twenty-two photos of 'Bailey' followed. A cousin of Maddie's had cooked a family roast. There were pictures of food, wine and smiling faces. A friend's girlfriend, called Freda, had updated her status with, 'don't know why I bother, men can be so selfish.'

I was unsure about Facebook since the break-up, but it really was a useful tool for any investigation these days, especially for younger people.

Amy's profile was private, though – there were a couple of accessible photos, her picture, a black and white selfie of her pouting in the mirror and one of her with a friend, Mina Burrows, at the local Garden Centre. After the Green household, this would be someone I would need to visit tomorrow.

5

I woke from a troubled sleep at about half six the following morning, a film of sweat wrapping my body. I got up and made a three-egg omelette, but I wasn't really hungry. The sadness and grief of yesterday made me feel nauseous. At least dealing with the Green's tragedy saved me, briefly, from dealing with my own.

My first stop today would be Twyford Gardens, to speak with the family in more depth. I knew they could never get over a crushing loss such as this, but it was a shame I couldn't give them a few more days to grieve. Sadly, police procedure wouldn't allow this. Any information that might be relevant, I needed to know immediately.

Alex, once more, let me in and motioned me into the front room. In what felt like a morbid re-run of yesterday, he again offered a drink and I politely declined. I sat down on the claret Winchester chair and took my pad and pen from my inner pocket.

'Alex and Jennifer,' I began. 'Again, I am so sorry for your loss. I'm just going to ask a few questions about your daughter if you don't mind.'

Jennifer softly sniffled into her tissue and nodded while Alex took up a chair by the window.

'Thank you.' I opened my notebook and took out my pen. 'Can you think back... did you notice anything different about

Amy in the last couple of weeks? Any strange behaviour or something that stood out?'

The couple looked at each other.

'No,' Jennifer said. 'She has, I mean had, just finished her exams and had taken on some extra work at the garden centre but, apart from that, it was the same old Amy.'

'What did she do at the garden centre, if you don't mind me asking?'

'They do all sorts, from potting the plants to staying late and bringing in deliveries,' Alex interjected.

'How late did she stay?'

'Well, if there's trouble on the motorway, or Operation Stack, sometimes the trucks don't get in until the middle of the night.'

'And, you didn't mind Amy staying there until then?' I asked.

'Amy always drove to work and we thought she was in safe hands there,' he said confidently.

'I see. I know this is tricky, but were there any family issues to speak of, any arguments in the home?'

'Officer, what are you suggesting?' Alex was brusque, his voice raised.

'I know it's difficult, sir. It's just that, girls of that age often have altercations, differences of opinion with their parents… especially a girl as bright and independent as Amy.'

'So that's it, is it? Good girl, gone bad?' Alex scowled and sweat covered his clenched jaw all the way up to his red-rimmed eyes. 'You think you know it all don't you? Well, there's nothing we can tell you, all right? She went to work yesterday and never came back. Check her room, there's nothing, absolutely nothing!'

Jennifer furrowed her brow, she ignored her husband's outburst and continued as if wandering through her own hazy nightmare.

'She was… bright, certainly, but Amy wasn't the most independent. She was a bit of a homebody. Alex had to convince her to take up the part time job…' she trailed off.

'What about friends or boyfriends, Jennifer?' I hoped to have more luck with her.

'Boyfriends?' Jennifer chuckled, 'No, Amy didn't have boyfriends. Like I said, she was quite family-orientated. Her closest friend at school was Mina. Mina Burrows, the girl from her Facebook photos, that is.'

I made a note in my book, as though it was a new fact in the case.

'Thank you. Did Amy have any health problems to speak of?' Alex grunted and sighed loudly, angered at this intrusion and willing me to leave.

'She had asthma, mild asthma. She takes her pump in the morning and at night…I mean she *took* her pump...' Jennifer did not finish her sentence. Her husband scurried to find some tissues and then hugged her close.

'Any more questions, officer?' he asked glaring at me.

'No,' I replied. 'I'll leave you for now. I'm so sorry,' I said. 'If I need to ask you anything else, I'll come back later.' I nodded at the man and let myself out.

As I got into the car, I wondered about Amy's home life. I often saw rich kids fall in with the wrong crowds because their Dad was not around, but this didn't seem like that. They seemed tight-knit and genuine, family photos in all the right places, everything seemed to fit.

So how did this good girl wind up dead?

6

My next stop was Mina Burrows who lived over the Downs in a sleepy village called Fulcombe that had a local pub and plenty of old detached houses.

The clock in the car read nine-thirty as I turned into a village waking from slumber: old ladies walking their dogs, the postman doing his rounds and folks waiting at the bus stop. I pulled into number 34 Lavender Drive, the Burrows' residence.

I knocked on the door. A tall wisteria plant grew up the side of the house. There was a pond hidden behind some weeping willows to the side of the drive and an old MG sports car parked on the pebbled drive. Two other vehicles, a silver BMW and a Ford Focus, sat proudly on the driveway.

'Can I help you?' A lady came to the door. Mrs. Burrows was younger than Jennifer Green, Amy's mother. She wore fitted jeans and a black camisole top. She had mid-length, brown, frizzy hair and looked at me with suspicious eyes.

'Hi, I'm Detective Sergeant Stone from the Kent Police. Are you Mina Burrows' mother?'

'Yes?'

'May I speak with her please?' I asked, showing my badge.

'What's this about?' She looked anxious, holding the door tightly.

'It's about one of her friends, Amy Green.'

Her brow furrowed. 'Wait there.' She pulled the front door open, motioning me inside.

'Mina, the police need to speak to you!' Mrs Burrows shouted up the stairs.

Mina came down in a nightie and a dressing gown. She wore a pair of pink slippers and held a steaming mug of tea.

The bags under her eyes did not affect her demure and serene beauty as she walked into the dining room and sat down.

She sighed, looking tired and somewhat irritated by my visit.

'Good morning, Mina. Sorry to bother you at this time. We want to find out what happened to your friend, Amy Green, and need to ask you some questions, if that's OK?'

Mina looked up at me with defiant green eyes. 'Go ahead,' she challenged, her manner unnerving. Why was she so defensive?

'When was the last time you saw Amy?'

'Yesterday afternoon. She gave me a lift home after work,' she said.

'Where do you work?'

'Garden Centre on Edgar Road,' she replied.

'Oh, so you both worked there?'

'Yes we both worked there.' she said.

'Is that so unusual, officer,' said Mina's mum. 'for best friends to work at the same place?'

'Well, no – um… '

'Amy's dad knows the owner and got us the jobs,' she retorted.

'I see. Can you tell me about Amy? What was she like?' I changed tack.

'Was? What do you mean, was?'

'I'm afraid we found Amy's body yesterday on the beach. She's dead.'

Mina looked at her mother and stared at me wide eyed. I waited for tears that didn't come.

She exhaled, troubled, 'Look, I don't know what you want to hear, OK…'

'Just tell me the truth about your friend please Mina,' I replied, her manner beginning to irritate me.

'Amy… she was a good girl, a great best friend. She worked hard at school and loved her parents. She didn't get into trouble… she wanted to be a vet.' Mina said the words as if she were reading from a script.

'Come on Mina, who are you trying to kid, growing up in a town like this? You're telling me an attractive girl like Amy never had boyfriends? Never went to parties?'

'Boyfriends?' For the first time, Mina looked up and gazed at me, then smiled a watery smile. 'No. Amy didn't have *boyfriends*. She came to the house parties now and again, but she often went early. Her dad didn't like her being out late. She was clever, like proper clever. She could have gone to Oxford or Cambridge.'

'What about you, Mina?' I asked pointedly. 'Boyfriends? *Drugs?*'

She smiled again with a glint in her eye. 'Are you investigating me officer, or the murder of my friend?' she asked, taking a sip of her tea.

'Who said anything about murder?' Our eyes locked.

She looked at me incredulously and laughed.

'Right. Perhaps it was an *accident…*' she said, looking me up and down.

'We can't confirm at this stage. Anyway, what do you mean by that?'

'By what?'

'The sarcasm. You don't believe it was an accident. Why?'

Mina laughed.

'No you're right, officer, it might have been an accident. I shouldn't jump to conclusions. Was there anything else? I'm quite tired.'

I tried to make her out. She had a strange confidence. I looked for signals or signs from her but it was hard. Her body was hidden under a blanket of clothes, and she masked her fresh, youthful face, no make-up, with a sheen of acerbic anger and contempt.

I passed one of my cards to her.

'No, I'm sorry. It must be hard losing a good friend like Amy,' I said.

She flashed me a quick glance.

'We're not your average teenage girls, officer. I know what you're thinking – late nights out drinking with boys – but there weren't any *boys,* really,' she said.

'Not really?'

'We sometimes used to meet up with a couple of lads from the rugby team, but that was a long time ago. They weren't really… our type,' she said smirking to herself. Memory of her lost friend quickly replaced that look, and the tears returned.

'I see, well thanks, Mina. If you think of anything which might be helpful, do give us a call,' I said, getting up to leave.

'She was a good girl, officer. I promise you. She didn't deserve this.' Mina drank the rest of her tea and headed upstairs. I saw myself out.

7

I needed to go to the station, so I checked in with the pathologists first, to give them a kick up the backside. I needed something to go on. Anything.

The car travelled smoothly over the Downs as I began the descent into town. The broad, blue sea came into view on the horizon, along with the many landmarks that gave Folkestone its unique character.

The Grand Dolphin Hotel stood bold and intimidating, whilst further up the coast, The Four Seasons and what used to be The Greenwich Hotel perched majestically on the edge of the Leas, just along from the Green' family home.

My mobile rang with an unknown number, I heard the call connect and shuffling on the other end of the line.

'Hello?' I asked.

'Officer? Officer Stone?' the female voice enquired.

'Yes, who's speaking?'

'It's Jennifer Green. Amy's Mum,' she said quietly. 'When you left, you asked me to contact you with any information I had and I thought of something.'

'Please go on, Jennifer,' I encouraged her.

'Well, it's probably nothing, but I thought it might be worth looking into…' she continued cautiously. 'Amy had extra English lessons just before her exams. Her English teacher would stay after school with her and help her study.'

'You mean with the class?'

'Well that's the thing, officer, from what I understood it was just her. I thought, I mean, I *assumed* there would be other students there, but now I'm not so sure…' she trailed off.

'Why's that?' I prompted.

'Well, it's just something my husband said…'

I paused for an explanation which didn't come.

'What did he say, Jennifer?'

She mumbled, 'I have to go…'

The phone went dead.

Despite an abrupt end to the call, I finally had a lead.

I visited the school hoping to catch them before Amy's death had become public knowledge. July was a good time as the students who'd taken their GCSEs and A-Levels had already left and only the younger students remained until the start of the summer holiday in a week's time.

The reception area was quiet and I was anxious not to draw too much attention to myself. The days of wearing a uniform were over for me but, as I neared the front desk, my suit, tie and appearance seemed to make the receptionist nervous. She shuffled papers and tried to ignore me.

'Good afternoon, I need to speak with the head teacher,' I said quietly.

'Do you have an appointment?' She was late forties with greying, curly hair and glasses resting precariously on the end of her small nose.

'No ma'am,' I retorted, showing her my badge. She recoiled slightly, forced into action.

'Please take a seat, sir,' she said as she rushed to grab the phone and her post-it notes. She mumbled into the receiver and jotted furiously.

'He will be with you shortly,' she smiled and nodded at me.

I took the time to make some initial notes.

The first name I wrote down was Mina Burrows. There was something about her that seemed curious; I wanted to speak to her again. The second was the garden centre. It was the last place Amy was known to be and why the late shifts? If it was Maddie at a similar age, I would do anything I could to keep her away from late nights out of the house.

'Officer?' A tall slender man approached me and offered his hand. His suit was well-tailored and he exuded an overpowering air of confidence. I couldn't be sure whether it was confidence or arrogance, but I gave him the benefit of the doubt. He looked more a businessman than a teacher to me.

He had piercing blue eyes, which never seemed to look down or away, just followed my movements as I got to my feet and shook his hand.

'It's sergeant. Sorry, I thought I was meeting with Mrs… '

'… Sergeant Stone, please come this way.' A second man, smaller with hunched shoulders led us to a corridor behind the reception area. He wore a bright, white shirt and had short dark hair and glasses.

He seemed beaten and defeated, faded perhaps, in the shadow of his colleague.

They led me into a large office. The tall man sat behind a desk in an upright leather seat. He motioned for me to sit in front of the desk, while the second man, sat to my right, just behind me.

'Mr Stone, allow me to introduce myself. I am Mr Smith and this is my deputy, Mr Tutton.' I remained quiet and waited for some form of explanation. The headmistress had been Mrs Jones for some years now and had built up a good reputation in the local community. She was often in the local paper which is why I knew about her.

'I've recently been appointed executive head teacher at the school and Mr Tutton forms an integral part of our senior leadership team.' The sound of Tutton's pencil furiously scribbling while Smith spoke, provided pertinent background noise.

'I know this may come as a surprise to you,' said Smith, 'but the governors and local authority thought it best for a sharp overhaul in time for the new academic year. Results have been dipping and it was decided a change of management was the best course of action,' he said.

'*Dipping*, you say? Excuse my ignorance, but I was under the impression that this was one of the best schools in the county?' I asked politely.

'It is. Kent County Council want it to stay that way,' he said leaning across the table, his blue eyes boring into me.

'I see.' I looked away. 'It all seems very sudden though. Shouldn't the press be informed, and don't the parents need to know?'

'We'll deal with that when we think the time is right, Sergeant Stone. That's not really your concern,' Smith asserted.

'There's no need…'

'How can we help you, anyway?' I was cut off in my tracks. It appeared futile to argue with such a belligerent person, so I kept things business-like.

'Mr Smith, I'm investigating the murder of Amy Green. She was a student here. Died in mysterious circumstances last night...'

'Yes, terrible thing that. We'll most certainly do anything to assist your investigation,' Smith said.

'Sorry, you know about the murder?' I asked. He looked at Tutton and back to me.

'We received a phone call this morning.'

'That's peculiar. Who was it from?' I asked, not giving this snake any chance to wriggle.

'I'm not sure who took the call and I don't really see why it's important - we can ask around the office,' he motioned to Tutton. 'Who do you wish to speak with?'

'Well, I think it's important since I'm leading this case and I didn't make the call,' I said.

‘Why don’t you take it up with your superiors? Now who do you wish to speak with? We’re very busy.’

‘I need to speak to Amy’s English teacher. It would be useful if he didn’t know what about Mr Smith.’

‘OK, I’ll check who that is. Mr *Wood,* I believe?’ He looked at Tutton who nodded in agreement. ‘Anything else?’ Smith asked.

‘No, that’s fine for now. Thank you for your time.’

Tutton led me out and into a small room along the corridor. I waited.

It was a typical school room, plastic chairs and primary colours.

I decided to check my phone. I had a message from my ex, Jo. I read it, steeling myself for its contents:

Court date set. Documents will be sent to you. Fill in your divorce papers and send back ASAP.

Charming. Jo all over.

I sighed and pondered how it came to this. There was a time in our lives where we would have done anything for one another. Now she couldn’t send a text message without it dripping with utter contempt.

I thought back to the Christmas, eighteen months earlier, when Jo and I had invited her parents to come and stay with us. We thought it would be homely and happy – a real Christmas for Maddie. However, this fantasy didn’t last long. Jo’s mum is French and insisted on serving duck hearts on Christmas Day – something that Jo and I, as vegetarians, refused. I found the production of food such as this cruel, and something we didn’t want Maddie being involved in, especially as we wouldn’t have anything to do with it ourselves.

It was a battle of generations – the typical, older traditional values versus our more modern, ethical stance. We won - she was irritated. Years of Jo's mother demanding her own way, downed with one swift shot.

Well, she wouldn't let it lie, and had invited us around for a meal on New Year's Day. Jo asked her at least five times whether she would serve foie gras, and each time she promised she wouldn't.

The day arrived, hope for a new year. Maddie was singing and laughing. I was upstairs in the bathroom when the foie gras arrived. Jo was furious. Raised voices. She wanted to leave immediately, but there was family yet to attend – people Jo and Maddie wouldn't see for a long time.

I urged her to stay. I kept Maddie in the front room while the family ate their foie gras. We left in the evening, rage written all over Jo's face as she drove Maddie and me home.

The next day I woke, Jo had hardly slept. She had handwritten a five-page letter to her parents about how she felt. It ceased to be about the bloody food – it was the utter betrayal and disregard for her feelings that resonated the morning after.

The letter was sent and we waited. I asked her if she was doing this for me. She said she wasn't, but I knew in my heart she was. Sticking up for my morals and beliefs. My wife was prepared to lose her family for this love, for us.

The letter was received with anger and tears. We met and discussed it – more tears and hurt. We drove home knowing we had done the right thing. But as I look back now, what good did it do?

When the relationship fell apart, the previous November, Jo went back to her parents. Of course they were overjoyed at this minor tragedy – I was the bad guy and they could resume their position as their daughter's providers. They were 'there for her' during the dark times of the break up.

It didn't change the fact that, at one point in our lives, Jo would have done anything for me and me for her. Nor does it change the fact that her parents lied to her face. Still, I'm the one alone now.

The darkness of our arguments and the words that came, filled me once more as I sat in the lonely, cold room waiting for Amy's English teacher, confirmed as Mr Troy Wood.

'You are, by nature, a tornado, Charlie,' she'd said to me once. I still couldn't understand how one moment she reaped that tornado, swept up in love and lust, the next she'd had enough and wanted out, taking Maddie with her. Now it was divorce and venom. Everything was happening so fast I couldn't keep my feet on the ground. In eight months since I had left the house in Faversham, my life had completely changed.

And *I* was the tornado?

I craved a drink and wanted to leave. Finally, I heard feet shuffling outside and muffled voices behind the door which eventually creaked open.

I looked at the man who walked in. He was in his mid-twenties, heavily set and with a handsome face.

'I'll leave you to it,' the receptionist said as she disappeared briskly, closing the door behind her.

'How can I help?' he said nervously.

'I'm investigating the death of Amy Green. What can you tell me about her?'

He bowed his head and looked to the floor.

'I can't believe what happened to her,' he replied with solemnity in his voice.

'What *did* happen to her?' I fired back, losing my temper with everyone here, seemingly knowing more than I did.

'Well, last night... ' he looked searchingly. 'Smith couldn't keep his mouth shut, could he?

'Yes, tell me what you know.'

'She was murdered,' he said. 'They found her on the beach,'

I made a note in my pad. 'Was she? Because this is my case and I don't even know that it was murder for sure.'

'A dead girl washes up on the beach… it seems pretty obvious… '

'Cut the hearsay and tell me about your relationship with her, please.'

'I taught her,' he said.

'English, yes, I know. Anything unusual about her? Any recent changes in behaviour?'

'Well no, she was a good student, but… quiet. I didn't really speak to her much; she kept herself to herself. I don't think she knew many people in the class.'

'I see. Was she more vocal in the private lessons you had with her?' His eyes met mine and he looked frightened.

'God, I... '

'It seems strange that you hardly spoke to her, but picked her out for extra lessons,' I continued.

'I didn't choose her, she chose me!'

'*Chose* you? What on earth do you mean?'

'What? No! You're twisting my words; I'm not saying anymore without my solicitor...'

'They're your words, Mr Wood. '*She chose you.*' What for? As her tutor? Or for something else? Come on Troy, now's your chance to get it all off your chest.'

'I'm not saying any more without my solicitor!' he said turning to the wall.

I paused and changed tack slightly. 'Bit sick this, Troy. Schoolgirls? Private lessons? A quiet girl too… '

'… She was eighteen, for goodness' sake!'

'She was still a student! You were her teacher. Did the school know about these… *lessons?*

'I'm not sure, why?'

'I just presumed that might be protocol, but I will check that with your boss. How many times did you meet her?'

He paused and breathed in deeply. 'Four times. We had four lessons.'

'Where?'

'I'm not saying anything else!' he shouted.

'Thank you, Mr Wood, this has been most enlightening.'

8

I left the school and got into the car, checking my phone. Dave had called, so I rang him straight back.

'Charlie, what can you tell me?'

'I'm just leaving the school now. I've been speaking with Amy's English teacher, Troy Wood. We need to get him in for a more formal interrogation.'

'Oh yeah? You think he had something to do with it?'

'Not sure. But I think there may have been more to their relationship than Shakespeare and poetry.'

'OK, I'll bring him in. Anything else?' Dave was never one for small talk.

'Not really. Just heading for an update on the autopsy results now.'

'OK. Get the hospital to email them to the station. After that, come in and we'll discuss this Wood guy.'

'Roger that, boss.'

I went back to the pathologists to see what they had found. I felt tense and my stomach was churning.

'What have you got for me?' I asked.

'A dead girl and a tragic end.' I supposed that dealing with the dead all day could make you become more realistic about your own mortality. 'It appears the girl was killed by asphyxiation,' he continued.

'She was strangled?'

'No. It appears she was killed by having something pushed into her throat that blocked her airway,' he continued, not removing his head from his note pad.

'She was also bound *before* her murder, which was at some point around two in the morning.'

'Where?'

'Arms and ankles.'

I winced as he pulled back the sheet covering her body to show me the deep cuts and abrasions. I had not noticed these properly when I found her on the beach.

Her face was pale and bruised, but there was a serenity to her that no-one could abuse or deface now.

'Incidentally, she had sexual intercourse on the night of her death.'

'With one person?'

'We'll have to wait for results on this one, same with toxicology. My guess is this was your typical party girl who got involved with the wrong crowd on the harbour. Although the object in the throat is peculiar… ' he said, drifting into his own thoughts.

'Leave the guesswork to me please. Are you from this area?' I asked.

'Peppermill, yes,' he murmured.

'Do y'know Primrose Gardens?'

'Yes…'

'That's where she lived. Straight-A student, went to the HG Wells Grammar School. Her parents are in absolute bloody pieces!'

'OK, sergeant, I take your point,' he said.

'Well don't assume things, doctor – do your job and leave the rest to me. When can I get those results?'

'Give me a couple of days,' he replied, burying his nose in his notepad again.

'OK. What about the stuff in her throat? You seen that before?'

The doctor paused. 'I've read about something like it. My guess, it would be some sort of message... '

'What, like some sort of... warning?

'I've heard about London gangs, blocking up airways... with, you know, cement and so on, when they have killed their own for turning away or going to the police?'

'But that can't be what we've got here. She's an eighteen-year-old schoolgirl from Folkestone!' I said.

'Well, you asked me what I thought, sarge. Come back in a couple of days.'

I returned to the car and drove up to the Leas, parked up and started walking. I needed to clear my head and this part of town took me back to a time where I wasn't surrounded by so much sadness.

I lit a cigarette and stared out to sea. I rarely smoked, but today I needed it. It was a clear day and the Channel was an aquamarine blue. If you squinted into the distance you could see France and the white chalky cliffs surrounding the town of Calais. It looked a world away.

I phoned Dave and updated him. He wanted me to come in, so I told him I would be there soon. The fresh sea air filled my lungs and I felt more human. I tried to rationalise the events of the last two days.

Did Wood kill Amy? I wasn't sure. It was likely he had strong feelings for her, but he didn't seem the type.

He erred on the side of confidence, but when I saw him he was rattled and flustered, not someone who I thought could murder.

Maybe he killed her by accident? It didn't seem likely though. The way she met her end looked professional. Washed up on a beach, so no evidence, the potentially symbolic asphyxiation, maybe this case ran deeper than it first appeared.

The phone rang and it was Jo's number. Despite my immediate desire to hang up, I reasoned it could be Maddie on the other end of the line. I took the gamble and answered.

'Daddy!' Maddie shouted. 'You forgot to call me! What are you doing?' She adopted the tone of a stern teacher disappointed in a naughty pupil. It was better than her being sad, but still made me feel bad.

I had been so wrapped up in the case, I'd forgotten the Monday night call.

'Oh darling, I'm sorry, I've been so busy at work,' I made the excuse, but knew once more I had failed her. By the end of our seven-minute chat, I'd won her round, but I needed to do better.

In my defence, this situation was new to me too. I also had to learn the new protocols, timings and arrangements. Jo had me at arm's length and kept Maddie close, just like during our marriage.

I returned to Folkestone police station, which was a large, old building from the 1960s. Plastic cream lino and chipped white plasterboard walls were the general theme.

Homicide was on the third floor and tucked away, which was often useful for keeping away nosy reporters and other distractions, but irritating when you wanted to get work done quickly.

Dave was waiting at the top as I walked the last flight of stairs, I was motioned into his office.

'Charlie! Good to see you!' he seemed happier than usual.

'Morning Dave, you seem chipper!'

'I feel it, now tell me about this Wood character.'

'Strange guy. He's in his late twenties, an English teacher, Amy's teacher, good-looking, confident. He organised extra lessons with Amy before her exams too.'

'One to one?'

'Yes. He also said something strange…what was it?' I reached for my pad and leafed through. 'Here we are, *'I didn't choose her, she chose me.'*

'Sounds dodgy to me,' Dave concluded.

'He probably developed feelings beyond his "professional boundaries." I know how it sounds, boss, but I don't think he killed her.'

'No?'

'I don't think so. He was upset and all over the place but I think it was mostly grief. My gut feeling is he didn't do it.'

'He's our number one suspect though?'

'He's our only suspect currently!' I couldn't help a wry smile.

'I guess you're right, Charlie. With that in mind, can you get down to the garden centre and check it out? See if anyone knows any more about this girl.'

'OK. Did they send you the initial report?' I asked him as I got up to leave.

'Yeah, what did you think?'

'Well I didn't understand the asphyxiation. It seemed like the killer had forced something down her throat.'

Dave looked up at me. 'Go on.'

'Strange way to kill someone, don't you think? No real signs of a struggle, she was bound anyway.'

'Hmmm…'

'I mean, she must have weighed nine stone soaking wet, why not kill her more…*conventionally,* I suppose? Why go to all the trouble and this weird message, when you'd think most people could easily overpower her?'

'So you think this 'method' of killing was planned?'

'Well, yeah, it seems like a message. Someone was making their point, to stop her breathing by blocking her airwaves,' I said, still slightly unsure of what I was trying to say.

'Interesting, Charlie. Whatever is going on here, I don't like it. This is beginning to look like a professional killing, an execution.'

We both sat solemnly for a moment, taking in the gravity of what we appeared to be dealing with.

Dave broke the silence. 'Anyway Charlie, get down to that garden centre. I want something concrete.'

'Oh, I nearly forgot. Dave, did you phone through to the HG Wells school this morning?'

'No, why?'

'That's funny. The new head teacher said he got a phone call from us. He knew about the murder before I got there. Said someone from the station called him.'

'No one here did. I'll look into it.'

9

I walked to the garden centre, as it was just around the corner from the police station.

The streets were lined with oak trees and large, beautiful houses, which had now mainly been turned into flats. Despite this, each building had its own individuality; imperious and magnificent in the golden, evening sunshine.

The garden centre was smaller than most I had been to before. A young man in a bright yellow helmet sped around the car park on a forklift truck, while octogenarians picked out their autumn hydrangeas.

I continued to the café towards the rear of the building. Behind the tills were two young girls of around Amy's age, giggling. One of them was chewing too intensely. I walked towards them. Despite their youth and immaturity, I was feeling more concerned with each step I took.

'Hi, how can I help you?' one of them said, slightly too enthusiastically for the quiet café. Her friend immediately laugh ed into her hand.

'Good afternoon.' I looked at each of them in turn. 'Do either of you know a girl called Amy Green? She worked here.'

The girls looked at each other and stopped chewing for a brief moment. They were both pretty in different ways. One had blonde curly hair and big blue eyes - but was plastered in foundation. The other had dark, straight hair and simple, feline features.

'No. I don't know her,' the blonde replied looking at her friend. 'Do you?'

'No,' the other girl replied.

'That's strange. She's around your age, just finished her A-levels at the HG Wells Grammar School...?'

'... Oh! We go to college, mate. We wouldn't know any of the girls from that school,' she said in a mock posh accent.

'Anyway, who are you?' the blonde asked. They had stopped giggling.

'Sergeant Stone, Kent Police. I'm investigating Amy Green's death.'

The dark-haired girl inhaled quickly and looked at her friend. Shock and fear.

The blonde girl just stared at me, twiddling the length of a blonde curl around a finger. 'We didn't know her mate. Sorry.'

I didn't believe them. 'Well, if you remember anything, here's my card. Please call if anything does spring to mind.'

I put my badge away and thanked the girls. I left to the sound of whispering and the feeling of concern in my stomach returned once more.

10

The day had shot past and it was now around seven in the evening. I needed a drink so stopped off at the Fiesta Bar on The Leas.

I walked downstairs to the entrance and was immediately greeted by the familiar sight of pink neon. I sat at the bar and ordered a double rum and ginger.

The TV screen fixed in the corner was blaring out the news - or the news they decided to report. These days, I preferred the news firmly with the sound off. I watched images of migrants entering the country through the Channel Tunnel, running with harrowed looks on their faces.

Cut to more people from foreign lands, this time on small boats trying to cross the sea. Next shot, the same faces looking somewhat relieved as they're detained or taken away by immigration police.

I gulped my drink, ordered another and went out for a cigarette. I couldn't resist picking up a copy of the *Folkestone Bugle,* our local newspaper, crisping in the heat. I read the front-page headline, *Immigrants flooding Folkestone.*

The so-called migrant crisis did indeed appear to be making the natives restless. The usual right-wing newspaper outlets printed these stories every day. Crime was increasing, jobs were decreasing and more benefits were being handed out. If I wasn't so tired, this skewed agenda would make me sick.

The newsreader appeared again, this time discussing the government's new plans to fast track trials for murderers and rapists. It seemed the prime minister in conjunction with the chief of the Met Police, wanted to reduce the media spectacle surrounding violent crime and convict the criminals in a less public fashion. Seemed like a good idea to me.

The sound of cackling laughter and clacking heels jogged me back to reality. The scent of a familiar perfume greeted me.

'Charlie, Jesus! Look at you!? It's been a while,' one of the voices said.

'Yeah, it's been an interesting few days. Hi, Polly,' I said, trying to raise a smile. We made small talk. Her friend, who stared at me aggressively, like a chained pit-bull terrier, went in and to the bar.

Polly was also in the police force. I'd worked with her in the Drugs Action department nine years ago and we had very loosely kept in touch, less so in recent years.

She wasn't what you would call conventionally attractive, but there was something striking about her appearance. She had a mousey-brown bob, her eyes were light blue - they always seemed to be searching for something when they looked at you. She wore a leather jacket, tight blue jeans and leather boots.

With a personality that could be spiky and abrupt, this made her an engaging and interesting person, perhaps not always for the right reasons.

'It's been a long, long time. Wow. How's the family?' Polly said, decidedly acidic. We'd had a brief fling just before I met Jo.

'Good question, we split about a month back.'

'Oh really?' she said. 'She couldn't handle Charlie Stone, "Super Cop?"'

I hadn't missed her fiery, antagonistic temperament.

'Something like that, Pol,' I responded curtly, hurt by her words.

'Sorry, that was a little harsh. Are you still seeing Maddie?' She said this more softly.

'Yeah. Once a fortnight,' I said. Polly frowned. 'Court order, so my hands are tied.'

Polly nodded; she understood the system.

'So, how is the old department?' I asked, trying to lift her mood.

'Ticking along. You know, it's Folkestone, always busy!' She smiled at her friend as she placed a drink in her hand.

'How's homicide?'

'Yep. Loving it so much I ended up here.' I gestured to the bar. She laughed.

'Oh dear. Well, we'd best let you get on. Good luck, Charlie Stone.'

'See you around, Pol,' I said, making my exit.

She was good at heart, despite her feistiness. She came from a difficult background, the poor part of Folkestone. East side. She'd worked her way up in the force and got under my skin and into my affections.

When our lusty passion for one another began to interfere with our professional duties, Dave moved me out to homicide where I went straight in as D.S. It was a sideways move but it was needed; we just couldn't work together anymore, I couldn't stop thinking about being in bed with her. Our working relationship had become toxic and damaging.

There were too many confused emotions, and for her to come into work and be bossed around by me couldn't have been easy.

I wondered where the night would go. I couldn't be at home now. I needed to feel numb from this case, from Jo and, ultimately, from myself.

I made my way further into town stopping at a few local pubs and bars. I knew some of the staff, so asked around about Troy Wood, the mystery English teacher. No-one knew him, despite this being a small town.

Two hours had passed but I wasn't ready to go home yet. I walked towards the harbour and heard a screeching voice from behind me.

'Charlie, wait!' shouted Polly.

I breathed deeply, apprehensive about where this would go. Time had moved on, divorce had made me a different man; scarred and volatile. I stopped and let her catch up.

'Where's your friend?' I asked.

'She went home. Had enough.'

'I don't think she's my biggest fan,' I smiled.

Polly grabbed my arm. 'Don't worry about her, Charlie. She is only looking out for me but, you know I make my own decisions,' she said smiling up at me and linking arms.

'Yes. Yes, I do,' I replied. In the aftermath of our nights together, Polly had grown angry and confused, and made it quite clear she didn't want to see me.

I was surprised she was even talking to me now, but I guess what they say about time must be true.

'So, how's work *really* going?' I asked.

She sighed, 'Hard - probably since you left, if I'm honest. Some of the years have been good but when you left, everything changed. New management, new team, all inexperienced. I was only a baby when you went, Charlie, and I didn't really know what to do.'

'I know, I know,' I said. 'But… '

'… You said you would stay and help me out. You knew I couldn't do it on my own.' She grew angrier and moved away from me, stopping still in the street.

'I couldn't stay, not after everything that happened. I wanted to… ' I lied. I didn't want to apportion blame and remind her of her threats against me, and how she made the department's life an absolute misery by refusing to talk to me.

'You didn't want to and you know it!' she shouted at me.

'Polly, calm down.' I headed towards her.

‘Get away from me!’ she said, eyes bleary and red, tears streaming down her face.

‘Polly, just let me put you in a taxi… ’

‘…Leave me alone, Charlie!’ I mulled it over and concluded she was a tough cookie and knew these streets better than I did. So I left her alone, as she asked.

I made my way down the old high street, towards Red Arrow pub for a night cap. I must have been in there for fifteen minutes, and when I came out Polly was waiting for me. That was her in a nutshell, you just never knew what was going to happen next.

‘I'm coming with you,’ she said. I realised I was going to need another drink, so took her by the hand and pulled her into the bar.

We sat and talked until closing time. She drank rose spritzers; I stuck with rum and ginger.

Most of the time she was a Rottweiler, picking people up and spitting them out at will. At others, she had the innocence and naivety of a child and I just wanted to protect her.

The barman rang the bell for last orders. She took my hand and led me to the taxi rank. I smiled, but inside I knew that this was probably a bad idea.

11

We got home and immediately started kissing. Polly pushed me up against the wall, unbuttoning my shirt rapidly and then moved on to my jeans. The mixture of smoke, alcohol and cheap perfume was a strong aphrodisiac for me.

I pulled off her top and unfastened her bra, releasing her firm, white breasts. I ran my hands over her nipples as she slid her hands into my boxer shorts.

I put my hand on the small of her back and led her to the bedroom. She pushed me onto the bed, aggressively tearing at my boxer shorts and jeans. The rest of the night became a blur; a beautiful drunken frantic one, but a sweaty haze none the less.

The alarm shook me awake at seven the next morning. I fell back to bed in a heap. Polly lay serenely next to me.

It was not that I'd done anything wrong, *technically.* I was separated from my wife, pending imminent divorce. It was just that Polly and I, I mean in a relationship could never work.

I liked her and wanted to understand her, but she wasn't able to let anyone in that far. My mind flitted back to last night and the angry, explosive sex. When we were in bed together it was more like exorcising demons than making love.

I got showered, changed and made my way for the door. I left Polly to sleep it off. She knew how seriously I took my work.

The car was at the station, so I walked there first. As I hurried along Brimstone Gardens, I noticed a gold BMW with a homeland anti-immigration sticker. On one of the windows on

Earl Street, there was a poster. I sighed and cursed the concept of groupthink. When the media pours its energies into creating fervour, nothing can stop it.

Then it dawned on me, where I knew the name Amy Green.

I scrolled through the number log on my phone and selected Jennifer.

A timid voice answered, 'Hello?'

'Jennifer, Sergeant Stone. I hope you don't mind me calling you?'

'No, not at all. How can I help?' she asked.

'I was wondering whether Amy did any work besides her job at the garden centre. Charity work maybe?'

'Oh, yes, she was always active with charities. Greenpeace, WWF, PETA and I think Amnesty,'

'OK, Jennifer, thank you. That's a real help,' I said.

'Any news yet, sergeant?'

'Not yet, Jennifer. But I'll call as soon as we have something.' I pressed the 'end call button'.

A few weeks back, a girl had come to my door collecting money for Amnesty International, raising awareness about the refugee and migrant crisis. Now I knew why I recognised the name and face, it was Amy Green.

I stepped into the local shop and grabbed a paper. Today's front page read, 'Folkestone teacher arrested on suspicion of murder.'

I turned to page five and read the implausible story. Wood had been arrested for Amy's murder. But why wasn't I told? What the hell was going on?

My phone had nine percent battery; I forgot to charge it last night. It was enough to make a phone call, so I rang Dave.

'Hello?' he picked up almost immediately, every time I called.

'Dave? Charlie here. I just… '

'… Charlie! Great news. Come in, I need to see you,' he said, sounding far too happy for this time of the morning.

'About Troy Wood, I'm guessing?'

'Yeah, nothing gets past you, eh?'

'No, not when it's front page news,' I said dryly.

I couldn't face going into the station yet. I was furious. Why did he go over my head? How had they got Wood to confess?

I picked up the car from where I left it in town and headed back to the hospital to check on the reports. A beleaguered nurse ushered me into an office with dark wood panelled fittings and a green banker's lamp on the table.

The doctor followed behind with a folder in his hands.

'D.C.I. Pensborough?' he asked.

'Sergeant Stone,' I offered my badge. 'I'm the lead investigator on this case, doctor.' Who the hell was *Pensborough?*

'I see. Not to worry… let's press on.' He continued, 'Let me tell you what we've found. The toxicology report revealed traces of MDMA and cocaine in her system. The amounts that were found indicated that Amy would have taken the drugs on the Saturday night before she died – maybe, up to ten hours before. There is also excess alcohol in her system. Again similar time frames.'

'She was using drugs?'

'Yep. Significant amounts. The report also suggests that Amy had sex with multiple partners on the night of her death.'

'*Multiple* partners? How can you tell?'

'Different strands of fabric on her undergarments, but we need to wait for one hundred percent confirmation. Also, her abdomen was severely bruised. She was bound tightly with twine, fragments of it found embedded in the skin. Abrasions on her face and neck were caused by biting,' he continued.

'Animal bites?'

'No, human. Probably.' He studied the papers for a while. 'There's something else. Odd materials found in her throat. Animal fur, splinters of wood. It appears that whoever killed her, wanted her to suffer too. Something was pushed into her mouth and throat, before being secured in place by rope tied around her mouth and neck.'

I had to take a seat. I was going to be sick.

The doctor sat next to me and put his hand on my arm. 'This is a particularly nasty case. I haven't seen one like this before, sergeant. This poor, poor girl.'

I gathered myself together, stood and thanked him for his time. He agreed to fax the main findings over to Dave immediately.

12

When I reached the police station, Dave wasn't there. A man I had never met greeted me.

'Ah, Sergeant Stone! Good to meet you! I'm DCI Pensborough. Sit down,' he said. *This was the same name the doctor asked for earlier*, I thought to myself.

'Where's Dave?' I asked as he offered his hand, which I briefly shook.

'He's on sabbatical at present. I'm looking after things in his absence.'

'But… I just spoke to him!'

'Don't worry, sergeant, Dave's fine. I know you two are big mates, and I understand it's a bit of a shock, but let's focus on the case shall we? Troy Wood confessed.' He assessed my reaction.

'What do you mean?' I said as blankly as I could manage.

'Exactly what I said. He admitted to murdering the girl. He's in cell two now.'

'We need to interrogate him. I want to speak to him!'

Pensborough chuckled. 'I've heard big things about Folkestone's number one crime fighter, Sergeant Stone. But it's done. He's confessed-'

'Yes, I heard you the first time, but, what if he *didn't* do it?'

Pensborough's face changed from one of joy, his brow furrowed and his lips began to quiver.

'Sergeant, if it smells like a fish, it's probably a bloody fish!'

'Wh-What?'

'It fits. The extra lessons, the relationship, the… *swagger*. My guess is it's his DNA we find on her clothes and on the rope from the night she died.'

'Have you spoken to him directly?' I asked.

'Well… no… '

'So how can you be sure he killed her?' I asked.

'He confessed, Stone! It doesn't matter what I think! Jesus Christ. We present the sodding evidence and he goes to trial, that's our job, done. If you can't do that, maybe you shouldn't be here!'

A low blow. 'Nice. And stuff all the consequences, eh? Who actually did the crime? Because, if it's not Wood, the killer is still out there!'

'Belligerent and truculent as ever, eh Charlie? Yes, I've read your files! You are beginning to give me a massive pain in the arse and I've only met you five minutes ago. Get out of my sight!' I hurriedly made my way to Dave's door, silently telling myself to shut up rather than say anything I might regret.

Who was this guy? And what had happened to Dave?

'Y'know she had sex with more than one person the night she died?' I spat out, unable to let it go.

'I bet you twenty quid one of them was Wood,' he replied.

'You're on. At least give me a chance to talk to him to try and make some sense of this, please?'F

'Don't you dare go in there and screw this up, Stone!' he shouted. 'Go take a walk, or have a pint or something! I'll see you later!'

I slammed the door behind me.

I went out front and lit a cigarette.

I tried to call Dave but his phone went straight to voicemail. I put out my cigarette and decided to sneak into the cell quickly, in case Pensborough suspected something. I only needed five minutes with Wood.

The cells were a collection of square rooms. Dismal, soul-sapping. The walls were originally whitewashed but over time had become stained with cigarette smoke and general filth and now had a dirty brown glow.

The custody officer was an amiable chap named Rod, who acknowledged me as I crept in.

Rod had large almost comical features. He was like a puppy dog with large feet and hands, but on a skinny, long body. Unfortunately, he had gone bald at a young age and what was left on his head he combed into a neat side parting. The issue was, he only had a few strands of hair left on top of his large, shiny dome.

'Evening, Sergeant Stone. How are you?' he grinned. It must have been lonely, a job such as his, so I daresay he was pleased to have the company.

'Hi Rod. How's he been?' I asked.

'Troy Wood?' Rod laughed. 'There are two types of criminal – guilty and not guilty. Do you know how to tell the difference?'

'Go on,' I said, interested in his thoughts. Behind his chirpy, youthful demeanour was a man who had checked in and dealt with more criminals than all of the officers put together.

'The guilty are the ones who are sleeping. Always. The innocent ones will be sitting up or pacing the room. Know why?'

'The guilty know the system and will need their energy?'

'Precisely! And the innocent are sitting there having panic attacks,' he said.

'And Troy Wood?'

'Come and take a look,' he said grabbing his keys.

He led me through a bolted, steel door and down a grey, dank passageway. The cells were silent. Normally there was the odd loud drunk, grumbling or protesting their freedom but not today.

'We thought, given the nature of the allegation, to keep him away from the others, y'know?' Rod said, scratching his beard.

'Probably for the best,' I said, checking for cameras in this part of the block.

The final cell we came to was Wood's. Rod opened up the shutter and invited me to look in. Wood was pacing the room, rubbing his hands together furiously when I looked through the gap.

'Hey, Woody, you have a visitor!' He opened the door and let me through.

Troy Wood was a different man to the one I spoke to yesterday. His face pale and gaunt, his eyes met mine with fear that I had not seen in a man for many years.

'Mr Wood, how're you doing?' I offered him a cigarette, which he took gratefully.

'Is that a serious question?' he said. He hadn't lost that air of arrogance after all.

'You didn't kill Amy Green, did you?' I asked.

'You've read my statement. It's all there.'

'Oh come on, Troy. It's a load of rubbish. I know you didn't kill her, so why are you doing this? Who are you hiding from? I can help you, Troy.'

He giggled. 'You can help me, right? You know *nothing* Sergeant Stone, you really don't.' He looked across the cell at the blank, white wall.

I slapped the cigarette out of his mouth and grabbed him by his shirt.

'Don't be such a smart bastard, Troy. I'm trying to help you. What are you so frightened of?' I let go of him and straightened him out, realising I needed to contain my anger. He stared at me un-phased by the threat of violence, while picking up his cigarette from the stone floor.

'It's bigger than you can imagine. No DS from Folkestone nick can stop this. I killed her,' he affirmed in a monotone whisper.

'Did you sleep with her on the night of her murder?' I asked. His eyes darted to mine and he breathed a little heavier, quicker. Anger.

'You didn't did you? Well someone did, Troy. More than one person in fact,' I watched his reaction.

'Why would I care who slept with her?' he replied unconvincingly.

'Because I think you loved her, Troy, that's why.'

Wood tried to hold it together, but his breathing sped up and, eventually, the tears came. I went to comfort him.

'I killed her, I was jealous. I did. I'm so sorry.' He drew deeply from the cigarette shaking in his hand.

'You're lying!' I screamed, grabbing him again, pinning him to the wall.

'I told you, I killed her! I was jealous… I… '

I moved back from him, just as the cell door burst open and Pensborough stormed in with two PCs and placed me in handcuffs.

I still couldn't comprehend why Wood had admitted to killing her, when I was convinced he hadn't.

13

This was the fifth time I had found myself in a cell due to my own actions.

The first time, I was fourteen years old and carried a knife in my back trouser pocket. We were young, cocky and out on the town in Sidcup, when the police pulled up and started checking us all. I was taken away, placed in a holding cell, and I cried and cried. I will never forget the look of disappointment on mum's face, now burned into my memory.

After the second, third and fourth time, I'd become accustomed to the silence and the solitude. I even sometimes enjoyed it. It was a chance to be at peace and to really think. What got me, though, was the uncertainty. How long would I be in here? What would happen to me? That was the hard part.

Luckily, now, I was on the right side of the law. It shouldn't take too long. Once Pensborough calmed down, he would no doubt be in to see me. I placed my head on the hard pillow and closed my eyes. I was so tired, but as Rod predicted, I was too agitated to sleep.

Hearing voices in the corridor, I stirred and raised myself up from the yellowing mattress. The door clanked open and in walked Pensborough.

For the first time, I took a good look at him. He wore a grey pinstripe suit and waistcoat. He had a short, grey beard and black hair, with grey flecks in it. He smiled at me, showing some yellowing teeth. His nose was red.

'Charlie? Are you OK?' he seemed friendlier than earlier.

'Been better,' I said.

'I think we should have a chat, don't you?'

'Where's Dave?' I asked.

'I told you. He's on sabbatical and will be for a period of time now,' he said.

'Did you? Why? What's going on?'

'Truth is, chief super is worried about what's happening here, doesn't want things getting out of hand. Tricky murder this one.' His nonchalance didn't convince me.

'When will he be back?'

'Don't worry about that Charlie. I'm looking after things now. Anyway, this Troy Wood. I'm struggling to see why you thought it best to take it in your own hands and accost the man. Why do you care so much?' he asked.

'This is my case. He shouldn't have been arrested without my say so,' I said, rage rising again.

'Charlie, he's guilty! He said so himself!'

'I don't think he is,' I replied.

'Is this why as a sergeant in the Kent police force, you felt it right to attack a suspect?'

'Well, I hardly attacked… '

'… You grabbed him and pinned him against a wall! That's an attack… '

'… He is innocent. I'm *sure* of it.'

Pensborough looked at the officers standing in the doorway and shook his head.

'Charlie, I want to show you something,' he motioned for the officers to move from the door and then I followed him out of the cell block and back to civilisation.

Moments later, I was in Pensborough's Jaguar, on our way to Capel-le-Ferne, a village just out of town.

'How long have you been a copper, Charlie?' he asked.

'Twelve years.'

'You sound tired of it all?'

'Not tired… just… the job has changed from when I first started it,' I said.

'Go on,' he urged.

‘I used to do it to catch the ‘bad guys.’ Now we just need enough evidence to make a conviction *stick.* It doesn't seem right.’

‘I see. You wanted to catch murderers, killers and rapists? You wanted to keep little children safe at night? That sort of thing, right?’

‘Yeah, something like that.’

‘The world's moved on, I'm afraid.’

He looked at me and smiled, before pulling the car into a gravel car park outside Capel church hall.

‘What are we doing here?’ I asked.

‘Follow me.’

We walked into the main hall and stood at the back. Light streamed in through the windows on either side and the wood of the church seemed to sweat with heat. The place was full with local people of all ages, mostly white, middle-aged, well to do.

The crowd quietened down and from behind a curtain at the back of the hall, stepped two figures, a man and woman. The man wore a navy suit, was red-faced and portly. The lady wore a pink, roll-neck jumper and a knee-length skirt.

They sat at a long, pine desk at the front of the hall and the man addressed the audience as the crowd fell silent.

‘Good afternoon to you all and thank you for coming,’ he said in a well-spoken English accent. Pensborough looked at me, before returning his attention to the speaker.

‘We are here today to discuss a problem, a scourge that is having a negative impact on our coastal towns here in Kent. We have come here together, to unite against the increasing crime, violence and danger on our streets,’ he said.

‘England, this great country, has always opened its arms to all faiths and creeds. Our nation is built upon the mixing of ethnicities and in the past we have welcomed this. However, in recent times, many of us have turned to each other and said,

"*Enough is enough!*" ' There were murmurings of consent within the crowd.

'Folkestone, Dover, Margate. These towns are littered with migrants, trying to make a better life for themselves. For years, we have tolerated this scourge, but now is the time to question, whether this has gone too far.

In Folkestone, the streets are dangerous. The parks are unrecognisable after dark. Prostitutes, drug addicts. In Dover, crime is at the highest point it's been in history, largely due to the influx of migrants, who argue amongst each other and disrespect the laws of this great land.'

People within the crowd were beginning to whoop and cheer as the man continued to speak. Pensborough gave me a nudge and motioned for me to make our exit.

'Now is the time, to stand up and stop our homes being overrun with this filth, these rats infesting the towns where our forefathers laid down their roots…'

The voice, although becoming more intense, trailed off into the distance as I followed Pensborough to the car.

'Thanks for the racist eulogising,' I said to him as we jumped back into the Jaguar.

'Why did I bring you here, Charlie?' he asked me while starting the engine.

'Erm, was it your brother's first speech and you wanted to support him? There are loads of racists around here? You tell me.'

'Very droll, Charlie, but don't be impudent with me, son.'

'Well get to the point. You bang me up for nothing, drive me out here, what do you want?'

'Have you ever noticed the ethnicity of Mr Troy Wood?'

'No, why?'

'Come on Charlie! The slightly swarthy appearance, that Adriatic cockiness…'

'Go on…'

'He's *Albanian*, Charlie. Well, at least his mother was. All over the area, meetings are taking place, people rising up against the 'migrant crisis.' We are getting called to angry protests in Dover and Ramsgate more and more frequently,' he continued.

'OK... '

'... And now they are becoming more organised, more powerful, more...'

'Middle class?' I offered.

'Precisely.'

'I see. So your plan is to finger Wood for the murder, as a kind of 'offering' to the pitchfork-wielding natives. Right?'

'Charlie, don't be so naïve. This is the right thing. It will help restore order. If the local people feel they are getting justice, especially in connection with the murder of a school girl, it will help settle things nicely.'

'Or make matters worse and cause anarchy!'

'Not if we design it so his community give him up. Imagine that, Charlie. The eastern Europeans, notoriously insular, criminal, apathetic towards our systems – law, education, order. However, in Folkestone, the local community give up the murderer of a white school girl, think what it will do to calm things down,' he said.

'But they haven't given him up, have they? Not to mention he didn't bloody do it!'

'Maybe not, but this growing mob will get their justice and be sated,' he said with finality.

'But what about *Wood's* justice?' I asked. Pensborough just smiled at me.

'But, Charlie, he killed the girl, he confessed.'

I turned away, knowing better, refusing to continue in this lunacy.

Pensborough took me back to the station and we walked up to his new office on the third floor.

'Charlie. You have a good heart, but sometimes in life you need to think with your head. I am going to give you the afternoon off. Report back to the station tomorrow morning. When you do, you will be off the case.'

I flashed a wry smile, 'Right, skip.'

'That's right, Charlie, because I'm your boss. You need to get your head around it! Now get out of here!'

14

Greater forces were at work right now and what could I do about it? I lay in my bed confused and angry but determined to work out what was going on.

I was too angry to do anything productive. I needed to speak to Dave and find out what the hell was going on. It was a quarter to seven on a Tuesday evening and I was drinking vodka in bed. I was off the biggest murder case in Folkestone's history and for what reason? I felt sick.

I called Jo's mobile number to talk with Maddie. It was hit and miss whether I would get an answer. Usually dependent on Jo's mood, I guess. I was in luck.

'Hello?' The familiar comfort of Maddie's voice, soothed me down the line.

'Hi Maddie, it's Dad. How are you?'

'Oh good, Daddy!'

'How was school?'

'School's boring!' she exclaimed. At once she added:

'Do you mind if we video call tonight, Daddy? I have homework to show you.'

'Sure. You want to do it now?'

'Yes, bye Dad!' The phone went dead and I waited in the empty silence of my bedroom.

Moments passed before the phone rang again. I accepted the voice call.

'Hi Dad!' Maddie's cheeriness was nourishment for the soul. 'Let me show you… '

Her work was amazing for her age. I couldn't believe how much she wrote. She was top of the class. Perhaps there was light in Jo's decision to ask me to leave.

As the conversation came to its natural conclusion, Maddie asked, 'Daddy, why are you in bed? It's just gone seven at night!'

The reality of my situation confronted me.

'Oh, Daddy's just tired, y'know… '

'You know when I'm tired,' Maddie added, 'I get up and do some exercise to liven me up. Come on, stop being lazy!'

She was right. I needed to do something. We said our goodbyes and the low glow of love returned to my heart, if only for a brief while.

I got out of bed and fixed myself a fresh vodka and coke. I tried Dave's phone but it went to answerphone.

In Maddie's room, there was a colouring pad and her pens which I quickly grabbed, before returning to the living room. I began sketching the crime scene and everything I knew about the case so far.

I woke up to the sound of my home phone. I grabbed it from beside the bed.

'Stone, get to your feet. Gaffer wants you,' the voice said.

It was Wednesday morning around seven fifteen, yet the room was dark. I supposed it was cloudy outside. Next to my bed was a dirty glass with a splash of vodka and coke left in it. I took it through to the kitchen and flicked on the kettle. I went back to my notes on the case from yesterday that were now stuck proudly on the living room wall in different colour felt pens.

Main points for today were to find out what had happened to Dave, my old boss. Also I needed more information about Mina Burrows too.

I got showered and changed and made my way on foot around to the police station. It was a brisk fifteen-minute walk and the fresh air on this gloomy day was a relief from the stuffy flat.

I got to reception not long after eight o'clock and walked up to Pensborough's office. Yesterday it was Dave's office. The window shutters were closed, so I knocked and opened the door.

'Good morning, Sergeant Stone. Please wait outside for a moment.' Pensborough's voice came from within.

I shut the door. Fifteen minutes passed before Pensborough called me in. He really knew how to make an impression this guy.

'Charlie, come in, sit down.' He motioned to the chair, while leafing through a manila folder.

'An interesting career you've had here, I must say,' he looked up at me. 'Would you agree?'

'I don't know what you mean,' I replied dryly.

'Oh, of course you do, Charlie!' he said, exaggerating for comic effect. 'Complaints by members of the public, issues with colleagues at work, 'a dangerous approach to law enforcement.' It does make interesting reading… ' He trailed off. I didn't give him the satisfaction of replying.

'What's this here? Allegations of "inappropriate relations with a PC in your unit?" Is this true, Charlie?'

I paused. 'Yes, but it was a long time ago.'

'I see,' he replied, writing down Polly's name. No doubt the old bastard would bring her in and grill her too.

Pensborough dropped the file on the table and looked across at me.

'Here's the problem, Charlie.' He breathed in deeply and looked out of the window. 'I don't trust you. Do you have talent? Yes, for sure. But you're a maverick. I can't afford a maverick in *my* unit.'

'That's fine, sir. I can always move units, go elsewhere, if that suits you better? It seems like you have the Amy Green case all sown up now anyway,' I added, not giving him the satisfaction of knowing how much I wanted to crack this one. Plus, I'd moved around a bit, London first, then through Kent and finally to Folkestone. I wasn't afraid of picking up and starting again.

'You will come back to it, though, won't you? You'll snoop around, trying to find something 'irregular,' and I can't afford that,' he said.

'Well, perhaps, if there wasn't anything "irregular," we wouldn't have a problem, would we?' Our eyes locked across the table and the blood rose in Pensborough's face. I wasn't sure he was used to this level of challenge; most of his subordinates likely bowed down and genuflected at his arrival.

'I thought this would be your response. You just can't let it go can you?' he said. I waited for his next move.

'Detective Sergeant Stone. Yesterday you physically attacked a suspect in a murder case. The suspect may well press charges, which would lead to your instant dismissal. There are many questions here over your past professionalism… indiscretions and indeed, moral turpitude. I'm afraid now you leave me no option but to suspend you from duty with immediate effect. Please hand over your badge and leave the station immediately.'

15

I walked home deflated and beaten. I hadn't eaten or drunk properly for thirty-six hours and my stomach churned with nausea. All I ever knew was this job and, as much as I hated the trivial side of it - the paperwork, speeding tickets and so on, it was serving justice that kept me going.

I once heard a story about a DC in South London, who used to wait outside pubs for people to get in their cars and leave. Depending on the type of punter he was following, he would stop and breathalyse them. No reason, except they had been in the pub and he wanted an easy nick.

He would pick on the older punters, the elderly. They were easier to target and wouldn't put up a fight, late at night through the old, quiet lanes of north Kent.

It was this same policeman who represented the Metropolitan Police every Saturday at cricket. It was at a high standard in the Kent league and was well known for being tough to beat. Yet every evening after the game, this guy would get steaming drunk until he couldn't walk. He would be helped into his car around eleven-thirty pm, start the engine and aim for home.

When asked, his team mates said that there was a rule in that area that they don't stop their own, no matter how drunk they are.

That's the system and what I hate about it. I wanted to avoid the corruption, which only seemed to provide for the elite.

I want to help bring about real justice. It appears they just want a scapegoat and to fuel the racial divide. It seemed that, no matter how hard you ran from the darkness, it would inevitably catch up with you. This time, it was dishonesty and the fact I wouldn't be part of this lie Pensborough seems to be spinning.

I called Dave again. Given what had happened with our respective suspensions, he didn't want me coming out to his house just yet. So he asked me to meet him at Gray's Hotel on the other side of town.

'One positive thing this job brought me, alongside danger, low income, nightmares, sleepless nights and the thirty-six-hour day, is intuition,' I said, two glasses of red down. Dave nodded in encouragement. He knew from his own experiences in the force.

'I can talk to a man and know within a few moments what's in their heart. Y'know?'

'Like a bullshit filter?' Dave asked.

'Kind of, yeah. Pensborough had it in for me from the first time I met him. There's something at work here, something unsavoury and he knows I won't rest until I know what's going on. That's why he took my badge and left me out to dry.'

'I'm still waiting to find out what's happening to me. I'm on enforced "sabbatical" but I've done a bit of sniffing around and sounds like they're going to suspend me for something too. What are you going to do?'

'In all honesty, I don't know,' I said, draining my glass and heading for the door.

'Thanks Dave.'

'Hey, try and get some rest, Charlie.'

I went back to my flat and sat in the dank darkness. I ran through the events in my head, trying to find some logic, but the Green case had become entwined and confused with Pensborough's takeover at the station and I couldn't make sense of anything.

I poured a large scotch, finishing the bottle, and headed for bed. It still hadn't been made from when Polly stayed. After the ecstasy, the laundry. I wondered how she was, alone again after another night with me. I guess that's how it would always end for me, fleeting affairs, one night things and, in the end, always alone.

I sat and sipped my whiskey, incarcerated by fatigue and emptiness. I chased shadows across the room and blinked the tears from my eyes. Eventually, the darkness won and I fell into an angry, restless sleep.

'I don't want to stay, Charlie. It's just a chest infection.'

I looked across at Claire, Dad's fiancee, and we both frowned.

'I believe you Dad, but d'you not think it's best to stay and make sure? Let the doctor's look at you and then go home when you're better?'

Dad coughed violently. 'I don't want to stay here. If I'm going to die, I want to do it on my own terms.'

Claire picked up where I left off and I thought about what my Dad had taught me, as he coughed and spluttered into his hanky, weakening by the minute. The walls of this institution weighed on him, weighed on me. It was a jail sentence, but one he couldn't avoid this time.

'I want to go, son. If it's my time, I'll walk away into the desert. I don't want to be a burden, a curse, I don't want this fuss.'

'But, Dad, these people know what they are doing. They can help you!'

'I don't want to die in here!'

'Dad, I think you should stay.'

I awoke in a pool of sweat, a surge of panic through my body. The sun was overpowering the weak metal blinds that covered my sash windows, failing to keep out the light, yet highlighting dust and dirt that filled the room.

I went to the bathroom, showered and brushed my teeth. I didn't quite know what to do with myself without my job. I checked the time, eleven – twenty-seven am. Dave was right, I must've needed the rest. I got changed, grabbed my phone and headed out for lunch. I thought this would be a good opportunity to see Maddie as she left school. If I left now, I could be there before three, when her day ends.

I sent Jo a text and told her my plans. I didn't anticipate a reply.

The Kent countryside seemed serene and peaceful from the comfort of the train. I watched the jackdaws glide from tree to tree and the occasional rabbit peek out of its burrow, before scampering back inside. The Garden of England - from a distance, everything looked all right.

I got to Morning View School at two fifty-five: I checked the time on my phone. There was no text from Jo; history had taught me that this was probably her way of reticently sanctioning my visit.

I looked around the school playground. There was a mural of a jungle scene on the wall. A smiling monkey was playing with an ostrich. There was a macaw in the palm trees, flapping its wings and feeding its babies. I wished we could bottle up this innocence and prevent the outside world coming in. I wanted to barricade the doors, press pause on Maddie's little life and keep her in this beautiful, imaginary world for as long as I could.

The bell rang and students came flying out of the gates. Maddie saw me and a big grin spread across her face. She hurtled towards me and I took her in my arms.

'Daddy, what are you doing here?'

'I had some time off and wanted to see my number one princess. How was school?'

'Great, Dad!'

I told her that I would take her for an ice cream and then to soft play in Tonbridge; she yelped with joy. Her mother could only get her at six today and so she normally stayed at the after-school club.

The sunshine warmed our backs as Maddie skipped towards the entrance with me.

'Excuse me, what are you doing?' A stern female voice came from behind.

'Maddie, who's this?' I asked.

'Mrs Smith from nursery,' she said dejectedly.

'Oh hi, Mrs Smith. I'm Maddie's dad. I'm taking her for a sandwich and bringing her back at six,' I said.

'I'm afraid you can't,' she said gruffly. Maddie began to whine, 'it hasn't been agreed with her mum.'

'I texted her mum today… '

'… Well she hasn't told us, I'm afraid,' the strange lady went to grab Maddie who held onto my hand tighter. 'Daddy, I want to go with you!'

'Listen, I am her dad. I have the afternoon off; I want to take my daughter. She's fine, she's not in danger.'

'If you take her, we will have to call the police,' she said definitively, as another lady from the school stood next to her in a show of perceived might. I didn't highlight the irony here, if only I had my badge. I remained calm and spoke softly to Maddie.

I told her I loved her, as the strange women I had never seen before, led my daughter away from me.

16

'After we split up, Jo found me a flat in Folkestone,' I told Katherine, the bar lady at the Fiesta Bar. It was the evening of the same day and I was slurring my words and pouring out my woes.

'She looked online and saw this flat - beautiful, grand, opulent. It had chandeliers and whitewashed walls. She said I had to see it; she told me it was too good to be true. She told me she would be moving into a house in Henlow or Tonbridge with Maddie. Although it seems far, at least it was on the train line.'

Katherine picked up a bar towel and began wiping around me.

'So I went down there, a bit confused. I saw the flat, loved it and phoned Jo. She told me to take it, said it would be the best thing, she said everything would be fine. I went and met colleagues in The Royal Appleton down the road, had a few beers, felt better and ended up phoning the estate agent to put a deposit down that day.'

'I see,' Katherine said, giving me the green light to continue my tale.

'In the evening, I got home, Jo was sat in the front room quietly. She asked me if I had put the deposit down, I said I had. After that, she told me she would never agree to joint custody of Maddie. She then told me that she was not moving to Henlow or Tonbridge and that she was moving in with her parents in Maidenhead! And she was taking Maddie with her!'

'You're kidding?'

'No that was how it happened. Here I am now, in Folkestone, trying to keep my whole life from falling around me,' I said.

'Charlie, you are going to be fine, you still see Maddie, right? OK, not as much as you want. But some dads never see their kids, y'know?'

The last thing I remembered was getting angry and tearful before Katherine told me to go home. I left the bar and walked out into the cool, Folkestone night and not even the sight of the sun setting over the sea could lift my spirits. I staggered back to the flat.

I woke up to the sound of my phone buzzing. I couldn't tell what the time was but it was still dark outside.

'Hello,' I attempted, my voice crumbling and cracking.

'Charlie, what's going on? Where are you?' It was Polly. I looked around.

'At the flat.'

'Stay there, I'm coming over,' the phone went dead before I could respond.

I checked the time, it was past midnight. My head was pounding and I needed some pills. I went to the fridge, grabbed a cold bottle of water and waited for Polly. I realised it must have been Thursday night. I guess she was out and had exhausted all her other options for any late night company, so I got the call.

Ten minutes later there was a loud knock at the door. I went down and let her in.

'Charlie, you look awful,' she said as she came in and sat down in the living room.

'Thanks,' I returned, admiring her, amazed at this full and vivacious young woman. She looked out of place in my flat, which hadn't seen any sign of life for days.

She had black knee-high boots, a short skirt and a red lacy top. Her face was made-up and she had moist eyes, probably the drink, which softened her looks. 'You look pretty good actually,' I said and we both giggled.

'I suppose one of us has to, Charlie. This place stinks as well, get some air in here,' she said, fumbling with the windows.

'So you've heard the news?'

'I just found out from Rod in the Prizz, I can't believe it.'

'Hang on, Rod still goes to the Prizz?' I asked.

'Tell me about it, you want to see his moves. He makes you look like Travolta.' We laughed again.

'Well, I haven't laughed for a while, thanks, Pol.'

'I aim to please. So, what're you going to do?'

I paused, I didn't know. What was I going to do? I doubted Pensborough would let me back on the beat, let alone the case.

'I… I… don't know,' I stuttered. She sighed, moved over to my chair and kneeled in front of me.

'Here's what you are going to do. You are going to fight this Pensborough guy, he sounds like a right prick.'

'It's not that easy, I'm suspended, remember?'

'Come on Charlie, you're a crime fighter - this is what you do. So what if he has taken your badge? Only a handful of people know you're off the case anyway. You need to get back out there and find this killer.'

'You don't think Troy Wood did it?'

'Not if you don't Charlie. I think he is a bloody perv and a bit of a weirdo, but no, I don't think he brutally murdered her.'

'Speak to Dave, find out what the hell is going on and find the guy,' Polly looked up at me.

'Thanks Polly,' I said, already feeling a sense of joy at her humbling words. My mind started mulling over all the things I needed to do, I grabbed my notebook and began scribbling things down.

'Ahem, Charlie? I know you have a lot of work to do, but that's for tomorrow. Now, you need to take me to bed or lose me forever,' I picked her up in my arms, powered by a wave of gratitude and headed for the bedroom.

17

I woke early, keen and ready to go. I turned on the laptop and my email box popped up. Thirty-six unread emails. I waded through the local, horny housewives and Argos special offers to find anything of importance. There was one from Jo sent late last night which I opened with trepidation:

Charlie, I'm so angry at what you did yesterday. How do you think you can just come into Maddie's life, unsettle her and leave again? Do you realise the damage you are doing to her? I am sick of your behaviour. You will be hearing from my solicitor. Jo.

What a pleasant start to the day. Now was not the time to get bogged down in her issues, I needed to stay focused. I checked out Smith and Tutton and found there were some extremely interesting articles about them. Smith had a number of different schools under his control before he took over at HG Wells Grammar School.

He is seen as a high-flying, businessman and for some unknown reason is trusted implicitly by Kent County Council. Reading deeper, it would seem he is brutal and antagonistic with those who do not agree with him, one report stating that he regularly shouted and swore at colleagues, male and female in meetings.

He also had a history of hiring and firing people as it suited him, as if the lives of the worker bees under his control, were entirely redundant – a term a number of his former colleagues came to know all too well.

Interestingly, Tutton had a grievance against Smith towards the back end of last year. He was going to be made redundant from one of his schools, then when the opportunity at HG Wells Grammar School arrived, he reinstated him to save money.

Something wasn't right with the school takeover, so I decided to do some surveillance there. I checked the clock, it was seven twenty-three, a little too early for the average school to lurch into life. I decided to respond to Jo and began typing when Polly walked into the living room, wrapped in a duvet.

She plonked herself down in the armchair. Despite the allure of her soft skin radiating the dark room, I could tell she felt a little worse for wear.

'How are you?' I asked.

'Awful. What time did we get to sleep?'

'It must have been past two,' I said. Polly groaned into the duvet.

I tried to continue typing but was a little stumped at what to say. I opened up a background page and searched Mina Burrows, who had a similar profile to her friend Amy, nothing major to report.

'Charlie? Can we talk?' Polly said, lifting her head from behind the cover.

'Sure,' I sat back in the seat.

'Is this right, do y'think?'

'What do you mean, Pol?'

'I mean, *this*… I don't want to call it a relationship because I'm not sure it is,' she continued.

'This mutually beneficial arrangement?' I offered, trying to lighten the mood. Polly completely ignored me.

'I don't think we're happy, Charlie. I don't think we're right together, y'know?' she continued.

I thought about what Polly was saying. I did like her but for all the wrong reasons. She was sort of like a wayward little sister. I wanted to help her and I think she wanted to help me, so maybe it did work.

'It works for me. You make me happy at the moment,' I said, turning from the computer screen and gave her my full attention.

She stared at me with those big wet eyes, angry and confused.

'Charlie, I make you happy because I come 'round late and leave in the morning. No hassle, no bother.'

'No, it's not that…'

'What about Jo? Your divorce? Charlie! I'm sitting here with you and you're emailing her! I don't want to be mixed up in all of that.'

'I don't know. I like it when you're here and...'

'What about Maddie? You have a kid, Charlie! I'm still going down the Prizz on a Wednesday night!'

'You seem to have made up your mind, Pol,' I let the words hang in the air. She looked at me. Her wet eyes had turned harsh and cold.

'We need a break, leave it for a bit and let things die down. I want to see how we both feel in a month or so.'

Polly got up went to the bedroom and threw on her clothes. She left without saying a word. That was her in a nutshell. Words of wisdom one minute, fleeing for the shore the next.

She was crazy and what she said hurt me, but I knew she was probably right.

I collected my things and headed for the school. A man with as much power as Smith would be in and out of there and I wanted to track his movements. I got in the car and stopped into the newsagent for the paper.

The front page was Wood's trial. A trial already? Pensborough wanted to speed things through, the court date set for next Friday, seven days' time.

Luckily, my 'suspension' had not made the local news, but on pages three and four there was a double-page spread about the Homeland Alliance and the increasing violence against Eastern Europeans.

The pictures made me feel sick, it was like the country had fallen back into the dark ages. White men with shaved hair, anger in their eyes, carrying St. George's Flags and shouting their programmed rhetoric.

I paid for the paper and drove to the school, parking twenty metres from the front entrance. I kept the paper in my lap so that I didn't look too suspicious. I had my binoculars and Canon-SLR on the passenger seat.

The school was not so much a hive of activity, but people came and went sporadically. There were smoking sixth-formers, caretakers emptying bins, dinner ladies arriving for their shifts. Nothing suspicious and no sign of Smith yet.

I heard the clacking of heels from behind me so I checked the wing mirror. In the glass I saw long, brown, lace up boots and a pair of full legs wrapped in skin tight, grey material.

As they approached the car, they came to a stop. I looked out the window to see a tall, slender figure and long flowing blonde hair. I wound the window down.

'Are you OK there?' a voice asked.

'Yes thanks,' I smiled, trying to look charming.

'Yeah, it's just that it's strange seeing a grown man waiting outside a school, I suppose,' she said, probing at what I was doing. Sadly, I didn't have my badge to get her to go away.

'I'm waiting for my daughter,' I said a little bit flustered.

'I see. With binoculars and a camera?'

'Well, I… '

'… Come on, what are you doing here really?' I looked up at her, she had dark sunglasses on masking a pretty, young face.

'Look, I'm a private investigator, just watching who goes in and out of the school,' I'm surprised I gave her so much information, but I wasn't sure I had much of a choice.

'Oh, really? How exciting! Anyone in particular?' I gave her a wry smile and she laughed. 'Well, I thought I would ask. Obviously with the news and everything. But you don't look that dodgy. So… '

'Dodgy, how dare you!' I said jokingly.

'I'm Tara, I teach Maths at the school,' she smiled a pretty, guarded smile.

'Charlie Stone, nice to meet you,' I shook her hand.

'Well, I better be going, classes to teach and all that,' she said and started to make her way, those high-heels clacking once more on the concrete.

'Hey, Tara!' I shouted after her. 'Can I ask you something?'

She came back to the side of the car and bent down to hear me.

'Do you know Troy Wood?' She looked away.

'Yes, I know him,' she said solemnly. 'I trained with him last year.'

'So you've seen the news about him, right?' She nodded at me sagely.

'Do you think he killed Amy Green?'

'Troy? I don't think he could kill a fly,' she responded.

'Then why has he confessed to her murder then?'

'Beats me. I guess you can never really trust anyone,' she said and began to walk away again. 'I've got to go, I'm sorry. This new head is quite strict; I can't be late.'

'Do you think, maybe, we should… swap numbers? Just in case… I need to ask you any questions or anything about this y'know?'

She looked back and smiled, 'Nice try!' she flashed me that smile again, before walking into the school, with her head bowed, clutching her folders.

As Tara walked in through the front gate, she stopped to talk to a female student making her way outside. They talked fairly animatedly, Tara didn't look pleased.

I grabbed the binoculars - it was Mina Burrows. She looked this way so I ducked down to avoid her gaze.

I slowly crept back up and watched her pull her phone out and walk down the road. She continued down Blooming Lane until she was out of sight, so I started the car and slowly followed her.

When she ended her call, a black Mercedes pulled up alongside her. She checked both ways again, before jumping into the back seat of the car.

18

I watched the car pull off slowly. It was a large, executive vehicle, the type that sounds like a purring cat upon ignition and moved like a shark through water. I remembered from Mina's house that this was not a car on her parent's driveway.

We stopped at the end of Blooming Lane. I grabbed the camera, holding it just above the dashboard and took a picture. The car had a private number plate which I'd check out later.

The car slid effortlessly onto Seagate Road and towards the town centre. As it turned, I noticed it frustratingly had blacked out windows.

My old Ford Focus jerked onto the road, two cars behind the Mercedes. I tried to keep my distance to avoid confrontation and to keep a good view of what was going on.

We turned onto Brimstone Avenue without signalling and took a number of unnecessary side streets towards the motorway.

My phone rang, lighting the audio display in electric blue. It was a private number - I ignored it for now. The car filtered left on the A2034 and onto the motorway. It was imperative I tailed this car as it was clear by now that it was not heading back to Mina's family home. Where was a schoolgirl going in such a plush car?

The phone rang and I ignored it again. The Mercedes accelerated onto the slip road, sparking into life and over the speed limit. If only I had my badge, I could pull them over and get a visual of the driver. But then again, I really needed to know where the car was headed and to stay hidden.

I weaved in and out of traffic, my old engine spluttering and straining to keep up. The phone rang again much to my annoyance and I answered.

'Sergeant Stone? It's Pensborough. I need you to report to the station right away.'

'I'm kind of busy, can it wait?'

'No, it can't. I'm expecting you here right away. No excuses, Charlie.'

The phone line went dead and I cursed my luck as the black car roared into the distance as I turned off for junction twelve and back to town.

'Sergeant Stone, come in and sit down,' Pensborough said casually signalling to a plastic chair he had positioned around a makeshift table in his office. This was new.

I also noticed a middle-aged woman I hadn't seen before. She had an aristocratic, unhappy face with pinched lips and piercing eyes. Her lips attempted an upward movement, an acknowledgement at my presence.

'This is Kate Skowalski from IIS,' Pensborough continued. The woman shuffled some papers.

'IIS?'

'Independent Investigation Services. Sergeant, I will get to the point. We have reason to believe you have committed gross misconduct and malpractice whilst employed by Kent police.'

'Really?' I smiled across the table at Pensborough, not really able to believe what I was hearing.

'Miss Skowalski is your investigating officer and will be in touch with you in due course to ask you some questions relating to the investigation.'

'What is it I'm supposed to have done?'

'The investigation is regarding your alleged relationship with Detective Sergeant Polly Ringwald, who may I add, was a constable at the time. You failed to report pertinent information concerning it,' Pensborough continued.

'That constitutes Gross Misconduct now?' I retorted.

'Yes, it is, if it brings other police officers or the general public into danger.'

'Mr Stone, if I may,' the woman spoke for the first time. I noticed how she didn't call me officer or sergeant. What was the agenda here? 'I will be in contact with you soon to meet and ask the questions we need to have answered. Until then you need to remain off-site and ready to take the call, when I make it. OK?'

I nodded my head and made for the door.

'Oh and Officer Stone, it would be prudent not to get yourself involved in any ongoing cases. No surveillance at the HG Wells Grammar School, nothing. Go home and wait for the call.'

19

Feelings of anger and rage pulsed through my body. The murder of Amy Green was unsolved and I was officially powerless to do anything about it. I called Dave but his phone went to voicemail as seemed to be the case every time I called these days.

I felt completely helpless. I wanted to press the destruct button and drink. Lots. It was too early in the afternoon to justify it though.

I thought of talking to Maddie but she would be at school. I decided to go to Dave's instead.

He lived on the Sea View, Harbour Bay Road, overlooking the hills towards Dover and the sea. I pulled up outside his house, jumped out and rang the doorbell. I listened intently but there was no sign of life from inside. I looked through the front window. His front room was understated and minimalist, how Dave approached most things in his life.

I could hear the sound of metal hitting concrete coming from the garage to my right and so I banged on the garage door. Silence. After a few moments, the door rose in a cacophony of clunking metal and there he was.

He looked tired and drawn. There were a few days of growth around the jowls and he was in an old, stained t-shirt and a pair of jogging bottoms. When he saw me, he couldn't help but raise a brief smile before succumbing to the masculine ego and suppressing it.

'Charlie, good to see you, come in.' He walked back into the garage. There was a small spotlight aimed at the engine of a

1960s blue Ford Mustang. The car was pristine. I wasn't really a car lover, but I had to admit it was immaculate, a historic piece of Americana hidden on the coast of south-east England.

I entered and he slammed the garage door quickly.

'How've you been?' he asked.

'Well I've been better. I've effectively been suspended. Twice.'

Dave harrumphed, 'join the club,' he responded, searching for something in his toolbox.

'What? You too? They said you are on sabbatical?'

'Misconduct.... when I brought you over from Drugs.'

'Jesus.'

'Let me guess. Misconduct for you too? Something to do with Polly Ringwald?'

'Bingo. Dave, what the hell is going on?' I asked. 'I've never dealt with anything like this before.'

Dave put his tools down and motioned for me to sit on a rusty, old chair to the side of the car. Dave leaned against the wall.

'Pensborough has been on the periphery for a few weeks now and has now taken over the running of the station.'

'But why?'

He sighed, 'that's what I don't know. He started off as an advisor, just making suggestions. Then things changed when we found the Green girl. He was the one who brought in Troy Wood.'

'But I thought that was you?'

'Before I met him I thought he was guilty. After interrogating him, I wasn't convinced.'

'Me neither. The problem is he's pleaded guilty.'

'Yeah and when I questioned Pensborough, told him it was your case, it all changed. An hour later I was relieved of my duties.'

We sat in silence for a moment, trying to grasp the bigger picture. A flock of seagulls flew by, their sound briefly soothing my troubled mind.

'I still don't think Wood killed her,' I said.

'No, I don't think so either.'

'What should I do, boss? Her killer's out there! When I went into the station today, they said if I go near it, I will be off the force.'

'What's more important to you Charlie, the job or the greater good?' Dave asked, for the first time turning his pensive gaze my way.

'You know I've never done it for the money... '

'And on the positive side, if they sack you, you won't have to pay Jo for a while,' we both laughed.

'I'll help you, however I can, but I think they've tapped my mobile. We don't want them knowing we're in communication. Pass me your phone,' Dave said. I guess that's why he wasn't answering my calls.

I handed it to him and he tapped some numbers in.

'That's a new number I have. Use that or the landline.'

'No worries boss, thank you.'

'Where are you going to start?'

'The black Mercedes... ' I said, already thinking about the best way to track it.

'Come again?'

'When I watched the school, Amy's best friend Mina Burrows got into a black Mercedes.'

'Her dad's?'

'I don't think so. Blacked-out windows and headed onto the M20 out of town. I lost it when Pensborough called me in. Do you think he knew I was tailing the Merc?'

Dave came closer towards me and spoke barely audibly, a faint whisper.

'Charlie, I reckon there's a connection between the new head at the school and Pensborough. Start there and stay in touch. Get going now, mate. It's been good to see you.'

I smiled back at him as he opened the garage door once more. Dave was already back in his toolbox, clanking away.

20

'If you can't be bothered to submit the documents to the court on time, it just shows you don't really care about Maddie's welfare at all,' Jo said as I listened to her gruff voice through the telephone line. This was once a voice full of warmth and love for me, now all I heard was hostility and fire.

When I got home I checked my computer. Jo had emailed and I'd responded by calling her back. Quite honestly, I wished I hadn't.

'It doesn't mean that at all. You know I love Maddie more than anything in the world. Do you ever think how it affects me that I no longer live with her?' I responded, trying to stay calm.

'And whose fault was that?'

'Both of ours, Jo! What if I had've gone for custody of Maddie?'

'How dare you say that to me?' She was fraught with rage. 'How could you do that to me? I'm her *mother!*'

'Yes, don't I know it? But you're not the only one who wants to have some input into her life. She is my daughter too, you know!'

This was what it had come to, arguing over sharing our favourite person.

When we were in love, sharing Maddie was easy. Now I was trying to cling onto something, in many senses, I had already lost.

'Charlie, you drink too much. You were not a good husband. You lose your temper. I've put it all in the application for custody.'

'Yes, yes, I've heard it, it's all me. You were blameless. Anything else you want from me or can I go?'

'Charlie, you need to get a grip of your life, otherwise you're going to be in breach of the court order.'

'How?'

'What happened when you were at the beach the other day? Maddie says you *left* her. Tell me this isn't true?'

'Don't get involved in my time with her. You either trust me to be her father or you don't. Like the hundreds of times you went out and I looked after her. Remember those times?'

'Stick to the court order. Don't let her down, otherwise I'll take it further.'

The phone went dead.

As if work wasn't enough I had the constant threat of Jo hanging over me as well. Hell hath no fury.

I left my pasta dinner and took a walk to get some fresh air. These days when I was home alone it felt as though the walls were caving in.

I walked along Dukes Avenue to the sea and thought about what Maddie might be doing. She was only five but she must have heard our arguments on the phone and sensed the bitterness emanating from her mum.

It made me so sad. A broken home is the last thing you want for your kids when you have suffered it yourself.

My dad was never around much and I think it made me more vulnerable growing up. He used to holiday in America every summer holiday, without the family, leaving us back in England.

Some years we could afford a week in Eastbourne or at Pontins. One year my mum and I went to Corfu. Most summers I sat on the sofa staring out of the window like a dog awaiting its owner, for dad's cab to return from the airport. It never did.

Sometimes he would be gone for four weeks, returning in the middle of the night and we would wake up the next day and he would act as if everything was normal. All would be well and we were a *normal* family again.

There would be a few weeks where we all got on well. Mum and Dad would be civil to each other for a while. Then the arguments would start.

My sister would nudge me to follow her upstairs and we would wait for the shouting. Actually, the shouting I didn't mind so much. It was the silence that bothered me. When it was silent, I wanted to go downstairs and make sure they were OK, but my sister wouldn't let me.

She would get out her guitar and play something or get out one of the pet gerbils that she kept in her room and we would play with it, hoping for it all to be over.

Maddie had to endure one night of Jo and I shouting. At least she only had one to remember. I made a mental note to never argue again with Jo. This would not be easy.

For a change, I decided to turn right on the Leas and head towards Seagate. There was a cobbled path that led down to the seafront.

It was balmy weather, a warm evening and people were out in numbers along the seafront walk. Cyclists weaved in and out of pedestrians as the waves broke meekly against the brown mossy rocks.

In the distance, amongst the evening strollers, I saw an elegant young lady in a brown fur-lined coat. Her long legs and thigh-high boots looked familiar.

She was walking with a young man who appeared to be in his early twenties. He was wearing a bow tie, a patterned shirt, a waistcoat and suit. As they moved closer, I saw he had a short beard and round, circular glasses.

The woman with him, although striking, moved tentatively and I realised where I had seen that gait before, it was Tara, the maths teacher, from the HG Wells school.

The evening air had lightened my mood, so I decided to engage her and her beau.

'Hi Tara, remember me?'

'Hi!' she said awkwardly. 'The weird guy who hangs around outside schools, right?'

'Yes, that's me!' I tried to think of something witty or clever to say, but as always, I failed in the heat of the moment.

'This is my brother, Richard,' he offered his hand and smiled warmly at me.

'Nice to meet you,' I said.

'Likewise.'

'Where are you off to?' Tara asked.

'Nowhere really. Just needed a walk and to clear my head. It's such a beautiful evening.'

'Yes, we're just heading back from The Ship. Richard's meeting his friend and I'm heading home.'

'Well, do you fancy coming for a quick drink? If I'm not intruding?' I didn't have much else to lose, given the day I'd had.

She looked at Richard. 'Go on,' he said. 'I'll see you at home later.'

He kissed his sister goodbye as she unlinked arms with him and we went our different ways.

Tara and I walked along the sea, as the sun slowly set to the east, past the large mass of land that housed Dungeness Power Station. Tonight the finger that jutted out from the Kent coastline was lit with an ethereal orange glow that felt strangely comforting.

We stopped in at the Seagate Hotel, along the seafront and ordered two diet cokes. It was a lovely setting, the large open fireplace sat proudly in the middle of the room and the dark oak chairs gave the place a cosy feel.

'Tell me about your job. It must be pretty exciting?' Tara asked, before taking the straw of her drink in her mouth.

'You would think so, but a lot of it is paper work and hanging around. Luckily, we don't have too many homicides in Folkestone.'

'Except poor Amy. The whole school is desperately upset. The new Head is having a memorial service for her next week.'

'That's good. The girl's family and friends need it. What do you think of the new head?' I asked. Tara rolled her eyes.

'He's a douche, really corporate and business-like. He runs the school so differently to how it used to be. The girls are terrified of him.'

'Really?'

'Well, yeah. He kind've has this icy glare when he looks at you. Like something out of a horror movie, y'know?'

'Yes, yes I do.'

'So Charlie, what's your story? How comes a good looking thirty-something like you isn't shacked up by now?' I laughed at her brazen chat. She was a real breath of fresh sea air, and I really needed it.

21

I couldn't remember the last time I'd spoken to a woman in such a relaxed way. Dave said to me once that there were too many strong women in my life. For the first time I could see how he was right.

'Been there and done that. Didn't work out,' I replied, gauging Tara's reaction.

'Sorry to hear that. Everyone gets a second chance though, right?' I watched her smile as she flicked her long blonde hair, revealing the tanned skin of her shoulder, highlighted by a white strapless top.

'And what about you, Tara? Any relationship woes you need to disclose?' I said, hoping she would take this as a joke, but realising halfway through my sentence that if she did have any skeletons, I may have made things very awkward.

'Me? Oh no!' Tara smiled. 'There was one guy… but it finished about a year back. I haven't dated since.'

I couldn't conceal my joy that she was single and a smile spread over my face. Luckily Tara was smiling too.

My phone buzzed and I jumped up.

'Sorry Tara, I really need to take this, it's my daughter.'

'No worries,' she said, sipping on her drink as I went outside.

Maddie was in high spirits, she had just returned from gymnastics club and was about to have dinner so it was just a quick call.

'Guess what, Daddy?'

'What, darling?'

'I've moved up a band onto Turquoise today!' she said proudly.

'Wowee! Turquoise!'

'Yep! Highest in the class. It's just me and Katie on it. No-one else!'

'Well done Maddie! I think you deserve a treat when you come down to Folkestone this weekend. What do you say to Funworld?'

'Yes, Daddy! Yes!' Funworld was a theme park recently re-opened in Margate. Maddie had seen the posters for it and was really keen to go. I had to admit, I was too.

'I will see you on Friday then, enjoy the rest of the week, I love you.'

'Love you, love you, love you!' Maddie replied before hanging up. It was amazing what a rollercoaster and a ride on the teacups could do to a child's affection.

I went back in and noticed Tara's empty glass. I swiftly ordered her another.

'Actually, I'll have a beer please,' she replied, beaming at me.

'Sorry that was my daughter on the phone, she calls twice a week.'

'Cool, how old is she?'

'Five going on fifteen!'

'Wow. I'd love to meet her sometime if that's OK. I love kids.' Tara suddenly looked to the floor, possibly realising the gravity of her request.

What she couldn't see was the growing smile which I couldn't seem to stop spreading across my face.

'Of course you can meet her. I'd really like that.'

Tara and I had a couple more drinks before I ordered us a taxi home. We both lived in the same part of town, she was on Terriwell Road, just around the corner.

'Well, I hope to see you soon,' I said.

'Me too, do you want my number?' she asked.

I fumbled like a teenager in my pocket, dropping the phone onto the taxi floor. The driver embarrassingly had to turn the light on before I could retrieve it and I nervously entered her number. Tara laughed at me, before kissing me goodnight and heading up the drive back to her front door.

'Back to Brimstone Avenue please,' I said to the driver. As the car pulled away, Tara waved from her front door and smiled her big smile. I smiled back while inside my stomach was turning back flips.

The driver dropped me off and I went back into the flat and closed the door. I could hear the sound of Jose upstairs strumming on his guitar. As much as it was quite relaxing, I knew I wouldn't be able to sleep while he was playing, so I decided to clean the kitchen and the front room a bit before I went to bed.

For the first time in a long while, I didn't pour myself a drink.

22

The phone buzzed and woke me at nine twenty-seven in the morning. I hadn't slept so well in months. The sun crept through the blinds and I went to make myself a coffee.

I felt enlivened. My head was light and I was ready for a day of work. Of course, not official work but as Dave had reminded me, I had a moral obligation to Amy Green's parents to try and find the truth about this case.

I stirred the steaming black elixir and went back to bed to check my phone. I had a voicemail from an unknown number.

'Sergeant Stone, hello it's Jennifer. I've found something I think you should look at. Please give me a call when you can.'

I phoned her straight back and arranged to meet in Twyford Gardens in an hour after a shave and shower. I put on a fresh shirt and a clean pair of trousers so I looked like I was on the job. I felt slightly uneasy pretending I was still an acting policeman when in fact I wasn't. But I kept reminding myself why I was telling white lies, to find this young girl's killer, which Jennifer Green would want me to do, by any means necessary.

I arrived at the house. Jennifer shepherded me in and shut the door behind me.

'Is your husband home, Jennifer?'

'He's at work, sergeant. Up in the city, Freeman's bank,' she replied.

'I see. He's back at work already?' She started walking up the stairs and motioned for me to follow.

‘Yes, he um, wants to keep busy, keep his mind off things. It doesn’t make sense for the two of us to be rattling around this big, old house.’

‘Are you *OK,* Jennifer? Because there are people you can talk to if you want to...’

‘Oh no, I am fine, y’know. It gets better every day,’ she said too quickly. I wasn’t sure I believed her.

We reached the top of the oak staircase and Jennifer led me to a room at the end of the corridor. The door was shut. She opened it and went inside.

It was clear that this was the bedroom of a young girl, Amy’s bedroom.

The walls were pink and there was a fresh, floral scent emanating throughout. Purple butterflies had been transferred onto the walls along with pink orchids and red dahlias.

There was a brown wooden wardrobe and the double bed was made perfectly. There was a white desk under an alcove, above it, framed photos of Amy with family and friends.

Jennifer walked to the white desk and opened the drawer.

‘I was cleaning up in here yesterday evening, when I noticed something peculiar. She showed me the drawer, which had a pencil case and stapler in it. Underneath though there seemed to be an extra compartment.

I pulled the drawer out and emptied the contents. There was a second, secret layer underneath which I prised open. Inside, I found a wad of twenty-pound notes and an A4 black book entitled, ‘Journal.’

23

I felt the money to see how much was there; I thought over a thousand pounds. I placed it back in the drawer and took out the journal, putting it on the bed between Jennifer and me.

'Have you read this?' I asked.

Jennifer shook her head in denial, biting her lip.

'Did you tell your husband what you'd found?'

'No, no. I didn't want to. I thought about it, but no.' She began to cry. 'I was scared of what's in it. If I don't have the courage to read it, how can I put that onto him and make him do it?'

'I'm going to have to read it. It could contain vital evidence.'

'If Amy was trying so hard to conceal it, it must have something to do with her death.'

'Probably. You need to be prepared to hear things Jennifer that... maybe are a shock to you, about Amy. There may be things in here that… '

'… D'you think I haven't thought of that, sergeant?' she retorted. 'It is probably filled with stuff about that animal… that scumbag Troy Wood!' she said reaching for a tissue from the sleeve of her jumper.

'Jennifer, be strong. I will do everything I can to bring to justice whoever killed your daughter. But, I need you to know that Troy Wood may not be the killer. I know it sounds insane and it's not what you want to hear, but I want to be honest with you.'

She looked at me with wide eyes, 'Then why is he in custody? Why have you arrested him? It's all over the papers?'

'Please Jennifer, trust me. Give me some time and I'll find out the truth behind what happened to your daughter.'

Jennifer looked at me, caught between anger and denial. In the end, her gaze fell to the floor and she sobbed quietly.

'Here,' she handed me the journal. 'Take this and find out who did it. Please, sergeant,' she said pleadingly.

As she showed me to the door, she didn't say a word. I felt bruised. Immediately, I picked up the phone to a counsellor we sometimes used. I gave him Jennifer's phone number and asked him to check in with her.

I went back to the flat. I was nervous about the journal. I knew I should really hand it in to Pensborough but I also knew what might happen to it if I did.

I went into the living room and sat in the comfy chair with the book. I opened it up and the first page read, 'The Diary of Amy Green!' There were love hearts around her name that had been coloured in pink.

I turned the page and noticed the first entry was from 2012, Amy would have been fourteen. It read:

23rd March 2012

Dear Diary,

This is my first ever entry! Yay! I thought it would be cool to have a diary and someone to talk too every night before bed to let you know what I have done. Eek! I'm rambling quite excited! I feel like a bit more of a grown up now!

Anyway school was boring. We had P.E. all day as Mrs Groves wants us to do a show in honour of the Olympics. I was soooo bored, I hate PE!

Mum cooked cauliflower cheese. I can't stand cauliflower, I would have been happy with just the cheese!

Mina split up with Rob today. I wouldn't be so bothered but it's like the sixth time this month. I don't know how she has boyfriends, I think all the boys from the Hemingway Academy are dull.

Anyway getting late,

Love Amy xxxx

I carried on flicking through, knowing it would take me quite a while to read this in depth. As I got nearer to the night of the death the entries became shorter and less frequent. One read:

13th June 2015

Hi,

I really find rugby boring. How can a sport make sense where you have to pass backwards to go forwards? Beats me.

My stomach hurts. Damn my ovaries! Boys are so lucky. Some days I want to just stay in bed all day, but I know Dad would never let me miss school unless I was dying.

A little scared about Friday but Mina says I will be fine.

Yours, Amy

I wondered what 'Friday' entailed. I would need to catch up with Mina as soon as possible.

I tried to read on but all of the pages from Wednesday 17th June onwards had been ripped out.

24

My instincts told me that there were too many unexplained events for this to be a cut and dried case of jealous homicide. What did Mina really know? Who was driving the black Mercedes? Why did Pensborough want Dave and me gone? Why did he want to take Troy Wood down? And most importantly, where were the missing pages to Amy Green's diary?

It was now Thursday and Troy Wood's trial. This had become a national media event and as I entered Canterbury crown court, I couldn't help but feel slightly nauseous at the whole unsavoury event.

Time seemed to go so quickly since Wood's arrest, but he was a prime candidate for the government's new fast track conviction scheme. The trial was simple, he had pleaded guilty and the authorities wanted the whole sordid incident put to bed. Unfortunately for them, I was convinced they hadn't got the right man.

The camera flashes were relentless. Whether it was Wood and his lawyer, or the Green family, the media shouted and bombarded them, throwing questions in their direction.

Inside, the court house was predominantly dark wood and leather. I didn't feel comfortable here. Whenever I saw Westminster or the House of Lords on the TV, I knew it was an alien place to me. It was somewhere for the elite of Eton, a class above. This courtroom felt no different.

I took my seat and there was a nervous buzz around the room. Reporters and photographers were talking animatedly, nervous onlookers, shiftily eyeing the press and the prosecution, the public gallery shaking their heads and scratching their chins in conversation.

Wood was in the dock behind a glass-fronted window. I looked across the courtroom and was surprised to see Paul Smith, the new head of HG Wells Grammar School. He was flanked by two middle-aged men in suits.

He looked unfazed as usual and when his eyes met mine, he didn't flinch or look away, just stared, until the judge's voice cut through the murmuring.

Despite this being a fairly cut and dried case, in that Wood had confessed, I could tell that this would take days. Wood may have taken the fall for her murder, but his lawyer was certainly arguing that there were further contributing factors.

The main points were that Wood was in a sexual relationship with the girl. They had met for after school lessons to help with exams and romance had blossomed. Again, I found this very difficult to believe. I had friends who were teachers and no matter what, they would ensure this could never happen.

Moreover, they would not even allow a situation where this accusation might occur. It would be career suicide. Still, this was Wood's story.

The plot thickened as it appeared Wood became jealous when Amy told him she was in love with a sixth-former from the Hemingway Academy. He followed her when she met him and murdered her in a white-hot rage.

Interestingly the boy was not at the trial, nor was he being called as a witness.

I stayed for the day and when the trial ended took a stroll around Canterbury's city centre. It was quite beautiful, ancient architecture, matched with recent investment and development. It really was one of Kent's major attractions.

The streets hummed with excitement; tourists, students, third-generation locals. It was a melting pot, an eclectic mix.

That said, it couldn't quell the sinking feeling in my stomach that something was horribly wrong with the Wood trial.

I stopped for a quick pint in The Apple Tree and let the human traffic die down.

I waited until six-thirty and when the crowds had died down, I got the car and drove along the old road to Folkestone to get an early night.

Maddie was coming tomorrow and it was our big day out at Funworld. I had not had a lot of recent practise when it came to the 'big day out' with the kids. I knew it would be wonderful yet exhausting so an early night was best.

I needed to piece the case together too. I wondered whether the missing pages from Amy's diary and the testimony of the missing boy could prove Troy Wood's innocence.

25

It was mid-afternoon on Friday, a few hours before I went to collect Maddie. Friday couldn't come soon enough. I was totally embroiled in the case, but I knew the minute I saw Maddie, my worries and anxieties would leave my mind. I had to try and get as much work done now and that meant locating Amy's missing diary pages.

Amy could have ripped them out, but why? Shame? Anger? If she didn't, who else would have the pages?

I sent Tara a text message asking what she was doing this evening and awaited her reply. I wondered if she would reply at all. It's difficult to know with some ladies.

For all I knew Tara was humouring me, though I felt something quite magical when I was with her. Like when I thought of Maddie, my stress just seemed to vanish. Tara had a similar effect on me.

My phone buzzed. Tara told me she was having drinks with her parents this afternoon but was free later.

I asked her whether she was free tomorrow and if she wanted to come to Funworld with Maddie and me. As soon as I sent it, I felt butterflies in my stomach. What was I doing asking a girl I barely knew to come with my daughter and I to a theme park? I hoped I hadn't blown it.

The ironing needed to be done, so I pulled out a couple of shirts for the weekend and busied myself in the kitchen. I can't stand ironing. I always put the iron on the top heat, no matter what item of clothing I'm doing, just to get the ironing over with sooner.

The phone buzzed. I had butterflies, steeling myself for a thanks but no thanks text:

That would be lovely! What time do you want to pick me up? Xx it read.

I smiled and made sure my shirt was very well ironed for the next day.

I drove to collect Maddie from Faversham rather than get the train. On Friday, in addition to a long week at school, she had gymnastics club in the mornings. So most of the time she was pretty tired and just wanted to relax at home, so driving got us back more quickly.

Jo didn't say a word to me or indeed make eye contact, so I focused on keeping things light for Maddie.

We chatted the half hour drive back to Folkestone.

'How was school?' I asked.

'Great, Dad, I'm one of the best readers in the class!'

'I know, darling, you told me, Daddy is so proud!' I was too. The only subject I could really do at school was English. I loved literature and to see it rub off on Maddie made me glow.

'What else has been happening?'

'Erm… ' Maddie paused, 'not a lot… '

'Maddie?' I probed, she could be quite lazy when it came to the details I craved to hear, from her life I was no longer part of.

'Well, it's the boys in the class. Sometimes they… '

'Go on… '

'Well, they try and kiss me… and I don't like it!'

'Err, kiss you? Why are they doing that? Have you told the teacher?'

Well, yeah but she just tells me to ignore them. I whack them in the face when they do it now.'

'What? Whack them?'

'Oh, sorry, Daddy. I meant whack them with my hair!'

We both laughed.

'Tell them, your daddy will come and tell them off if they carry on!'

We arrived home and Maddie was tired so we stayed in the flat, had dinner and played games. Tara and I had been texting throughout the evening and as we sat for dinner, my phone vibrated again.

'Is that a text, Daddy?'

'Yes darling.'

'Who's it from?'

'A friend. Someone you might meet tomorrow…' I hung the words out to gauge her response.

Maddie put her fork into a piece of ravioli on her plate.

'Is it a boy "friend"?' she asked.

I looked at her and raised an eyebrow. 'No Maddie. Daddy does not have a boyfriend!'

She laughed hysterically at the thought. I decided to leave the concept of same-sex relationships until she was a little older.

'So it is a "girl friend?" ' she asked again staring into her bowl of pasta.

'Erm, well… I suppose she's a friend… who is a girl?'

Maddie continued to turn her fork in her food, stirring slowly. I waited silently for a reaction, pretending this was normal.

Maddie, without looking up, smiled and nodded before finishing her bowl of food.

We played a quick game of 'Coconut Drop,' one of Maddie's board games, before it was time for bed.

The usual routine I loved followed. Some days I kept Maddie up a little later just to drag it out. My father told me anticipation was nine-tenths of the pleasure in most cases.

Maddie got into her pyjamas, brushed her teeth and I read her a story. She then, through half-open eyes, told me she wasn't tired. Then she would negotiate some music from the iPad to sleep with, usually Justin Bieber or Ed Sheeran. I would arrange it and in two minutes she would be asleep.

The morning came around quickly and there was a lot to do. This was my favourite part of fatherhood. Not the theme parks, or rides, or football games. It was watching her fall asleep, surrounded by pink butterflies, knowing she was safe from any harm.

I put Maddie in charge of tidying up and she strolled through the rooms with her duster, mercilessly attacking any surface she could find.

I got the picnic bags ready for Funworld. The weather was set to touch thirty degrees, so I packed Maddie's factor fifty and some lotion for myself and Tara who I was picking up in half an hour.

We scuttled around filling bags and tidying away until it was time to leave.

Tara was already waiting outside her house when we pulled up. She had on big, brown sunglasses, a black strappy top and denim shorts. She sat in the front seat with Maddie behind me.

'Maddie, meet Tara,' Maddie smiled as Tara turned around and greeted her with her own big smile. Maddie paused from chewing on her cheese string for a second, to smile and nervously say 'hello.'

The drive to Margate was longer than I anticipated. We made small talk in the car while Maddie picked the music and encouraged us to sing along with her, much to my embarrassment.

When we arrived, I already felt exhausted. The heat matched with the drive was tiresome and I was glad just to get out of the car. I went to grab a parking ticket from the machine and as I did that, Tara smiled and was already immersed in full dialogue with Maddie about what rides they would be going on first.

I queued and eventually got the ticket, turning and making my way back to the car. I couldn't see Tara or Maddie and immediately started to panic. My instincts kicked in, I didn't know whether they were paternal or from the job, yet I steeled myself.

In the distance though, I could hear a voice shouting 'Daddy!' with what seemed like a level of annoyance.

Maddie and Tara sat on a wall underneath the multi-coloured Funworld sign, both waving in my direction. The rides were whirring and clunking behind them and the hubbub of the growing crowds and children's voices provided a delightful backdrop.

I looked at them, Maddie urging me to hurry with extravagant hand gestures and thought to myself that there is hope for the future, even for me.

Funworld had been demolished some years ago during the decline of Kent's seaside towns. It used to be known as Bembom Brothers. It was fun for a while, but eventually got left to rust and delapidation.

However, following a resurgence in Margate's tourism, the high-speed rail link and the Turner Art museum, a group of local businesspeople invested in it and opened it again.

Now, Funworld was like going back in time. The entry gate was dotted with little booths and it churned out paper tickets like an old American movie theatre.

There were girls on roller-skates in pleated miniskirts, bringing food to diners, while the sounds of the arcades whirled furiously in the background.

Looking onto the park, it was a magnificent achievement. The wooden frame of the old rollercoaster stood proudly above the rest of the rides while the blue sky was tainted with multi-coloured flashing lights. Oohs and aahs provided the soundtrack as rides dipped and soared.

Maddie grabbed us by the hand and led us through the rides. When there was only room for two riders, we would take it in turns. Sometimes she wanted to ride with Tara, sometimes not. But what was merciful was the lack of animosity, the mercurial ease with which the day passed and the joy on Maddie's face as we skipped from ride to ride.

I felt a glow of joy and stood watching as Tara strapped Maddie in, nervously sitting with butterflies in her stomach, waiting for each ride to start up. I videoed them both as they rose up into the bright, blue sky, Maddie yelping with delight as the rides bounced her here and there.

The heat of the day was debilitating so as lunchtime approached, we headed to the cool of the American Diner and Roller-skate Park that was undercover.

Tara ordered soft drinks at the bar and we waited for them to arrive at our table.

A teenage girl with bright, soft skin and permed, blonde hair came skittering over excitedly as we sat down.

'Hey, Tara!' she said.

'Hi Lucia, good to see you!' Tara got up and they hugged. 'I knew you had a new job, but I didn't know it was here!'

'Yeah, started last week. I have three jobs now! How are you?' The pretty girl kept looking at me awkwardly. Tara eventually cottoned on and introduced us.

'Lucia, this is Charlie,' she smiled at me with a big, pretty grin.

'Lovely to meet you,' I said.

'Likewise,' she returned, slightly flirtatiously, but all in jest.

Maddie stared, twiddling her straw, immersed in the quick-fire conversation of the two young women. I tried to look interested as they caught up and made tentative plans to meet up in Lucia's next holiday.

'How old is she?' I asked once she had said some polite, hurried goodbyes and went back to serving the customers.

'Seventeen,' Tara replied.

'She looks older. You are going to have your work cut out, if you're going to keep the boys away from her,' I said.

Tara gave me a sideways glance before smiling and nodding, she knew what I meant.

Maddie was growing restless and grabbed my arm.

'Daddy let's go on those arcades, over there,' she was already sliding off her seat and over to the machines.

'What about the rides?'

She looked at me sideways, 'maybe later. Come on Dad!'

Tara paid the bill and came to find us afterwards. We spent the rest of the day trying to earn as many tickets as possible from the two pence games. Maddie watched transfixed, hoping and praying the tacky toys and the orange bits of card that filled the glass cabinets would fall, so we could take them home for later.

Maddie was growing tired as dusk arrived and informed us she would like 'fish n' chips' for dinner. I immediately looked at Tara, ardently wanting her to stay, but suspecting she was probably exhausted from being run ragged by an excitable five-year-old.

'I know a really good one in town. It's the best in Folkestone,' Tara said.

'Well we best get going then!' I said, as Maddie sat in the front seat this time, playing DJ once more and dictating the homeward bound sing along.

Tara's favourite takeaway chip shop turned out to be in the centre of Folkestone, opposite the Old Wetherspoon's. It was awkward to park, so we left the car in the NCP around the back of the old amusement arcade.

Evening had arrived and there were people milling about outside the pubs and bars. Outside the pub, old men were smoking and groups of lads began to congregate for their Saturday night shenanigans.

The take-away was busy, but we all got what we wanted. As we left, I noticed a black Mercedes parked further up the road, near the masonic hall. I couldn't tell from the distance but it looked like the one from yesterday. There were a group of four men, all in suits, standing nearby and talking.

'What's wrong, Charlie?' Tara asked, as the mood changed and I picked up my pace towards the car.

'I'm pretty sure those guys have something to do with Amy Green,' I whispered.

'What? Really?'

'Yeah. I recognise the car. I saw Mina Burrows get in that car the other day from school.' I replied.

'What? Mina? With those… *old men*?' Tara seemed shocked.

'I know, seems weird right? I need to go and check it out. Do me a favour would you? I know it's a lot to ask but can you take the car and head back with Maddie? I really need to check this out,' I asked.

'That's fine, Charlie. Don't do anything… y'know…'

'I'll be back in half hour… promise. This could be really important to the case,' I smiled at Tara, handing her my keys.

'Daddy, what are you doing now?' Maddie asked.

I quickly opened the boot and pulled out a tracking device and a small, battery-operated microphone from a bag of P.I. paraphernalia I had.

'I want you home with an empty plate by the time I get back, OK?' I said, kissing her on the forehead. Out of the corner of my eye, I watched the men enter one of the buildings further up the road.

Maddie harrumphed, 'typical Daddy. He *always* does this…' her voice trailed off as Tara put her back into her car seat and shut the door.

I kissed her and Maddie before creeping towards the masonic hall.

26

I ran around to find out exactly which door they had entered. Butterflies raced around in my stomach. I was once again caught between being a good father and the line of duty.

In essence, I had left my daughter with someone I barely knew. I thought about all the news stories about missing children and wolves in sheep's clothing and wanted to go back.

On the other hand, I knew Tara was good at heart, that there was a connection, a bond between the three of us. It sounded crazy, but I could sense it would be OK.

I trusted my gut instinct and prayed Jo wouldn't find out about this.

The men had entered the masonic hall on Under Hill, in between Rover taxis and The Angel pub. I loitered outside the front door and tried to gauge what might be going on inside but without success.

I checked that no-one was on the street and swiftly placed the GPS tracker under the wheel arch of the black Mercedes. I got to my feet, heading west up the road and away from the front of the hall.

I broke into a jog and went to the back of the building, past Lidl and into the car park. There was a great deal of overgrown shrubbery and waste to contend with but, I managed to get onto the drainpipe, to climb up the back of the building.

I jumped onto a flat roof and moved towards the windows at the back of the masonic hall.

I noticed where the lights were off and pulled myself up onto the ledge nearby. The window was difficult to open from the outside, but I managed to wedge the vent open and reached inside to open the large window and squeeze in.

I dropped onto a red-carpeted floor in an empty room. A stone fireplace sat against one wall but there was little light as the shutters were down on the bay of front windows opposite me.

I crouched in the darkness for a moment, straining to hear voices anywhere nearby.

I went to the door of the room and noticed a bar of light leaking through the bottom. I slowly opened the door onto a hallway, with a staircase leading downstairs. I crept down anxiously. If I was spotted, I could face criminal prosecution. I knew there was something strange going on and I had to get to the bottom of it.

I took a deep breath and made it to the foot of the stairs. Voices grew louder coming through a large oak door at the end of a narrow corridor. I crept towards it, aiming to hear as much as I could. There was a door adjacent, which I tried and opened, just in case I needed to make a hasty exit.

I knelt by the door, put the microphone against it and flipped it on. It picked up the sound of the voices but they were muffled and distant.

'The message has been sent and they know what we are looking for now,' one of the voices said.

'It couldn't be clearer. Anyway, let's not dwell on this. I want to look towards the next one.'

There were muffled noises and the sound of chairs scraping upon the wooden floor.

'There is a type and I think really the new girl is more… what we're looking for. Very English and y'know charismatic, but also a bit more in line with what we desire… '

'Well she can't be worse than the last,' there was a murmur of laughter.

'When can you bring her?'

'She's ready. Can come this weekend for the first time if you want?'

'Good, yes. The usual setup, well done on the turnaround Paul, after the last… hiccup,' then there was silence.

'Anything else?' I recognised Paul Smith's voice. Movement started on a greater scale now. I grabbed the microphone from the door and quietly crept into the room next door, shutting it behind me.

The men bustled out and I watched them get into their cars and leave through the window. After they left, I sneaked out through the front door, covering my coat with my face and ran back home.

27

The feeling of fear and trepidation stayed with me the whole way. The walk normally took me twenty minutes, but it was only fifteen this time on account of the adrenaline still coursing through my body. I was glad I let Tara have the car, I didn't feel I was in the right frame of mind to be behind a wheel.

I could hear the sound of laughter coming through the door as I put my key in and turned it. It was Maddie, running through the hallway. Tara was on her knees with a big grin on her face as Maddie dived into her arms. They must be playing some silly game, both enraptured.

I wished I could make parenthood look that easy.

'Hey, Daddy's back!' Tara said.

Maddie turned and dived into my arms.

'Daddy, we've got a great new game! You sit at one end of the corridor. That's it, like that.'

I moved and sat how Tara was and waited for Maddie to come sprinting down the corridor and throw herself into my arms.

'This is great, but I'm sure Tara needs to get home at some point,' I said half-querying, half hoping she would want to stay.

'Yes, Lucia is home alone tonight and I promised her I would go over,' she replied, Maddie and I both visibly sank. 'But, I'll come and see you again soon, Maddie. I had a great time today!'

Tara gave Maddie a big hug.

'Thank you so much for today,' I said to Tara.

'It's no problem. I had a lot of fun. Anyway, what did you find out?'

'There's something weird going on, something very unsavoury.' I tried to keep what I said vague.

Tara gave a quick nod. 'Escorts and prostitution have always been a problem down here. Now with the Eastern Europeans coming in, more gangs, more competition. I hate it. It gives Folkestone a bad name.'

'I don't know if it's that, something else I think,' I tried to change the subject. 'Anyway, I'd like to see you again soon?'

'You better make sure you call me, Charlie Stone!' Tara said, her mood changed once more as she put her arms around my neck and gave me a lingering kiss on the lips; butterflies and trepidation once more.

'Are you sure you can't stay?'

'Well… I really should see Lucia…' she mulled over her options.

'Don't worry, see your god-daughter. I'll see you soon.'

'I'll make sure he calls you!' Maddie shouted from her bedroom.

We all laughed before Tara left and I put Maddie to bed.

28

The school holidays were a peculiar time as a parent. All routine seemed to go out of the window and I was totally at the mercy of Jo's whimsy.

She had decreed that she wanted Maddie returned to Faversham station by ten am today, which was Saturday. There was no reason why, it should have been later in the day. To prevent further animosity, I agreed to what she wanted.

If I kept her in any unplanned way, Jo had told me she would tell the police I had kidnapped her.

Maddie and I didn't have time to do much this morning, so as it was another warm day, we went over to the park and played a bit of cricket.

She was getting better at hitting the ball and yelped with joy whenever she gave it a good whack.

Sadly, her bowling needed work. I needed the feet of a ballet dancer to get anywhere near her wayward and indiscriminate deliveries. Still, at least this was a sport she would let me play with her.

We went back inside after a while, a little puffed out and packed Maddie's bag for home. I made sure to grab my iPad so I could keep an eye on the GPS tracker attached to Tutton's car.

One positive outcome of having to say goodbye to my daughter was that I could continue with the case.

I had a sickening feeling in my stomach and I wanted to tail Tutton's black Mercedes straight away and find out how deep the rabbit hole went.

We drove back to Faversham, stopping for petrol and sweets along the way, then chatted the rest of the journey home.

Maddie brought up the boys in her class, Max and Olly, who always tried to kiss her when her teacher Miss Smith was not looking. I couldn't quite believe all this was starting at the age of five. I thought I would have at least another ten years before I needed to start vetting over-excited boys, wanting to kiss my daughter.

Jo was waiting as we pulled up. She seemed fairly pleasant and amicable, which was an enjoyable change. I kissed Maddie goodbye and watched them drive off.

I felt more together than I had for a while about leaving my daughter. I still felt blue, but instead of wanting to destroy and sink into darkness, I wanted to go to work.

I took a deep breath and opened up the tracking app. It always took a few moments, so I texted Tara.

I sent her a message thanking her again for looking after Maddie and hoped she had a good time with Lucia. Did I send a kiss at the end? If so, how many?

I went with one, there was never a right answer. One could be accused of being too forward or indeed too cold depending on the recipient. The sadness of the modern age was that there was always doubt. One thing that was not in doubt though, was my feelings for Tara and that I wanted very much to see her again.

The app finally fired up and it showed that Tutton's car, the black Mercedes, was in Hythe.

I put my foot down and headed as quickly as I could to his location. He seemed to be heading slowly in the direction of Folkestone, so I headed across country, through the lanes, where I would hope to head him off. Before I knew it though, the tracker was back in Folkestone and then onto the M20, speeding west.

I was caught trapped in a spider web of lanes, leading me through little villages; nowhere fast.

By the time I had got back on the M20, the tracker was heading up towards Maidstone. I got on at junction ten, a good twenty miles away. Tutton was doing a solid eighty miles per hour, so I floored it to try and get in range of him.

The motorway was clear and by the time the Mercedes had taken the M26 turn off, in the direction of Surrey, I had him well within my sights.

I eased off the accelerator and stayed a safe distance.

My phone buzzed with a text and the Bluetooth read it out for me. It was from Tara thanking me for the day out and hoping we could meet up for dinner again soon. Two kisses, or 'X, X' the automated voice told me. I smiled to myself.

A few moments later, the phone rang and it was Dave.

'Hi Dave, what's going on?'

'Listen Charlie, I got some news.'

'OK…'

'I got a message from Pensborough earlier; he's not happy.'

'What now?'

'He knows we've been talking and that we're working on the case together.'

'Has he tapped the line?'

'He can't have tapped this one, I'm sure of it. That's why I'm calling you now. Things are bigger than we thought. There seems to be some sort of ring, I'm sure of it. It's been going on some time.'

'Like a sex ring? Prostitutes?'

'Like that, but different. It goes deep Charlie; I think they're all involved. Pensborough, Smith, the lot of them.' He started to break up, as we moved through the mid-Kent countryside.

'I'm following Tutton now. I tracked his car, I'll see where he's headed.'

'Be careful, Charlie. These people are dangerous.'

'You too, stay indoors, Dave. Don't do anything, I'll come see you when I'm back.'

It felt strange telling Dave what to do. He had been my boss for years and when I tried to take the lead, he always subtlely put me back in my place. Maybe he was beginning to trust me a bit more these days.

We continued onto the M25. The traffic was heavy but moving.

I flicked on the radio just in time for the news. War, immigration and the football took centre stage, but then I heard the familiar name of Troy Wood and I quickly turned the sound up.

'At Canterbury Crown Court today, Troy Wood was found guilty of the murder of Amy Green. The body of the seventeen year-old was found on Folkestone beach earlier this year. Troy Wood has been sentenced to life imprisonment, with a recommendation that he serve thirty years.'

Tutton eventually pulled off the motorway at junction ten and made his way to the village of Godalming. It was a beautiful, unassuming, middle class enclave. I drove through it feeling uncomfortable, like it was too good to be true.

The roads became quieter, so I pulled further back. I was turning corners as Tutton was navigating the next one and so on, so he wouldn't notice me.

He turned onto a narrow lane and I slowed so that I couldn't even see the Merc in front of me. I watched it on the tracker as the landscape around me became more natural, woody and sparse.

Large oak trees, with deep green leaves, lined the road and as we twisted through the countryside. Up ahead, I watched the black Merc, pull down a very, narrow private road to the left.

I carried on driving past and brought the car to a standstill about three hundred and fifty yards further on at a passing point up ahead. I got out and decided to catch the car on foot, sprinting through the trees and undergrowth, listening for the ominous purr of the black Mercedes in the distance.

29

Despite my life having become pretty chaotic over the previous twelve months, I had managed to keep my work life reasonably intact. In fact, it had been a refuge from the hail of grenades and bullets coming relentlessly from Jo, since we'd gone our separate ways.

To keep my mind from its troubles, I dedicated myself to the job with meticulous detail. I bought a watch with an accurate compass and stopwatch, notepads with expensive writing pens and accessories to make the job easier.

I was prepared, dark outerwear and my size eleven CAT boots. They crunched through the shrubs and twigs louder than I wished, but gave me good purchase.

I was blessed with a good sense of direction and had an inkling as to where Tutton's car would be in the distance. I sprinted forward nervously trying to be as quiet as possible, but the ground was fierce and thorny.

Eventually I reached a brown dirt track wide enough for a car and followed it as quietly as I could.

In the clearing up ahead, I could see the black Mercedes, with its brake lights on, sitting in front of an old detached manor house.

The area had cleared significantly and I was acutely aware that I was becoming more visible the further I approached. I swerved from the path and back into the undergrowth. I was about fifty yards from the car, hiding behind trees as I drew nearer.

I sidled up behind a stump and noticed that despite the blacked-out windows, I could see the silhouette of the driver, talking animatedly on the phone. The sun shone directly at the window and I could see the man take the key from the ignition, throw his phone passively on the passenger seat and then exit the car.

As he got out I could see it was Glenn Tutton. He looked flustered as he exited and immediately reached for the back door. He opened it and motioned for someone to get out.

I watched as Tutton used his arm to lever the female figure out who was clearly unstable and wobbly on her feet. She was dressed in a short black knee length skirt, a red tight fitting top. She was about eighteen or nineteen years old, I guessed. Her head bowed and her legs gave way once more as Tutton tightened his grip on her.

He was so engrossed in helping her look presentable, his voice raised trying to shake her back to a sober state. I was able to edge closer, right to the edge of the clearing and only a few feet from the other side of the car.

The girl's eyes could barely stay open. She appeared drugged, dressed in designer clothes, looking the part, but unable to stand without assistance.

Tutton grew further infuriated and laid the lifeless figure against the car. He slapped her around the face as the girl whimpered and slowly tried to regain her senses, but to no avail.

He took her by the arm and shifted her so that her face slammed against the side of the car. Her eyes opened and I knew I had seen those eyes before. Lucia.

Tutton, grown tired of trying to get her to walk of her own accord, had put her arm around his neck.

He carried the teenage girl to the door, as her legs continued to slip and give way, like a young pup trying to walk in a cruel world it was not quite ready for.

30

I felt a surge of rage sweep through me. I wanted to destroy Tutton with my bare hands.

He was man-handling Lucia, the girl from the Funworld diner, Tara's god-daughter. Vibrant, beautiful, intelligent Lucia, reduced to limbs and body parts at age eighteen.

Not if I had anything to do with it.

I waited for Tutton's inquisitive eyes to scan the area before he slammed the big, old oak door shut. Then I made my move towards the old house.

To the left hand side was a cast iron gate, surrounded by brick work that led into a garden. I slid the latch open and used the apple trees to cloak my visibility, as I tried to find any sort of conspicuous entrance to the house.

I took a breath and went to my pocket to check my phone; no reception and only thirty-seven percent battery. It seemed that I was on my own out here.

It was remarkable how fifteen minutes from the motorway, in the heartlands of Southern England, we were in the middle of nowhere, a world away from the rest of civilisation.

I ventured forwards and noticed an open door at the back of the house. It was only slightly ajar and creaked somewhat as I pushed it further open and headed inside, into a kitchen area.

There were muffled voices so I edged further forward, crouching behind the cabinets that guarded my view. I peeked around the side and could see a pair of white double doors leading into a large reception room.

The right hand door was open and there were three figures in the room. I needed to get to the wall of the reception room, but realised I wouldn't be able to without becoming visible through the double doors, if only briefly.

I sat quietly and tried to hear the voices from afar but it was futile. The backdoor creaked making my heart pound to the sound of birds tweeting in the idyllic Surrey heartland.

I waited a moment then crawled slowly past the open door, where Lucia's barely conscious body sat slumped on a cream chaise-longue. I paused as one of the men in the room paced slowly; the other had his back to me watching the girl.

I continued crawling and saw that the man pacing was Paul Smith and the other was Tutton. As quietly as possible, I leant against the wall and was now mercifully out of view. The men whispered but were audible.

'But Glenn, she's barely bloody conscious!' Smith said.

'I know; she didn't want to go. I had to do something… '

'This isn't the deal, you know that! How can we take her upstairs, if she is hardly awake?'

Lucia murmured something incomprehensible.

'The salts are in the car; shall I get them?'

'And then what? How will she react if she comes to?'

'I don't know. She did sign up to this. Mia promised she knew what she was getting into,' Tutton pleaded with his boss.

There was a pause.

'Get the salts then. Be quick!'

Tutton scurried in the opposite direction, while Smith's footsteps against the wood floor grew closer. My heart pounded as I tried to push my back further against the wall, as if to make myself invisible.

The door crashed open and Smith stormed past me into the kitchen. In the thunderous anger of his actions he didn't notice my cowering frame as he strode past.

He had his back to me as he turned on the water tap and grabbed a glass. The noise of the falling water hitting the sink gave me time to move against the opposite wall and out of his view.

He placed the glass down and stormed back into the reception room, slamming the door as he went. The closed door gave me more cover and if I listened carefully, I could still make out what was being said.

'What? Where am I?'

'Lucia, you remember us, don't you?' Smith spoke.

'Yes, but what happened? I don't remember, are we at the house?'

'Yeah, you're here now. I think maybe Glenn was too… generous with the spray and you fell asleep,' he chuckled.

Silence.

'Do you remember, what we agreed, Lucia?' Tutton eventually asked.

Silence.

'Because our friend will be here soon and I think it's time to go upstairs and get ready...'

'OK, but I have such a headache… ' Lucia slurred.

'That's OK. Glenn can get you something for that, don't worry. Go with him now and he will make you feel… comfortable. There's a little time.'

'But, I… I'm not sure that… ' Lucia trailed off.

Smith's voice became clearer and assertive. 'Go upstairs with Glenn now, Lucia.'

There was a murmuring and the sound of bodies moving, before the sound of heels on the wooden floor, followed by voices and then silence.

31

I waited a couple of minutes, before poking my head around and looking through the double doors. It appeared empty, so I quietly pulled the handle and entered the room.

However, there were floor-length windows on either side. To my left the rest of the garden was vast and empty and to my right the front of the house and Tutton's parked car.

I checked to see that there was no-one outside and then moved swiftly to the other side of the room. Through the doors was a wide hallway and carpeted red stairs to the left.

There were three other doors leading from the hall, but they were shut as was the front door to my right.

I started making my way slowly up the stairs. As I crept quietly, trying to work out the upstairs layout, I was jolted by the sound of a car pulling into the front driveway.

The car stopped and there was the sound of jangling keys and slamming doors. If the front door opened now, I would be in full view, I had to do something.

I scampered to the top of the stairs and put my ear against the first door along the hallway. Nothing. Downstairs, the front door had opened and the sound of two men's voices laughing and joking wafted through the house.

I turned the handle of the door quietly and entered, shutting the door behind me. Mercifully, the room was empty.

Feet softly padded up the stairs and past my room. I heard a door open further down the corridor.

'Ready?' the voice said. I was certain it was Smith.

'Five minutes,' a female voice returned.

I heard the door close and two male voices, as they walked past me and back down the stairs.

I had to move quickly. Every sound was amplified, the door handle creaked open and I made my way further up the corridor to the next room. Again, I listened in and heard nothing but silence.

I opened the door swiftly to an empty bedroom. There was a four poster bed and something caught my eye just to the back of it. It was an old-fashioned safe.

I looked closer at the lock which took an Abloy key; impossible to pick. They were very rare in England, but they were highly reliable locks; often used in Scandinavia. I had only ever encountered one in my whole time on the force. I went to look more closely at the safe and pulled the handle. Unsurprisingly, it was locked.

I shut the bedroom door quietly and moved further along the corridor and around the corner to the final room upstairs, opening the door and creeping inside.

In front of me on a four poster bed, Lucia sat bolt upright. Her eyes widened, there was a sharp intake of breath and I knew she was going to scream.

I rushed towards her and covered her mouth just in time. She was shaking, petrified and began to cry.

I soothed her and tried to calm her but her heart was pounding furiously. She was wearing stockings and suspenders and a pink, figure-hugging negligee. It was disturbing seeing a girl, not even a woman, in such forced attire.

Her thick black eye make-up had run down her face and, as her breathing calmed, I removed my hand from her mouth, taking a layer of powdery make up with it too.

Lucia looked at me with her big, blue innocent eyes and whispered, 'help me.' Tears streamed down her face.

I reassured her and quietly went to lock the door of the bedroom from the inside. We only had a couple of minutes before Smith would return, but the locked door could buy us a few precious seconds.

She sat on the bed anxiously as I grabbed a bath-robe I found on the back of the en-suite bathroom door. Lucia put it on, tied it tightly while I searched the wardrobes for sheets, finding none.

I quickly stripped the bed that was made with red and white silk sheets. I tied them together, creating a long extension of rope. I went to the window and opened it, throwing the rope down the side.

Footsteps came up the corridor outside, so I pulled Lucia close to me. I reached into my pockets and grabbed my car keys and my phone.

'Run through the woods, my car's on the main road. Go back to Folkestone. *Now.*'

'Wh-what about you?'

'When you get there ring Dave Marsh, his number's saved on this phone, go and see him, straight away.' I said, bustling her towards the open window.

There was a knock on the door and the handle slowly turned.

'He lives at 44 Sea View, go straight to him…'

'Why don't you come with?' she pleaded.

The locked door rattled behind us, Lucia improvised and in her sweetest voice said, 'one minute, just give me one minute.'

She climbed onto the makeshift rope of sheets as the door continued to rattle louder and louder behind me.

'Quick, Lucia!' I said. She looked up terrified and mouthed the words 'thank you.'

'Hurry!' I watched her hit the ground with a thud and sprint off in the direction of the woods. I ran to the door of the bedroom and held my body weight against it.

The voices outside were confused and angry now and the door was being forcibly opened. I pressed my weight against it.

I checked out of the window and she was long gone. The house wasn't far from the main road and every second I distracted the men, the closer she was to the safety of the car.

The door was beginning to give and then there was silence. I was worried they might have seen her running away, so I sprinted for the window and threw myself over the ledge, hanging off the side.

I jumped and tried to grab the ledge of the window, missing it and crunching into the ground.

The door of the bedroom crashed open so I tried to sprint as fast as I could for the main road. My legs were heavy though, the fall had done some serious damage.

I made it into the wooded area and safety was near. I could hear a car in the distance over-revving, just as voices surrounded me. I tried to turn, but before I could, I felt a thump on the back of my head and the sunshine of the summer day faded to black.

32

Our old house in Bexleyheath was just that, an old house. It was on a beautiful wide road, more like an American boulevard than an English, suburban thoroughfare.

Dad and Mum had left our home to rack and ruin. Not that my Mother didn't want to keep up with the Joneses, but my Dad had other… interests.

I am eight years old now, running around the house, a bored kid in north Kent. I am pestering people. If I wasn't outside, playing football on my own, I was indoors nagging my Dad to come and play with me.

He wasn't in the mood. But then again he hardly ever was.

I would ask and ask, but to no avail. He just sat in his chair, chain-smoking fags and reading his paper.

Eventually, he would put the paper down.

'Son, go into my jacket pocket and get the wine gums.'

I scamper, a diligent lad at the behest of his father's whims. I remember his big, blue shapeless overcoat, South-East London - market cheap, plastics and padding.

I rifle through the pockets, dirty hankies, fisherman's friends, lighters,

a cardboard packet, which I pull out. It's red and I don't know what it is.

Mum is cooking a meal in the kitchen.

'Mum what are these?'

She turns and looks. Then she drops the plate she is using and crumples into a heap on the white and red peeling laminate floor.

The dream leaves me clammy and hot. I wake on a cold, stone floor in the centre of a dark cell.

There is tape around my mouth and my arms and feet are bound.

I panic and start shouting, writhing and retching. My head pounds. Then I remember, Lucia and the manor house. God, I hope she's safe.

I knew I was slow and would have been seen heading towards the woods. I must have been caught and hit by one of Smith's henchmen.

The cell was dark with a small window at the top bringing the occasional crack of light. I imagined I could slip through it if I could only get free from my bindings.

I must be under the house I thought. If I can get free, I can find a way out.

The door to my cell clanked open and Smith stepped in with two other men in suits, so I closed my eyes pretending to be asleep.

'When will he come to?' a voice said.

'Anytime soon,' Smith said.

There was a sigh from one of the men. 'Kill him now, while he's out.'

'He's a police officer,' Smith stated.

'… a suspended police officer, in our man's nick. It's not worth the risk, especially after the Green girl. Get Tutton in and be done with him.'

I allowed my eyes to open into slits and watched the two men leave and close the door behind them. Smith remained.

He moved towards me quickly and planted his shoe firmly in my gut.

'Wake up, Stone. I know you're not asleep.'

I breathed heavily and opened my eyes.

'Couldn't help yourself, could you Charlie? Had to be the bloody hero, yeah? How did you find us? Eh?' He kicked me again, this time under my ribs, winding me in the process.

He knelt down and took the tape from my mouth and sat me up against the wall. I regained my breath.

'How did you find us?' he repeated. 'And Charlie, don't try and do the right thing here. You don't want to be responsible for another girl's death do you?'

I looked up at him confused.

He laughed, 'that's right, Lucia's dead. We caught her in the woods and brought her back here. A few of our… 'associates' gave her quite the send-off.'

'You're a liar, Paul. I heard her get away. I heard the car… '

'… You heard *a* car, Charlie. She's dead now and it's thanks to you. That's not going to go down too well with Tara now, is it? How did you find us?'

'Go fuck yourself, Paul.'

'Quite the brave man, eh? It would be horrible if anything were to happen to dear Tara while you're here. She gets on well with your daughter doesn't she? Maddie isn't it?'

I shouted with rage, writhing, trying to get free and tear Paul Smith's head off.

'Relax, Charlie. But you need to start talking.'

I calmed down and tried to think logically. I didn't want to implicate anyone, but also couldn't risk any more lives.

'It was luck. I saw Tutton's car outside the Freemasons' Hall a few nights ago.'

'How did you know it was Glenn's car?' he returned, holding my gaze.

'I… I followed him. Intel from my old boss…' my lie was totally unconvincing.

'Glenn!' Smith shouted, 'bring her in!'

There was struggling and the sound of a whimpering girl outside the door. Smith opened the door and Tutton threw in Mina Burrows; Amy Green's best friend.

She was in a black corset and suspenders, bound by her arms and taped around the legs and mouth. Her pale, youthful skin was covered in bruises and grazes. Her black, greasy hair hanging over her face.

'It was her wasn't it? She led you to us?' Smith asked.

She looked up from the floor for the first time and directly at me. She whimpered repeatedly.

'It's OK, Charlie. I'll save you the guilt of this one. You're already responsible for one girl's death today,' he said, nodding at Glenn.

Tutton looked nervously at his boss, before pulling a small blade from his belt and grabbing Mina's hair and pulling up her head.

'Please don't... please... I... ' she pleaded, her voice cracking as she spoke.

'Don't do it! I'll tell you whatever you want to hear, *don't do it!*' I bellowed.

Tutton paused and looked once more at his boss, who nodded and turned away from the helpless girl.

She stared at me, pupils dilated as Tutton sliced her throat from ear to ear. The crying ceased and her body flopped limp and lifeless into a pool of dark blood. Tutton wiped his knife on a white handkerchief from his pocket. Smith turned back around and looked directly at me.

I hung my head and sobbed. I prayed now that the same fate might befall me, as the guilt felt worse than my murder at this moment.

'You really don't understand what you are involved in, Charlie Stone. This is the tip of the iceberg. Mina's death is a message. Just like Amy Green's was and yours will be. Hopefully no-one else will be stupid enough to get involved again.'

Smith made his way to the door of the cell, but before leaving he spoke.

'...Just something to think about Charlie. You've been responsible for two deaths today, I'm going to spare Maddie, I'm not sure about your squeeze Tara. Glenn, over to you.'

Smith left, slamming the door behind him. I watched helplessly as the blood of Mina Burrows spread towards me and the figure of Glenn Tutton loomed ominously nearer.

33

I sat in Dad's Capri and he told me the news. Mum had kicked him out and my sister was going to uni. A house of four was now a house of two. I didn't even really know my mum. It was always my sister and mum, my dad and me.

I was now fourteen, in an old, spluttering Capri on a rabbit warren estate in Slade Green. My dad was in low spirits. He said he needed to talk to me, to help him. But only three times a week, Tuesday, Thursday and Sundays. The other days he would have 'other' things to do.

He took me to his new flat. We drank vodka and diet coke and Dad told me his woes. Tonight was a sleepover night, so he pulled out the creaky, sofa bed and turned off the light.

I waited in the darkness for half an hour, then slipped out and sat outside my Father's bedroom door. I always checked that he was breathing when he slept. I don't know why; it was a habit I had gotten into.

I came to from my dream and realised the gravity of my situation; I was going to die.

Tutton had moved the body of Mina Burrows to the side of the cell and was standing over me.

'D'you enjoy this, Glenn? Is this the life you wanted?' I croaked desperately.

'I'm going to enjoy this,' he muttered under his breath, before cracking me across the jaw with his fist. Blood rushed into my mouth, which I spat on the cold floor.

'You are just a bitch, Glenn. You do realise this don't you? You can kill me, but you will always be Paul's go to man, a nobody, doing his… '

The punch came harder, this time an uppercut, crunching my jaw together.

'I can see the headlines now, "Tutton the Butcher." They'll have fun with you in prison.'

'Shut up, will you? Shut up!' Tutton picked me up by my armpits and threw me against the wall, the back of my head cracking against the brick work.

The bindings on my arms were slipping now from all the movement. I continued to rub the rope against the brick, desperate for it to catch and break. It was no good though, Tutton pulled out his knife once more and towered over me.

I had made my peace; I knew what was coming. All I could think about were the dead girls. I wept. But I felt at peace and welcomed the oncoming blade. The light in my eyes went white and I saw Maddie's face smiling at me. I saw my father too and he told me, it was OK, I would be all right.

The world seemed to move in slow motion now and the bright, white light was dissipating. I was back in the cell and Tutton had slumped to his knees and was clutching his right leg. He had dropped the knife.

The door was now open and I saw bodies flood in. God knows who it was, but I remember smiling before my sight crystallized and I lost consciousness.

34

'I've something to tell you son and it's not easy to say.'

At his side in the hospital in Sidcup, I would've done anything for him.

'There's someone else besides Claire, another woman... I need you to look after her, she wants to come and see me. Take her number and organise it, so as Claire and your sister don't know,' he said, lying on his deathbed.

'OK, Dad,' I did what he asked out of blind love and duty.

I made the call. I watched Claire and my sister go in and out visiting my father; I waited with his mistress.

At one point, I asked Claire if she wanted to go for a coffee or pint over the road. She said yes.

As I walked away, I turned to the car and nodded.

I heard the door of the car open and watched the girl less than half my father's age, scamper up the stairs and into the hospital.

When I woke, I thought I was in heaven. I never really believed in heaven, nor was convinced that if it did exist, I would end up there. But when I tried to force open my eyes, everything seemed so white and brilliant.

Slowly the figures around me began to gain clarity.

Tara was there, along with Dave and Polly. I hoped this was a dream because if it was real, Tara and Polly in the same room would be terribly awkward and would more closely resemble hell.

If this was a dream though, where was Maddie?

'He's waking up, he's waking up!' I heard voices gather momentum.

'Am I dead?' I asked. The searing pain suggested otherwise as I creaked back into life.

Dave laughed, 'no, you're not, Charlie. You're in the Walter Tull Hospital in Ashford.'

I moved and tried to open my eyes further.

Tara motioned for someone else to come into the room.

'Maddie?' I croaked, Dave passed me a glass of water.

'No. But she's fine, she's with her Mum,' he assured me.

I drank the water and it tasted like nectar. As I guzzled away, I heard a pair of high heels click-clacking slowly into the room. My eyes followed the black, suede boots, up the black leggings, to a grey figure-hugging cardigan.

Her hair was blonde, naturally frizzy and her pretty made up face beamed from ear to ear.

I smiled, 'You're supposed to be dead!' I exclaimed.

She laughed, 'well here I am, thanks to you.'

Lucia came over to the bed and gave me a huge hug, whispering 'thank you' in my ear. She smelt wonderful; of life.

She eventually released my neck and I leaned back into the hard pillows. She beamed at me with tears in her eyes. Those big, beautiful eyes looked happy and confident once more.

'What happened?' I asked, looking up at Dave. 'Did you get them?'

Dave went to the door and shut it firmly.

'We've got Tutton. When we got there, Smith and all the others were gone.' Dave said.

'When *you* got there?'

'When Lucia arrived at my house, she told us the story. There is a lot she needs to fill you in on, Charlie… but maybe not now.'

I looked at Lucia and that youthful confidence was lost briefly as she looked down at the hospital floor.

'So you escaped? In my car?' I asked her.

'Yes. Just like you said, Charlie.'

Dave continued, 'I contacted Polly. There was a drugs link from what Lucia told us. Plus, Polly is the only one of us who can actually make an arrest at the moment!'

I had briefly forgotten about mine and Dave's suspension, but it was beginning to come back to me.

'We headed straight to the Manor House and there was no-one there. Smith had gone and we thought that the house was empty. Polly heard some movement under the floorboards and we found a trapdoor, leading down to an underground corridor of… cells.'

'That's where I was… '

'Yep. There was some pretty sick stuff down there and at the end of the corridor was your cell. We heard your voice through the walls.'

'We thought you were dead, Charlie,' Polly added.

'We got to the cell just in time it seems,' Dave added.

'So Tutton's in custody?'

'Yeah. He's been charged for the murder of Mina Burrows.'

'What about kidnap and drugging?'

'We don't think it's wise, Charlie. Lucia would have to give evidence… we've got enough… '

Dave trailed off.

'OK. One thing Smith said to me was, *'you don't know what you've got yourself into.'* Then he made Tutton kill Mina in front of me.' I said, beginning to feel nauseous.

'It's Smith pulling the strings, Dave. Organising and running the girls through the school…' I responded, but shooting pains in my side, left me short of breath.

'Rest up. Then we'll figure out what we can do. OK?' I looked at the concerned faces around the room.

'Fine,' I said dejectedly.

'Great work though, *Charlie Stone!*' Polly said provocatively, flashing me that wicked smile. Good old Polly, always inappropriate. It was probably for Tara's benefit and not mine anyway. So I was glad she was making for the door.

'Come on, let's give them some time,' Dave cut the tension and led Polly out of the room shutting the door behind him and Lucia.

Tara came and set next to me on the bed.

'Hello handsome,' she said. 'I was worried about you.'

'Yeah?'

'Yes, *very!* And you saved Lucia's life, thank you Charlie,' she said, giving me a hug. I smelt her hair, as the long blonde curls fell around my face and chest. It felt like home.

'It's got to be worth a second date, surely?' I said.

Tara laughed, 'Definitely, *Charlie Stone!*' she said, mocking her love rival, not much got past her.

'Excellent, let's go,' I went to get out of the hospital bed, but it was no use. My legs were heavy and I felt dizzy.

'No, no, no! Not *now!* You need to rest.'

I slumped back in my bed.

'I'd like to speak to Maddie,' I said.

'Ah, that reminds me,' Tara reached into her bag and retrieved my mobile phone, placing it by the bed.

'Yeah, Jo's not very happy. You missed a couple of Skype sessions and stuff, so… maybe… let me talk to her?'

'Right. Does she know I nearly died?'

'I doubt it. You don't need the stress now; I can sort it out for you.'

'Honestly, you don't want to,' I warned her.

'Leave it with me and get some rest. I don't care what she thinks of you, it doesn't interest me. I just want you to be able to talk to your daughter and you don't need the grief of all this now. You just need to get better, Charlie. I have plans for you!'

she said, kissing me on the forehead, before bouncing towards the door.

Perhaps it was time to try something new and actually trust someone for a change.

'OK... ' I said tentatively.

'I'll be back in a couple of hours, see you later!' she said, blowing me a kiss.

As the sunshine of Tara's aura left the room, I immediately felt sadden by Mina Burrow's death. It was a tragedy, that poor young girl. What sort of horrors had she seen and had been forced upon her before her gruesome death?

For now I needed rest, but afterwards, I would make sure justice was served.

35

The call came in the middle of the night.

'I think it's happening, he's not good.' Claire said.

I drove the journey from Carshalton to Sidcup in record time, it took sixteen minutes.

I got to the hospital. By now I knew where ITU was.

Dad was like a husk in his bed. This strong, powerful, passionate man was reduced to skin and bones. He looked like an old man, far older than sixty-two years.

An air supply was thundering oxygen down his throat and his eyes were shut.

The nurses whispered in the corner.

I held Dad's hand which was limp and lifeless. It was no good. The rest became a blur but still I watched the life support machine like I did when I was a fourteen-year-old boy, listening for my Dad's breathing. I couldn't hear him breathe.

His hand always felt like leather but, this time, there was no grip. He always gripped your hand hard. Not anymore.

The machine was running down now. Claire was crying. I think I was crying.

I watched the machine drop to zero and the lines that moved before, were now flat.

I woke suddenly to the feeling that I was being watched. I was covered in sweat; the bed sheets soaked through.

My eyes blinked open and the figure of DCI Pensborough stood at the far end of the hospital room.

He wore a grey suit with a waistcoat and a bright pink shirt. He held his hands behind his back and as I came to, he smiled a big grin and laughed to himself.

'Hello Charlie.'

'What time is it?' I asked, still slightly confused.

'It's ten am on Tuesday the second of August. If you're interested, you've been in hospital now for about twenty-six hours.'

I sat up, sensing a threat from Pensborough, as he unfolded his hands from behind his back and moved slowly towards me.

'Quite the hero, Charlie. The papers are full of it. "Local cop uncovers sex ring." Very… impressive.'

'Thanks, but I'm sensing a slight lack of sincerity in your words, Inspector… '

'Not at all! The public obviously want you reinstated. Despite my efforts, the Bugle did not run with the story that you are in fact a rogue cop acting outside of the law since you were suspended, much to my disappointment.'

He continued to pace the width of the hospital room.

'I still don't like you, Charlie Stone. You've proved my point that you are a maverick, out of control. But you saved this girl's life. Another died, while you were there mind you… ' he mused.

'Well, I did my best. It's kind've difficult to protect people without a gun and a badge, when you're chained to a wall.'

'Here's what we're going to do, Charlie. I'm going to reinstate you when you're better. Once you're fit and well you can resume duties, as was. But...'

'...Let me guess, leave the Green case alone?'

'It's done Charlie. Troy Wood is a confessed killer at Her Majesty's Prison Banstead now. You will forever be the cop that saved the girl, a local hero. I *need* you to let it go now.'

I mulled over his proposition and for the first time since meeting him, I realised I was in a position of ascendancy. Yes, he was my boss, but he knew I got close, close to uncovering something dark, something evil.

'Why do you need me to let it go so much? What's the problem?'

'Charlie…some things have been going on for years that quite honestly will never change. There are people, born into power and money. They run *things*. And it's always been that way. We do our best with what's left, but honestly? No-one can change things at the top for good. And those who have tried, wind up dead. It's that simple. You're a good cop, Charlie, but do you really want to leave Maddie behind? Or that pretty, new girlfriend of yours?'

'How do you know about her?' I said defensively.

He laughed again, 'relax Charlie. She's out in the corridor, waiting for me to leave. I merely said hello to her.'

'What about Dave Marsh?'

'DCI Marsh has been relieved of his duties. Fear not though, he's on full pension, significant pay-off.'

'What? He wouldn't have wanted that!'

'Well, it is the way it was wanted. He has signed a compromise agreement to keep quiet about these recent… events.'

'And you're to continue, right?'

'That's the plan.'

'I see.'

'Listen Charlie, this is getting tiresome. You can come back and fight crime as you *so* desire to do, lawfully, whilst getting paid. Just how it was. No, your big mate Dave, won't be around, but you're a big boy and I'm sure you can handle it. But you *must* leave this case alone!'

'And if I don't?'

'You will be gone. No severance, no pension, nothing.'

I paused for a moment. 'And what about Tutton?'

'He will stand trial for the murder of Mina Burrows.'

I thought of all the other girls he may or may not have drugged, kidnapped, maybe even raped. I thought of all the lives he would have affected, a surge of rage powered through me.

'Let me talk to him and we have a deal.'

'No chance.'

'Well then no deal. I just want ten minutes, come with me if you want. If not, no deal. I'll tell the Press exactly what I saw and what happened to me. It could make an even bigger mess than you might want.'

Pensborough mulled it over.

'Ten minutes Charlie and I'm in the room with you, but do I have your word, you leave this case alone now?'

'OK, Skip. We have a deal.' Whether I liked it or not, I was getting better at telling white lies.

36

The nurses wanted me to stay in for a further few nights but I did a quick appraisal of my injuries and decided to check myself out.

I'm not sure anyone particularly likes hospitals, but since the death of my father, I hated them. I was convinced they could make you worse.

Two of my ribs were cracked, they would heal in time. The rest were cuts and grazes that were mostly on the way to healing.

I collected my wallet, keys and phone then headed for the door.

Despite my distaste for hospitals, it gave me time to mull things over as I drifted in and out of consciousness. I dreamt of Maddie and Tara, I think sometimes they might have been there but I couldn't be sure.

I thought of everything that had happened and despite my new found 'hero' status, I felt disgusted about Mina. I felt guilty that she died and I couldn't get it out of my head. Some hero.

I made a lot of sense out of what had happened. This was a sex ring, but nothing I had seen before. What struck me were the profiles of the girls. Young, white, English.

Having worked to lock up drug dealers, pimps and murderers, this group and their 'tastes,' were something I'd never seen before.

I thought about Amy and how she died; her naked body, when I found her, did not look too dissimilar to Mina's when she died.

That's why I needed to see Tutton and look into his eyes to help with the answers. I also needed to find the missing pages of Amy Green's diary.

I went home and was anxious to start on the case. If Pensborough thought I was letting this go, he knew less about me than he claimed. I knew I had only touched the surface.

If I lost my job so be it. Recent events had given me a little more perspective.

I checked out Mina's profile on Facebook. Sifting through her pictures posthumously made me feel sick, but it was necessary, unfortunately.

I was fairly confident that I had found the group of boys Mina and Amy were hanging around with at the time of Amy's death.

My phone was charging in the next room, so I got up to grab it and had four new messages. Not now, I thought as I typed in Jennifer's number.

'Hello?'

'Hello, Jennifer it's Detective Sergeant Stone. How are you?'

'Oh, hello. I am better since… since… the trial.'

'Yes, Jennifer. It must give you a great deal of closure,' I thought it best not to tell her that I didn't believe the convicted man was not the killer of her only daughter, not just yet anyway.

'It does. I know you had your doubts sergeant, but there was something about that man that gave me the creeps. I know that he was the killer.'

'Yes, Jennifer, I do now believe you are right...'

'And thank you for everything you've done, we've read the papers and…'

'Thank you Jennifer, that's very kind.' Now was not the time for platitudes. 'I was wondering if you knew of any boys that were dating Amy at the time of her death?'

'W-Why? I thought the… '

'… It's just he might have been involved in other crimes. Y'know just a few loose ends we need to follow up.'

'I see. Well like I said to you before, she didn't have any boyfriends as such… '

'I know Jennifer, but any boys whose names came up?'

'Well there was one boy who went to the Hemingway Academy. He was the only boy who ever came to the house. I think my husband scared him so much, he never came back!' she laughed to herself, reminiscing about happier times.

'Can you remember his name?'

She paused, 'I think he was… a… Harry?'

'Harry Wise?' I asked.

'Yes, that's him. Harry Wise.'

I looked down my lists of potential suspects and found the name halfway down the list.

37

It was a Tuesday night in the school summer holidays. What would Harry Wise be doing? My guess was playing PlayStation with his pals or drinking at a house party.

I went to his home on Dring Road and knocked on the door.

A middle-aged man answered. He had a short, grey beard and a smiling, affable face.

'Can I help you?' he asked.

I flashed my badge, 'Hi, does Harry live here?'

'Is he in trouble?'

'No, not at all. I just need to ask him a few questions. Are you his father?'

'Yes. What's he done now?' his affable demeanour faded.

'Honestly, nothing. He might have witnessed a crime and I need to speak with him. Is he in?'

His father sighed. 'No, he's at his friend Bill's house. Lower Seagate Road.'

I checked my note pad, 'Bill *Durham?*'

'That's him.'

'Thanks very much, Mr Wise,' I said before getting back into the car.

Bill Durham lived along the Leas in the West End of Folkestone. The old, Victorian houses had now mostly been converted into flats, yet this was an expensive part of town to live, especially for a young man like Bill Durham.

I found the number and pressed the doorbell. It was a flat block that had an outside door which would need to be opened manually. I waited and then rung again.

A sash window slid open at the side of the building and out popped a curly mop of brown hair.

'Can I help you?' a deep, plummy, English accent asked.

'Are you Bill Durham?'

'Yeah, who's asking?'

'Sergeant Stone, Folkestone Police. I'm looking for Harry Wise.'

In the background I could hear loud house music, it sounded like a party, or at least gathering.

'I'm afraid he's not here.'

'Can you let me up please?'

'I told you, he's not here!'

'Do you know where I might find him?'

'No idea, sorry. Actually, now I think about it, he might be at the gym. You know Balladown's Gym? He's normally there in the evenings.'

'OK, thanks for that.'

I walked away from the ornate, yellowing building. The light was fading in the old town as dusk settled, bringing with it a purple melange of colours.

I waited for the sash window to close before turning around and heading back to the flat block.

Bill was lying. His story about Balladown's may have been true some days, but as an afterthought? No. Also, if Bill Durham was having a party, my guess is, his good mate Harry Wise would be there.

The door was old and oak framed with a moderate Yale lock on it. I had learned once to pick a lock such as this, but it wasn't easy and I didn't have the correct tools with me.

I jogged to the back of the building where there was an overgrown garden and a back door. The door was wide open, presumably due to the warm weather. I headed in and went up the stairs.

The music was constant. A thundering house beat was all you could hear from outside. It wasn't deafening, but louder than it should be. I rapped the door hard and took my black leather gloves from my pocket.

Bill opened the door on the latch.

'I told you, he's not here!'

As Bill went to close the door, I barged it open breaking the latch and knocking him off his feet. As he stared up in disbelief, I offered him a hand.

'You're lying, son, and this is a police investigation. It's in your interests to tell me the truth.'

Bill looked very flustered.

'And turn that bloody racket down!' I said, as the endless thumping of computerised drums finally fell silent.

I scanned the room. It was grand and old with whitewashed walls, sash windows and wood laminate flooring; not dissimilar to mine. I wondered how this young man who'd barely finished school could afford it.

Squeezed into a two-seater sofa, sat three teenagers, two boys and a girl. They looked forlornly at me. One of the boys was desperately trying to hide cannabis paraphernalia.

'Don't worry. That's not what I'm here for,' I said.

None of the people in the room matched Harry's description.

'Where is he?' I concentrated my efforts on Bill once more.

'I… I told you… '

'… Stop lying to me and tell me where he is!'

'He's in the bedroom!' The girl on the sofa shouted, much to Bill's disapproval.

'I'm going to call my father and have him come here. You can't just break in; do you have a search warrant?' Bill said.

'This isn't the movies, kid. And we are investigating a murder. Maybe multiple murders, do you understand?' The young man became decidedly pale and was lost for words.

'If you keep your mouth shut and let me speak to Harry, then maybe I won't let your father know about the drugs and booze that I found here, OK?'

The young man stopped talking and stared out of the window defeated.

I made my way into the bedroom. As I did there was a flurry of white sheets and a blonde-haired boy poked his head out.

'Are you all right mate?' he asked. A teenage girl also raised her head from under the covers. She took a deep gasp and returned back under.

'Harry, get dressed. We need to have a chat.'

38

I didn't really like to use force, so I softened my approach when Harry emerged, ruffled and dishevelled, from the bedroom. His defences were up understandably, so I took him for a walk along the Leas to calm his nerves.

'Harry, you know Amy Green, right?'

He looked at me with a deep fear in his eyes. I felt my pockets, I knew I had a packet of cigarettes in there somewhere. I offered him one, which he took gratefully.

'You're not in trouble, Harry. I just want some more information, not everything seems… right about her death, y'know?'

He took a drag and looked out across the sea, 'you're a brave man snooping around in this.'

'Why?'

He looked at me, 'no reason, sergeant. It's just…' he pointed out towards the Channel. 'A lot of water out there. From what I hear, a lot of problems, get dropped in that water.'

He put his cigarette out and I gave him another.

'Was your friend Amy one of those "problems?"'

'She wasn't really a "friend". I only met her a couple of times.'

'Tell me what you know.'

'I met her through Mina. They were best friends and like, complete opposites. Mina was a party girl, always out, really extroverted y'know, but Amy was… quiet.'

'Go on.'

'Well, Amy never came to the parties, really. I hardly knew her. The thing about Folkestone, everyone knows everyone.

Same circles, same people. Amy was…off the radar, she was different to the other girls.'

'She was *sweet?*' I said, searching for the right adjective and failing. Harry looked at me and laughed.

'Something like that! Maybe, innocent is more accurate.'

'The reason I say that, is because she had a diary. A secret one.'

Harry's face dropped.

'It doesn't say anything about *you*, Harry,' his face changed and he relaxed once more. 'But it does concern me why you're so… worried?'

'Are we off record here?'

'Of course, Harry. As far as I'm concerned, we never met. And if your pals can keep it quiet, I think that's better for all of us.'

He sighed, 'people know me, know our group. It's just little things, we can find things for people, y'know?'

'Drugs and so on?'

'Yeah, only weed and stuff, nothing major. But, my dad wants me to go to one of the Red Bricks. If he found out…'

'… I understand, don't worry. He won't. But you do need to cut that stuff out,' I turned Father figure for a moment.

'I know and I will when term starts, it's the summer and old habits die hard. You stop trying to take drugs and you get dealers cold calling you. You try and stop dealing and people are always asking.'

I felt for him, he genuinely sounded like he wanted a way out.

'What about Mina, is there anything else you knew about her?'

'She had the same problems I do. She was caught up in a lot of stuff. Once you're in, it's difficult to get out.'

'Like what?'

'Drugs, sex. Not just us either, she had bigger things going on but she kept that very, very quiet. I don't really know anything I-'

'Don't panic, it's OK. I kind've have an idea what she was doing and who was behind it.'

'It's strange. Mina was never like that when she was younger. She used to come and play in my garden. She was quiet too. Her Mum and I were friends. It was only in the last couple of years or so, things changed. She became louder, more boisterous. I think it was more of a front, or a cry for help, or something.'

Perhaps he was right. Everyone had their own way of protesting. Perhaps Amy stayed quiet and suffered alone and Mina's effrontery was her cry for help.

It was cooling now on the Leas and I wanted Harry to get back to his friends and cool *them* off. They would be panicking.

'Harry, some pages have been taken from Amy's diary around the time of her death. Do you know who might have them?'

'I told you, I only like dated her twice… '

'Did you go to her house?'

'He looked at me and sighed. 'Yes once. She brought me home for dinner, but I'm not sure I really… fitted in.'

'What do you mean?'

'What I mean is, if you're looking for the missing pages to her diary, my guess is that you should start with Amy's dad. That guy is weird. Now, I've told you what I know, I want to go back now.'

Before Harry went, I shook his hand and told him to stay out of trouble. It was beautiful, if for only a moment, we could talk like adults, honestly. In a minute, he would be back in his druggy haze showing off to his pals.

Still, Harry's honesty made me happy and he had given me another lead, back to the Green's house, where all of this started.

39

Night was falling and the hour for social visits was swiftly passing. However, time was not on my side. I was a fool to think Pensborough would not have his spies out watching me.

If I wanted the truth to unfold, I had to work quickly.

I walked around to Twyford Gardens which was only a few hundred yards away.

I could see the warm glow of artificial lighting through the curtains and decided to knock on the door.

Alex answered, 'Sergeant Stone, how can I help you?'

He seemed calm and relaxed.

'I know it's late, but I was in the area and wanted to ask a few questions if possible?'

'Really?'

'I'm just following up a few loose ends with Amy's case.'

'Well I'm not sure there is much more to say, but… ' he clearly didn't want to have this conversation on the doorstep, so I was ushered in.

Alex went to the kitchen door and shut the sound of activity inside, before taking me into the front room. I followed him in.

'How can I help you?' he asked, offering me a seat.

'I was wondering whether you can tell me what you know about Harry Wise?'

'Harry came around once. He was a no good sort, lazy, moneyed. I wanted more for Amy.'

'What do you mean?'

'Well I thought Amy could certainly do better than that… type of boy… '

'But he is a bright boy, going to a top university… '

'… He'll waste his talent, like they *all* do. Drugs and partying. Amy wasn't like that and I didn't want her to… go down that road.'

'I see. Sounds like you and Amy had quite a close relationship?'

'Sergeant Stone, as far as I am aware, Amy's case is closed. Her murderer has been tried and sentenced. So what my relationship with Amy was like is of little importance now.'

'You see, I think it is, because some things don't add up...'

'Has DCI Pensborough not closed Amy's case, sergeant?'

'Yes.'

'And how would he feel to find out you've been here again?'

'Well, that's not really...'

'He wouldn't be happy would he?'

I smiled at him, 'no of course he wouldn't.'

'Anything else then?' he smiled back.

'Amy's diary. We found it locked in her room but there were a few pages missing. You wouldn't know where they might be?'

'Yes, I heard you found that. Very distressing for Jennifer that day. And no, I have no idea. I presume Amy ripped them out. Probably some embarrassing date with a boy, or an argument with Mina or something.'

'You said she didn't have boyfriends?'

Alex paused, 'I think you should go now.'

He ushered me out of the front door and after some empty courtesies, I was gone.

Back at the flat, I checked the text messages I had earlier. One was from Tara:

I spoke to Jo, she said you can Skype Maddie tonight xx.

I checked the time and it was coming up for eight o' clock. If I was quick, I could reach her before she went to bed.

I grabbed the laptop, cursing how long it took to fire up. As it did, I grabbed a glass of water and then turned on Skype.

It took an age to ring, but eventually she answered.

'Hello Daddy!'

'Hello honey, how are you?'

'Good, Dad, I haven't spoken to you in ages. We're supposed to talk every Tuesday and Thursday!' I was being told off, but I was so glad to speak with her, I didn't really care.

'Let's make sure we keep to those times from now on, OK?'

'Yes, Daddy. I have lots to show you.'

Maddie ran me through bits of writing she was completing and arts and crafts pieces she'd done. After fifteen minutes we decided to say goodbye and I promised that we would see each other soon.

I couldn't promise much more, as I didn't know what was going through Jo's head. It was only thanks to Tara that I was able to speak with her that evening.

I texted Tara to say thank you and she immediately responded.

It's OK. Are you at home? Xx

Yes, are you around? X.

By the time I had had a quick tidy, the doorbell rang.

Tara was wearing her thigh-length grey boots and a tight black dress. She never wore a lot of make-up; she didn't really need to.

'Hi, I thought you might want some company?' she said.

'Sure, come in and have a seat,' she sat on the sofa and crossed her legs. I went to the kitchen and opened a bottle of white wine, pouring two glasses.

I came in and placed the drinks down.

'Thank you for speaking to Jo. What on earth did you say?' I asked.

'It's a woman thing, Charlie, don't worry. She's just protective of her daughter. She doesn't understand what you've been through recently.'

'Will Maddie be coming down next week?' I asked. Tara nodded and I grinned so hard, I couldn't stop. Tara smiled too.

'Thank you,' I said again, trying to hold back the tears. I couldn't really believe how kind she was being to me. I'd forgotten what it felt like.

She moved forward and kissed me. She lingered somewhat and I suddenly felt a surge of lust I had been suppressing for quite some time.

Luckily as I moved towards her, it became clear she shared the same passion.

I put my hands on her smooth long leg and slowly up her thigh. She kissed me harder and began unbuttoning my shirt.

Eventually she pulled away, took my hands and led me towards the bedroom.

40

We made love twice. She was a gentle lover and far more sensitive than I'd expected. Her slender, lithe frame navigated my body with curiosity and an effortless grace.

Afterwards we sat in bed nervously. Sex can be free and easy, if your feelings don't run too deeply. But I think we were both falling for one another and didn't want to make any mistakes.

I offered her a drink which she declined. I asked her if she was going to stay, she wasn't sure.

While Tara was in the bathroom, my phone rang. It was quarter to eleven at night.

'Hello, Sergeant Stone? It's Jenny Green.'

'Hi, what's the matter?'

'It's my husband. Something's up, can you come over?' she sounded panicky.

The loo flushed in the next room. I didn't want Tara to leave but I was sure she'd understand.

'I'll be there in ten minutes.'

Tara came tentatively out of the bathroom.

'Hi, I just got a call from Jennifer. She needs me to go over there now. Walk you home?' I said.

'Oh, I see…'

'It's just that it could be something very important about Amy's death… '

'Sure, no problem. I'll get changed.'

I made further apologies while she dressed. The relationship with Tara had blossomed fairly quickly and I didn't want to upset her.

I walked her back to her parents' home on Terriwell Road. She said I didn't have to, but I insisted.

I kissed her good night.

'Call me tomorrow, OK?' she said.

'OK.'

I watched her hips sway easily up her drive as she turned back to me and smiled. I knew I was a very lucky man.

For the second time that evening, I walked up the Green's driveway. This time Jennifer opened the door before I had time to knock.

'Sergeant, I… oh… goodness…' she started, there were tears on her face.

'Where is your husband?'

'Out. Where he always is this time on a Saturday night.'

'Do you know where?'

'No, he never tells me. That's why I wanted to see you. I heard you two talking earlier today. He is hiding something, I'm sure.'

'Like what?'

'I think he knew about the diary. A few times I saw him in Amy's room when she was at school. He always said he was tidying or returning a CD he'd borrowed, but I knew he was lying.

'Every Saturday he goes out at about this time and comes home around four in the morning. What married man *does* that?' she sniffled into her sleeve.

It seemed like a minor epiphany for her. The power of denial is remarkable in the human psyche, she seemed to be realising some frightening truth.

'Do you think your husband might have those missing pages from the diary?'

She nodded at me.

'Do you know where?'

'Follow me.'

Jennifer took me to her husband's study. It was mostly regular, with a banker's lamp on the desk and paperwork littering the dark oak table top.

I thumbed the papers but they were legitimate, mostly headed letters from the banking company he worked for.

The drawers of his desk were unlocked and I looked up to Jennifer. She gave me a nod and motioned to me to continue. There were pens and pencils, post-its but nothing incriminating.

I looked around the room for a safe, but the room was lined with glass cabinets filled with framed photographs and sports trophies. I recognised a number of the politicians in the pictures. In most, they were shaking hands at some party, sharing drinks. I scanned the cupboards, testing to see if they were unlocked. All of them were, except one of the sport's trophy cabinets.

'Any reason why this one's locked?' I pulled at the hinges.

'Wait! Don't break it! He'll know… ' she replied.

'Do you know where the key might be for this one then, Jennifer? Seems strange that all the cabinets are unlocked bar this one.'

Jennifer seemed agitated, shuffling from one foot to another.

I stared at her. 'Jennifer?'

She looked away and scratched her head. 'Try the third drawer in his desk.'

I looked at her and she pointed down to the drawer. This time, I took out the contents, spreading it across the floor. There were folders and A4 envelopes. Old documents that seemed innocuous. I ran my hands over the documents to spread them out and in between my fingers, I felt the cold, smooth metal of keys. I grabbed them and went to the cupboard. The lock, although being old and a bit stiff opened easily. I began lifting out the trophies one by one, but there was nothing there.

Behind them though sat a smaller cup that appeared to be hidden behind the rest.

As I lifted the cup out of the cupboard, something fell out and onto the floor. I knelt to pick it up and found a long black key. An Abloy key.

'I think I know what lock this key fits,' I told Jennifer. If I was right, this would mean Alex had a hand in what was going on at the Manor House in Godalming.

I knew he might even know more than he was letting on about his own daughter's death.

41

I went home and slept soundly until the light streamed through the blinds and woke me.

Jennifer let me take the key, which was great, but posed a number of problems. If the key opened the safe in the Manor House, it would be coveted by Alex. I didn't have long before he knew the key was gone and when he found that out, there could be severe repercussions.

Jennifer had placed everything back as carefully as possible, but still, I needed to work quickly.

The second problem was how to get into the Manor House. I could go myself but that was going to be difficult. Smith would have his operations tightly monitored after Tutton was arrested and of all the people he would not want to see, I was guessing I would be high on the list.

I had to talk to Tutton, even more so since the boys at the station said he hadn't uttered a word since his arrest. He had been in custody for four days.

I went to see Dave first though.

When I arrived, the garage door clanked open and Dave was in there, a cup of coffee steaming next to him.

He offered me one, but I politely declined.

I brought him up to speed, but most importantly, about the safe and the key.

'You need to find out what is in that safe, Charlie,' he asserted.

'I know, but how will I get into one of the bedrooms at the house?'

Dave took a sip of the dark, brown liquid. He put the cup down, picked up a cloth and wiped his Mustang's bonnet. He really did love that car.

'How are things with Tara?' he asked.

'She's amazing. Sorted things with Jo for me, she's a real angel,' I gabbled, the words coming out before my brain had time to censor them. I felt slightly embarrassed.

'Good. She's good for you. Look after her,' I marked Dave's words as he looked wistfully into the distance.

'You need someone who is going to get in under the radar. Not Tara. Anyway she works at the school with Smith, so he would recognise her. We need someone with the skill to handle it, but with the... *assets* to get in.'

'We can't risk it, Dave. Think of what happened to Mina. What could've happened to Lucia! We can't send a civilian.'

'Not a civilian,' he waited for the penny to drop.

'Polly?'

Dave nodded.

'It's too dangerous!'

'It's less so for an officer, who also has a vested interest in the case.'

I mulled over his proposition.

'She came with me last time, not only does she care about you, but there is the link to these drugs they're using on the girls. Lucia said something about a spray?'

'Yeah, she was definitely given it. MDMA, it's to keep the girls happy... pliable... I guess.' My skin crawled at the thought.

'So we're covered, professionally and personally. I know it's risky, Charlie, but if you want to solve the case, she's your best bet.'

'I guess I'd better make a phone call then,' I reached into my pocket.

Polly agreed to meet us at Dave's and hear me out. I felt a bit strange and guarded talking to her. I was now in a new relationship and I didn't know how Polly felt; she never made it clear.

The reality was that she had finished things with me that morning a couple of weeks back and wanted a break. But what does a *break* mean to her?

During that time, I'd met Tara.

Either way, if Polly was harbouring amorous feelings towards me, she was hiding it well. She stuck to brief, one word answers and spoke mostly to Dave as he explained how we would infiltrate the Manor House.

'I've been intercepting and tracing some of the phone calls in and out of Smith's home in Serafin Heights, Seagate. It used to be Glenn Tutton who organised the girls for Smith's clients, but now it's a female called Anna Gibson.'

'Where have I heard that name before?'

'She's the manager of the garden centre on Edgar Road.'

I remembered now, when I went in to speak to the two girls about Amy, her name was written on the chalk board. 'For any enquiries speak to Anna Gibson.'

'There is something about the garden centre that's not right, I think some of the girls work there. I think for now, our priority has to be getting that safe open.' Dave was back at work again, his reading glasses on, streaming through information on his old computer screen.

Polly sighed, 'I can see where this is going, Dave. You want me to pose as one of the girls, right?'

Dave and I looked at each other.

'I think it's the only way. Charlie and I can try and break in, but Charlie was lucky last time and look what happened. They won't leave the compound so insecure, this time around.'

'But, not being funny Dave, how will Polly get in and is she not a little…' If she was upset with me already, I might as well make doubly sure.

She cast a glance my way, 'I know what he means. The profile of all the girls is young teens. I'm twenty-eight.'

'True. But all the other girls so far have been English and from Folkestone, like you. It's the best plan we have,' Dave said.

A silence hung in the air for what seemed like an age. I felt awful and I knew Dave would, asking Polly to do this. I also knew she didn't do things if she didn't want to.

'How do I get in contact with this *Anna Gibson?*' Polly asked, arms folded.

'I have her number here. Basically, she calls Smith with the details of any new girls she has, but I don't know how the girls are...selected, so to speak.'

It was tricky. If Polly cold-called her, we could blow the whole case. An organisation like this would be watertight.

'We need a backstory, a recommendation from one of Smith's clients or something,' I said.

'I'm not a bloody whore, Charlie!' Polly shouted.

I looked at her sensing her frustration. 'You don't need to do this, Polly; we can find another way,' I reassured her.

'I can hardly tell you to solve the case, then let you down at the last minute, can I?' she smiled at me, warming for the first time.

'This isn't a joke, Pol. These people are really dangerous,' I said softly.

'I know. But I want to get these bastards just as much as you two, so I'm willing to do what it takes.' There was a steely resolve to her words. I sighed with relief.

'What about Tutton?' Dave asked.

Polly and I looked at each other bemused.

'Why can't Tutton give the recommendation?' Dave grew excited.

'He's nicked, pending trial! That's why!' Polly said.

'Exactly. It can't be verified. How can Smith check it out, if Tutton is behind bars? It's perfect,' Dave tapped away on the old computer.

'Why can't you be an old friend or an ex-girlfriend of Tutton's who told you to contact them?' he continued.

'It's worth a shot. What's the worst that can happen? They either say no and if they say yes, we will be at the house if there are any issues anyway.'

'Well then, it sounds like I have a call to make.' Polly walked outside with her phone and her cigarettes.

42

The more I thought about it, the more the plan was fraught with difficulties.

I agreed with Dave, the organisation was weakened by not having Smith's right hand man around. That said, we would be very lucky for them to buy this story and let us in through the front door.

We were running out of time and options, and that safe was important to finding the truth.

Polly returned from her cigarette.

'Dave, can you get any information on Tutton, like his family or friends, something? Anything that can give Polly a story, something believable?'

Dave finished tapping and turned to me.

'Way ahead of you Charlie, take a look at her. This is Glenn Tutton's step-sister, Ellie.'

Polly and I looked at the photo.

'Hmmm… she doesn't really look like Polly… ' I said, a little concerned.

'Similar figure, skin tone, a wig and some make up. What do you say?' Dave turned to Polly.

'It's doable,' she said sounding moderately more upbeat.

'Good. She lives in Manchester, where Tutton's from. It's not beyond the realms of possibility, she could have moved down here for work. When Smith gets his goons to check her out, as long as your back story matches, we are golden.'

I had to admit, it was very clever. But there were so many parameters that could let us down. What if Smith knew Ellie's step-sister? What if she showed up for real? What if she was dead and Smith went to the funeral?

I tried to put these thoughts from my mind and focus on keeping Polly safe. If all else failed, it would be down to Dave and I to save her and I could live with that.

'Shall I ring now?' Polly asked.

'No time like the present,' Dave responded. 'Remember, *Glenn told you to get in touch. Ellie Simpson, you've come from Manchester, you've spent your last twenty pounds on travel,* lay it on thick!'

Polly steeled herself, then went to make the call. We sat nervously, waiting for her return.

'This is going to be OK, right Dave?'

He turned and looked at me, taking off his glasses.

'I don't know, Charlie. But we've worked a long time together and I took a lot of what you said to heart about charging Wood for Amy Green's murder. Looks like you were right and you've taught me an important lesson.'

'You're the best cop I know. It was Pensborough and the pressure… '

'… Either way, I should've stuck to what I felt was right and if I'm being honest, I was never sure Wood was the killer. That's why we've got to make it right.'

I'd never heard him speak like this. He was always my guide, my role model. To know that I had helped him made me glow inside. Then I reminded myself, I was leading two of my closest friends, into a volatile and dangerous situation. The glow turned to trepidation.

Dave could sense my unease.

'It's the right thing to do Charlie and that's all that matters.'

The door opened and Polly bustled in. I still found the scent of her leather jacket mixed with cigarettes and cheap perfume strangely alluring.

'She's going to call back to confirm but it looks like we're on at the Manor House this Saturday.'

43

Polly had to leave, so Dave and I decided to take his newly-refurbished Ford Mustang out for a drive.

It was the first time he had driven it since he started work on it and was a little nervous, but with a bit of friendly coercing, he agreed.

It was a balmy August evening, or at least as balmy as Folkestone got. This area seemed to have its own micro-climate; slightly cooler in the summer and warmer in the winter.

'Come on mate; put your foot down a bit!' I urged.

Dave clasped two hands to the wheel, like a hawk's talons and made sure to check left, right and then left again before turning right onto Tintern Street. It was quiet, as it often was at the harbour, eerily silent.

He finally opened the car up a little, driving up the hill and the deep rasp of the engine reverberated against the ghostly buildings that surrounded us.

Some parts of Folkestone stood with Victorian, elegant majesty, others like Tintern Street, were desolate.

'There's still a problem with the fuel injector,' Dave said, putting his foot down.

My hand hit the back of the leather seat, 'Seems all right to me!' I said, enjoying the wind hitting my face. I felt as if the clouds were lifting. The hole I had gotten myself into after the break up with Jo seemed long gone. Things were looking up. All we had to do was finish this case and the future looked bright.

'You happy being retired?' I asked. I watched his face for signs of sadness or joy; he remained motionless at the wheel.

'It seems strange being told what to do. That someone else has come in and turfed me out. It's been twenty-seven years Charlie!'

'Sure. But you know the boys miss you and appreciate what you did?'

Again, he gave nothing away as the Mustang squeaked to a halt at the traffic lights, much to his disgust.

'The brakes aren't quite right either. Bugger! I spent £200 on the discs!' he tutted and muttered under his breath.

Perhaps he *was* happy being retired, I thought to myself.

Dave dropped me off at my flat. With the case on hold until Saturday night, I rang Tara.

We organised to meet that evening at La Caverna, a short walk for both of us.

She met me on the corner of Seagate Road and Brimstone Avenue, her broad smile the first noticeable effect as I clumsily ambled towards her.

She had on a black dress with her hair in a bun. She looked gorgeous but it was the scent of her that really got me, fresh, clean, subtlely exotic.

Marriage and childbirth can change a woman's allure. In all honesty, Jo gave up on any physical aspects of our relationship after Maddie's birth.

I still loved her but it was like a part of our relationship died, the part that wanted to make *us* happy. Everything became all about Maddie, she filled the void our marriage had become. The problem was the daily tasks were never shared. Jo pressed Maddie so closely to her chest and was never going to let her go. I was left out on my own.

The rare nights Jo had plans meant I got uninterrupted time with my daughter; precious, treasured time.

Tara was a blast of fresh air from all of these difficult memories. She was like riding in the passenger seat of Dave's Mustang. She was the sunshine on your skin. She was the cool sea breeze.

I hoped she knew what she was getting herself into.

La Caverna was fairly busy. We had to go a few steps down into the old-fashioned building. It was silver service and the waiter wasted no time taking a drinks order.

'I'll have a Sauvignon Blanc,' Tara said.

'What about a bottle?' I responded.

'Sure, why not!'

Dinner was great and I enjoyed watching Tara order what she wanted and drink her fill. I've spent many dinners watching women not order what they want, feeling obliged to order the salad and drink soda water. Tara was free of those inhibitions, as I watched her clamber into her steak and dauphinoise.

We finished the meal and we went for a drink and a chat at the Frenchman pub around the corner from the restaurant. Once we became giggly and cuddly, I hailed a taxi.

Tara asked to come to mine which I happily agreed to. We sat and watched a survival documentary on the sofa with a glass of wine, before Tara started yawning and we went through to the bedroom.

Her presence had a soothing serenity that I'd never experienced before. Her aura was light and her soul was free from Marley's chains that wore down even the lightest of spirits.

We made love carefully. It was early relationship sex, no-one wanting to make a mistake, no-one wanting to disappoint. Afterwards she wanted to stay and I was more than happy to have this warm body, I was falling in love with, to hold on to.

She was a beacon in the night, something solid, pure and good, in a world too often swallowed up by disappointment and disillusion.

Her purity of spirit was overwhelming. I just hoped her innocence and my experience, could last.

44

We slept late and I was woken by loud, diesel engines and a cacophony of estuary English from the dustbin men below. Tara's golden hair lay in ringlets on the pillow as she slept soundly, facing the window.

I raised the sheet we were sleeping under and admired her naked presence. I pressed myself against her to feel her warmth. She stirred, before I kissed her on the head and quietly raised myself from the bed.

I checked my phone and noticed a voicemail.

'*Hi Charlie, it's Polly. We're going tonight with Anna to the house. There's an evening party from what I understand, we won't be the only ones there. Call me when you get this.*'

It was Friday morning. I thought we were going on Saturday? I returned her call straight away.

'So from what I could understand, they have some sort of party tonight, lots of men, lots of girls. I'm happy to do it, but might make things tricky.'

'Yeah? I thought they wanted you on Saturday?'

'She said that it's tonight, is that OK?'

'Yeah of course. Are you?'

'Well yeah, but think about it Charlie. If there's lots of people, that's more people who could know me or *Ellie*.'

'Shit, you're right. Still, it's got to be worth a shot, don't you think?'

'We haven't got time to waste and, if we call off now, we might blow our chances completely,' she said.

'Have you thought about… what you're going to do… y'know… ?'

'… When I'm in the room with some random old pervert? Yes, Charlie. I have thought about that kind of a lot actually!'

'You know what I mean… '

'Don't worry. I've got something up my sleeve, literally.'

'Clever girl. What time are you getting picked up?'

'Seven.'

'OK. Let's meet at five around Dave's. OK?'

'See you at Dave's.'

The phone went dead and Polly was gone.

I turned around and Tara was standing behind me. She was smiling, wearing nothing but my sky blue polo shirt from yesterday.

'Hello handsome,' she said. It made me smile and I gave her a big hug. She went and sat in the front room, putting on some generic daytime TV, while I went to the kitchen to make coffee.

Once she finished her drink she made her excuses to go. I'm not sure she wanted to, but we both had things to do.

I had to get back into work today. I had hardly been in since I had been reinstated, using the excuse that it would be easier to work from home, rather than come in. I was still technically on light duties and medication.

I wanted to gauge Pensborough and give him an update as to what I'd been doing. I knew he would be in touch soon anyway.

Jo had tentatively agreed for Maddie to come to Folkestone this weekend. I asked Tara if she wanted to stay over. She said she would let me know, but couldn't see a problem. We kissed and she left. The road ahead did not appear as tough as it once did.

45

I arrived at Dave's house early and he made coffee. Anxiety was high as we weren't expecting a number of other people at the house that evening, too.

If Polly was to get in, open the safe and leave with its contents, it seemed nothing short of a miracle.

Polly arrived at quarter to five; she was obviously nervous. She had her get up on for tonight, a pair of stockings and a little black dress. Her make-up was thick yet subtle, she looked younger, but there was fear and determination in her bright eyes.

'Pol, we're going to be listening out for you on the receiver. The device picks up conversation within about ten feet. Obviously, if you need to speak to us directly, we will be right there, in the woods to the front-right of the Manor House,' Dave said, attaching the wire to Polly's chest and taping it down.

'Where exactly?' she asked.

Dave looked at me, 'I'm thinking in the woods near the main road. It's only a couple of minutes from the house through the woods. We'll be out of sight, but on hand if anything… you know… '

'Make sure you keep us updated on what's going on. Talk to us when you're on your own, but lean forward and whisper. OK? Right you're done. Anything else?' Dave asked.

There was silence.

'It's going to be OK, I promise,' I reassured her.

'Yep. I need to get back home. Anna will be here in half an hour. I think I need a drink.'

Polly left without saying a word. I looked at Dave and he reached into the bottom drawer of his old, oak desk. He pulled out an old Enfield revolver and loaded it with six bullets.

We dropped Polly at her flat in Dallas Brett, five minutes west from where we were.

I knew where she lived from the hazy nights and throbbing mornings I had spent with her in the halcyon days of our 'relationship' before things became complicated.

We sat in silence in Dave's 'adult' car as he called it, a blue Honda Accord, tucked in-between the many vehicles parked along Polly's road. I looked around at the overhanging buildings, the high-rises and the kebab shops as they rose up into the South Downs. It was a world away from the ancient tranquillity of west side Folkestone; there was a hustle and bustle, the streets were real. Alive.

Polly was a good girl. Her family set up was difficult. Her mother, whom she worked to support, was a heavy drinking, recreational drug-taking trouble maker. I doubted her drug use was still recreational, but I knew a major part of Polly's monthly salary went to support her.

Her father was barely around. He rocked up occasionally, when his money was low. He had let Polly down. He had let the family down. An all too familiar story these days.

Polly was trapped, which was why she was angry. The police was a way out of the darkness for her. Her heart was good, she meant well. A fact that became abundantly clear to me as I watched her click-clack towards a black Mercedes that was pulling up a few cars ahead.

She jumped in and I suddenly felt a stab in my stomach. I wanted to get out of the car and tell her to stop. Dave saw me flinch and put his hand on my arm.

'Are you all right, Charlie?' I looked at the thick veins as he held me. It was comforting, but he let go.

I stared at him, dead-eyed, as he started the car and we followed the Mercedes through the Folkestone streets to the motorway.

46

The microphone device Polly was wearing buzzed into life. Although the conversation was chilling; I listened to Polly lose her effrontery and arrogance and act in a churlish, innocent stupor, playing her role.

'So let me run through how this works,' Anna Gibson talked in a warm, slow voice. 'We are going to drive to the house where my friends are staying. It's only about an hour or so, a lovely big house in the middle of the country.'

'Yes,' Polly responded.

'When we get there, I will introduce you to the rest of the girls and you will be checked.'

'Checked? What do you mean?'

'Well… it's just to make sure you're dressed properly for our friends and smell nice and so on.' There was a pause. 'I'm sure you'll have nothing to worry about, darling,' she chuckled to herself.

'After that, we will offer you a little something to take the edge off and you'll go in and meet the men.'

'Take the edge off? Like a drink or something? I would murder a glass of wine!' Polly said edgily.

The woman laughed, 'yeah something like that, but maybe a bit stronger y'know. To take the edge off.' she repeated.

I looked at Dave.

'That's the MDMA. How's she going to get out of taking that?' I said.

'Have faith, Charlie. She'll find a way. Be quiet though, we need to hear this!'

The woman's voice faded back up.

'You meet the men; you mingle with them. Make friendly conversation. Tell them what they want to hear. Ask them about their jobs, what it's like living in London, how many dogs they have, whatever. And… when they're ready, you'll go upstairs with them. OK?'

'Yes, sure,' Polly said nervously. 'Can I ask about payment?'

'Of course, darling. We don't do this for free! You'll be paid tomorrow, after we've dropped you home. Once the party's over and everyone's…happy with the service.'

'OK. And… how much?' Polly asked.

'It's your first time, seven fifty. But if everything goes well that will rise to a thousand pounds for the night.'

Polly said, 'wow,' but this indeed, could've been a collective response from Dave and I too. I watched his eyebrows rise as she repeated the figure.

'Well there's an incentive. No wonder these girls are being lured in. That's more money than their parents probably give them in a year,' Dave said with disgust.

'Yep. But what did Amy Green do that was so wrong, I wonder?'

'Maybe, tonight we'll find out.'

We followed the car which seemed to take an age to reach its destination. It was twenty past eight when the Merc took the last left turn and onto the private road towards the Manor House.

We slowed almost to a halt and waited for it to disappear out of sight, before accelerating slightly and parking in the bay on the main road. I shuddered, remembering the last time I was here.

Dave immediately dimmed the headlamps and I could see the warm, golden glow of fluorescent light, providing a warm façade. Unfortunately, I knew the grim realities that awaited inside.

'At half past eight we can go in and get ready. They'll do the check and you'll have time to do your last minute preparations before the men come in at nine.' Anna confirmed.

'Sure, it will be fine,' Polly said, sounding anxious.

'Honestly, darling, you'll be fine. Just smile and be friendly. But listen, these people are gentlemen and want you to listen to them. If you do as they say, you will be much, much richer come tomorrow morning.'

'Sure,' Polly returned.

'It's nearly time now. Let's go in and meet the others.'

We heard car doors slamming and the sound of a hubbub growing nearer. Dave pulled out his binoculars.

'Can you see anything?' I asked.

'No I can see an upstairs window, but the view is obscured. Let's head closer.'

We had headsets for Polly's device so we could listen to it remotely, but I decided against it, for now.

'Let's stay in the car just for a little while, until the party gets going. We're bound to encounter some of Smith's henchmen if we go now.'

Dave seemed unsure, keen to stay near Polly, but after thinking about it, he closed his car door.

'OK. Put on the headset and kill the radio. Drop down in your seat, as if no-one's in the car.'

I did as I was told and we listened to Anna say various 'hello's' as Polly and her walked further into the building.

'Paul! Paul! Come over here, this is the new girl,' Anna shouted.

There was a kerfuffle and then the clear and confident voice of Paul Smith came over the microphone.

'How do you do? You are… ?'

Polly spoke for the first time in the house, 'Ellie… '

'… You remember, Paul, the new girl we spoke about yesterday on the phone?' Anna interrupted.

'Ah, yes! Glenn's cousin?'

'Err… no,' Polly chimed in. 'His step-sister.'

'That's right! I'm sorry. Well, welcome. Welcome! Has Anna been looking after you?'

'Yes, fine thanks,' Polly said quietly.

'Well, good. That's marvellous. There are some important people here. Some people who I'd really like you to meet. Someone who I know is going to make sure your brother is back with us, as soon as possible.'

Dave and I looked at each other, a little worried.

'Erm, is it OK, if I just pop to the toilet please?' Polly asked.

'Yes, Paul.' Anna interjected. 'We can meet at nine, when the rest of our friends have arrived. We've had a long journey, let the girl use the facilities,' Anna said.

The noise faded out from the radio and there was the sound of clacking heels and slamming doors.

'Charlie? Dave? Can you hear me?' Polly whispered.

'Yes, we can hear you,' I said.

'We have a serious problem. *Pensborough* is here. This guy wants to *introduce* him to me!'

'OK, relax Pol! Take your time in the toilet, take a minute to breathe. Describe to us what it's like in there.'

'OK… so… I've come in through the front door like last time. There's a group of about ten girls, young girls mingling in the hallway. Most of these girls are bloody teenagers. Like eighteen or nineteen!'

'Stay focused, Pol. Don't get angry and we will.' Dave affirmed.

'Through the double doors in the main room, there is a group of men, drinking and chatting,' she continued, taking a deep breath.

'Polly, when you finish here, go back outside and mingle with the girls, be a wall flower. Talk to one of them, blend in.' Dave said.

'But, what if he sees me!'

'How many times have you met him? You would be unlucky if he recognised you... as you are... ' I tried to reassure her.

'Jesus!' she said. We heard a rustle of clothing and then silence.

'Right, I'm going back out there,' Polly bustled out of the bathroom and back into the hallway. There was silence.

'Oh god!'

'What's the matter?' I asked.

'There's no-one here anymore. Everyone's gone!'

Dave and I piled out of the car and made our way quietly through the woods to a safe and covered vantage point.

'Ellie! Where've you been? We've been looking for you!' It was Anna's voice.

'Sorry, Anna,' she replied, as doors opened and the sound of female voices grew nearer.

'It's time for you to get checked, come into the dressing room, with the rest of the girls.' A door opened and there was an awkward and eerie silence from Polly's mike.

Male voices, some with London accents, dominated and I thought I could make out the voice of Smith getting nearer. Polly shuffled.

'The new girl, what do you think boys?' Smith said. There were at least two other men there and they leered and laughed to each other. I could hear the sound of heavy breathing in Polly's mike, unsure of whether it was Polly or Smith.

'Darling, you smell gorgeous.' Smith said, 'Good girl, give her the spray.'

'Open your mouth, love,' a voice said.

'Won't be the last time she hears that today,' another joked.

Jesus.

'Oi, open your mouth!' the voice asserted angrily.

'No, its fine. I'm fine,' Polly said shakily.

'Listen, Ellie. Do as you're bloody told. It makes life much easier. OK?' Smith said angrily.

I heard the sound of the spray and a loud whimper from Polly cutting through the dark murmurs of the men in suits that awaited her.

47

'Right, come in, I've someone who wishes to meet you,' Anna said as the rumblings of conversation grew nearer.

'Rowley, this is the girl I have been telling you about, Ellie.'

'Well, hello there! My, my, aren't you quite adorable!' Rowley said.

'Yes, she's a new girl. First night tonight, so I thought you would be keen to meet her,' Anna said.

'Yes, yes how lovely indeed! So whereabouts are you from, pretty lady?'

'I'm from Folkestone,' Polly said nervously.

'Oh, how marvellous. The West End, I hope?' Rowley continued, chuckling as he spoke.

Polly lied and told him she lived in Brimstone Gardens. I'm not sure why her current residence made such a difference to dear Rowley, but then there was not a lot of this whole set-up I did understand.

They continued to make small talk for a few minutes. Anna seemed to have disappeared. Dave checked that his gun was loaded. I rearranged my earpiece to see if I could get a better sound; I couldn't.

More minutes of small talk passed; where Rowley worked, the thirty-five years he had been at his corporate firm, the three cars he owned (one for the weekend of course), his grandchildren that made him happy.

'Excuse me, I just need the ladies room,' Polly said.

'Well don't be long!'

I could hear Polly shuffle off before the doors cracked shut and the sounds were much quieter.

'Charlie, I think I can make it up the stairs now,' she said. 'Let me just wait a moment to see if the coast's clear.'

She was right, people were still mingling at the party. The chance of anyone being upstairs was slim.

'When you get to the third or fourth step, you can look up and pretty much see the breadth of the hallway. Check if it's clear,' I said.

'OK… I'm going now… it's clear. Right, I'm going up… '

'Careful Pol,' Dave added.

We heard the sound of her covert movements as she crept. I could also feel my heart beat in my chest like a drum getting louder and louder.

'Which door was it?'

'It's the third on the left as you look down the corridor.'

'OK.' We heard the shuffling of feet and voices now far in the background.

'I'm at the door… sounds empty behind… I'm going in.'

'Shut it behind you,' I said as we heard the sound of the door opening and then shutting quietly.

'Brilliant, I'm in. I'm sweating though… I think it's the drugs... but I can see the safe… yes, now the key… can I find the key… yep, in my bag… OK, here goes!'

'Keep your voice down, Pol!' Dave said.

'It won't open!'

'Try it again anti-clockwise. Turn it hard, those locks can be stiff,' I told her.

'… Got it! It's open, there's a brown box inside… '

'Anything else?'

'No… '

'OK, take the box, put it in your bag then get back down to the party before Anna wonders where you are again,' Dave said.

'Right, OK. We did it, I can't believe it!' she said.

Suddenly there was quiet and the sound of a toilet flushing. I remembered, the en-suite bathroom. There was one in each of the bedrooms.

I could sense Polly freeze. She hadn't time to hide or get out of the room before the door of the bathroom slowly creaked open.

'Oh, *hello.* Follow me up, did you? You naughty, little girl!' Polly remained silent but it was the voice of Rowley from earlier.

'I was watching you from across the room, you were watching me too, *yes?* I knew that's why you came to speak to me!' he said, chuckling to himself.

Polly shuffled and giggled, 'Yep… '

'Sexy, little bitch… you wanted to see me? How very naughty! I come up here for a little… you know party powder. Keeps me going, now I'm not as young as I once was,' he chuckled to himself. 'But how rude of me, would you like some, a little livener?'

'I'm fine thanks,' Polly said.

'No, I insist! You'll love it once you try it!'

Polly's voice melted, 'well… I had, you know… other plans instead for you.'

'Hmmm. Yes, yes… you are quite something… very… alluring. A little on the more mature side but, a change is as good as a rest, I suppose. Let me join you on that bed.'

Polly was obviously on the bed, pretending to be waiting for the creep as he came out.

'Let's have a good look at you… and a nice feel of you… lovely, nubile flesh. Good… good… give me a kiss now… that's right… '

I felt nauseous.

I turned to Dave, 'shall we go in now?'

'Have faith, Charlie,' he said, clearly becoming more agitated.

I tried to stay calm, but wanted to jump out of my skin. One of my old lovers, old friends, was being molested and I was doing nothing.

'What a good girl… yes, yes you are… now spread those legs for me... mmm, a sweet scent. Let me take a closer look… '

'*Dave!*' I was losing it.

'Stand down, Charlie. We can't get in there. *Wait!*'

'Yes… let's pull these down… ' the sound of kissing and the ruffling of clothes reverberated through the earpiece.

'Good… good… girl… ' the old man purred.

'Come up here, I want you to taste this,' Polly said.

'Ooh… sounds exciting, what is… ' then there were was a sound of muffling, choking, before silence fell.

'*Polly?*' I said.

'Yep, Chloroform. He won't be bothering anyone for a while,' Polly asserted.

'Chloroform? How did you get that?'

'I borrowed some from the police lock up, anyway why are you worried, would you rather he carried on?'

Dave and I looked at each other, eyebrow's raised.

'Polly, can you hide this guy under the bed or something? Buy yourself a little time?' Dave said.

'Way ahead of you. He's going in the wardrobe. It locks and the key is in the door.'

'Good work, hopefully no-one will miss him for the next half-hour or so. How are you feeling?'

'Surprisingly sober now. I need to get out of here. Any ideas?'

'Get back to the party. Get a drink and check for an escape route. Anna said through the double doors out the back, right? Through there, towards the back there is a little kitchen and through that is a door to an orchard. You can follow that back to the front of the house,' I said.

'How do I find you guys?'

'If you can get to the front of the house, where Anna's car is parked, we will see you and can motion you over. Be careful, perhaps crawl. You will be in full view of the front of the house.'

'Lovely, Charlie. Jesus. There better be something worthwhile in this bloody box.'

'Get in the bathroom, Pol. Sort yourself out then back downstairs. If anyone asks, you were with someone upstairs, but keep it vague. Then out the back. OK?'

'Sure, I'm going!'

She went to the bathroom and then made her way downstairs and the rumble of voices grew closer. I could see the warm, orange glow of the house in the distance and couldn't believe how something could look so innocuous, yet house such evil.

Sure enough, Polly engaged someone in conversation, making small talk about their job in the city and their interests. She lingered for a few minutes before making her excuses to get a drink.

'Not too much mind you, I might want to see you later on, Ellie!' the voice shouted after her, guffawing away.

Polly laughed back and we heard the double doors open and the sanctuary of solitude.

Polly said a few more 'Hi's' and 'Hello's'. She clearly wasn't the only woman seeking the solace of alcohol. We waited, presumably until the women had gone back into the main room.

'OK, I'm in the kitchen. I see the door. One moment… it's locked!'

'Jesus, what about the window? Whatever you do, do it quickly!' Dave urged.

'The window it is,' Polly climbed out and we could hear the sound of the outdoors in our ear. She came around to the front of the house and I saw her figure in the distance.

'We're ahead of you, in the woods. I can see you. We're about fifty yards away across the drive! Stay low, Pol, come over!'

Polly got on the floor and crawled across to the woody undergrowth.

'I'm going to start the car,' Dave said, getting up and handing me his revolver. I looked at him, praying I wouldn't have to use it. He turned and ran backwards, while I waited for Polly.

She made it to us and got to her feet, looking over her shoulder.

'Quick, Pol, twenty yards this way,' I urged.

A few moments passed which felt like an eternity and I heard Dave turn the engine of the car. The end was in sight. Polly found me and fell into my arms. She was limp, like a poorly child and I held her as she recovered her breathing.

'One last push, Pol. The car is through those trees.'

We got to our feet and started running. Dave was ready to go; he had even opened the car doors for us to get in. I dived into the passenger seat, Polly in the back as he sped off, leaving the delusive glow of the Manor House firmly behind us.

48

The car sped away and it didn't look like we were being followed.

Polly was woozy, her head bobbing up and down, her eyes rolling back into her head. I had read about MDMA, it had a habit of taking a while to kick in and really only when you were relaxed.

'Charlie, open the window… '

I opened it for her and she promptly vomited out the side of the car. When she finished she lay back exhausted. I passed her a bottle of water which she declined.

I grabbed her bag and took out the brown wooden box. It was about twenty centimetres by ten and was held together by a gold lock. I shook it and turned it over, but it was no use.

'Leave it 'til we get home. I can open that,' Dave said.

He was right. We didn't know what was in there and I didn't want to damage anything. Dave drove home at great speed and we were back at his house within an hour.

I carried Polly inside and put her on the sofa. She was clammy and murmuring in her half-sleep. Dave covered her in a blanket.

'Right, pass me that box,' I handed it to Dave and he put on his glasses to take a closer look. I grabbed us a couple of beers from the fridge as he wiggled the lock open.

After a few minutes, the latch clicked and the lid unlocked.

I opened the lid and in the box was a folded plastic wallet, which housed the ripped pages from Amy Green's diary. Along with it, was a pair of dog tags. I took them out to see what they said. On one of the silver sides read the words, '*I love you to the moon and back.*' I turned it over and there was a crescent moon with a face smiling up at me.

I took the plastic wallet and sat in one of Dave's armchairs. He started thumbing the dog tags, trying to find any further clues.

I opened the plastic wallet and unfolded the sheets of paper. The large girly swoops of Amy Green's handwriting immediately hit me, sending a pang of sadness through my bones.

I steeled myself and prepared to read. They were folded directly in half at the earliest entry. I took a deep breath and read the crumpled papers:

July 7th 2015

Dear Diary,

The summer is coming soon and I can't wait! The exams are pretty much over, I have one left, Public Services, which shouldn't be too difficult. Then I'm free! Yay!

There are things about Mina that I am worried about. She seems to have a lot of things going on. She always wants to get stoned, but I think she is getting into harder drugs too.

I tried to talk to her about it but she just fobs me off saying 'I wouldn't understand.' I keep telling her I want to understand but she just says to not get involved. We hardly ever go out anymore, the last time was like a month ago when we went out with Harry and Chris. Most weekends now she's got other plans, god knows what that means.

Anyway, it's the summer soon so I'm hoping I can pull some money together and go away for a holiday. Mina says she wants to go too. Hopefully there I can talk to her and try and sort our friendship out a bit.

I've also got to find some money from somewhere – maybe Dad will lend me it? Yeah right, who am I kidding?

Bye, Amy x

I sifted through the papers and saw that there were four more entries, all spaced over the final three weeks of her life.

I looked over to Dave and he was looking at me.

'Do you want me to read these out?'

Dave was wiping Polly's brow with a cloth. She was sleeping on the sofa.

'I'll read them after, you carry on.'

10th July 2015

Dear Diary,

Strange day. I finished my last exam (thank god) and then met up with Mina. She looked really tired, I mean like super tired. Her face was pale and she wasn't wearing any make up. This is a bit of a pattern now. She always used to love getting all dressed up and chatting with the boys on the way home but she doesn't ever bother now. She's taken to wearing tracksuits and trainers. Trainers! She's never worn trainers to school!

Anyway I asked her how she's going to afford the holiday and she told me money wouldn't be a problem. She told me that she could introduce me to someone who could get me work, like really well paid work.

She said she had been spending the weekend with new 'friends' she had made. Friends who it turns out are middle-aged men!!! She said she had been going away with these men for the last three months. Three months! One weekend she said they gave her £1200!

Then it clicked, she was basically being a prostitute! Anyway we ended up having a massive row and she said she predicted I would be so prudish. Prudish!? For caring about my best friend? For not wanting to have sex with random men for cash? She said they weren't random and they were rich and treated her well.

I told her I thought she should go to the police and she just laughed at me. Now I'm scared because she's not talking to me.

Maybe it wouldn't be such a bad idea? Mina says after the first time, it's not difficult. You just have to get used to it.

Confused.

Amy

July 12th 2015

Diary,

So I found Mina at school today and told her I wanted to speak to her in private. I think she was a little taken aback by how abrupt I was but I wanted to show her I'm not the little girl she sometimes thinks I am.

I told her I would be interested in meeting her 'friend' and I thought she was going to die! She was so surprised but I think also a little pleased and relieved. It must be hard living this life without anyone to talk to about it.

She asked me whether I was a virgin, but she knows I am. I've done a few things with boys (as you know diary), but never full sex.

She says being a virgin will mean I could earn a lot more. Anyway she made a phone call and we went to meet her friend. She told me I was in for a real shock and that I needed to be completely open-minded. Well, I nearly fell down when the man she meant was Mr Tutton, the new deputy head teacher at the school!!!!!!

I thought it was all a bit weird and sick but she said he doesn't do anything with you, he is just the driver and looks after you and stuff.

I am going with Mina on Saturday to do my first weekend. I have told Mum and Dad we are going away to Center Parcs so I hope they believe me! I'm going round Mina's on Friday to beautify and pamper and then Glenn (that's Mr Tutton's first name) is picking us up at 10am. Eek!

It's all happened so fast, but Mina keeps saying to think of the money – I think she's right, especially with holiday and uni coming up. I cannot wait to be in Falaraki on the beach!

17th July 2015

Dear Diary,

Off to Mina's and first day tomorrow so I won't be able to write to you for the next few nights. I'm going to hide you in my desk so NO-ONE finds you. Wish me luck,

Amy x

19th July 2015

Diary,

Something awful has happened. I didn't want to write this entry but felt I had to. It's bad, really bad. My Mum thinks I'm ill but I'm just numb, I feel so sick.

I went with Mina to this old house somewhere in the country. When I got there I met this really nice man. He was a bit old, but really kind. They gave us champagne and some mandy, which I've done once before, but it was much different to last time. It was easier and the come up was a lot smoother. It made me feel all gooey and dizzy.

I remember going upstairs and into the bedroom with the old man who I will call 'John' (but that's not his name) and we had sex. It felt more like making love, probably due to the mandy. He was really gentle and caring and kept asking if I was OK.

Anyway, we finished and he went downstairs and I was in the bath, when I heard a knock on the door. By the time I had gotten out of the bath and put a robe on, Mr Smith the new head of school was in my room!

He stared at me and then, told me I had done really well. He then put me on the bed and told me to relax. I didn't want him to touch me or do anything I told him to stop and he just kept looking up at me and smiling. It was vile.

He kept doing things to me, I didn't like and he became more and more aggressive with me. He turned me over held me down and raped me. I was still sore from earlier and this was just agony. I was crying and shouting but he kept telling me to shut up and he kept hitting me.

Eventually he finished and left. I cried and cried for hours before Mina came in to find out what had happened. She said that Smith was mean but he was also in charge of everything. He organised all of this and he could do what he wanted.

I was so angry with her. Why didn't she care? She told me that this was bigger than I could possibly understand. I said, I didn't care and that I was going to the police.

Then I started shouting and shouting. I ran downstairs and found Smith and slapped him. I told him, I would tell the police about all this. He just laughed at me.

The next thing I knew everything went dark and I woke up back at home in my bed.

I went downstairs and Dad was there. He asked me how Center Parcs was and I just started crying. When I looked up, he was crying too, I don't know why. But he couldn't stop. I told him I felt ill and that I was going to bed, but truthfully I was covered in bruises and didn't want him to notice.

I'm going to the police. I don't want Mum and Dad to know but tomorrow I'm reporting this whole thing. It's sick.

Until tomorrow,

Amy

49

When I stopped reading, I noticed my eyes were very watery. A tear dropped onto the page and I was quick to wipe it off, so as to not damage the evidence. I passed the papers to Dave and the anger inside me forced me to my feet.

I went out into the cold, dark night and lit one of my final cigarettes. The stars were clear tonight and the roar of the sea was fierce down below.

I felt empty. The death of two bright young girls, the danger Polly had put herself in, the perverted behaviour that had gone on under our noses.

How have these people been undetected for so long?

It was obvious that fear played a pivotal role. Amy Green was murdered because she threatened to tell. Her symbolic killing was a warning to anyone else. But what confused me was the speed at which Amy Green was introduced and then within a month, she was gone.

Perhaps she was the wrong type. Perhaps Mina Burrows' fatal flaw was confiding in her best friend a month ago. All I knew was that we had to get Smith and get him soon.

I went back inside and Dave had finished reading.

'That's evidence, right? That's enough to get Smith, yeah?'

Dave pondered the question. 'Maybe, but it's a handwritten document from an eighteen-year-old. It's not watertight.'

'But we've got the diary and it's clear these pages come from that…'

'We can get him on rape charges, there is nothing about murder, or about the fact he's running all of this.'

'We need to get him now; we must have a case!'

'Maybe, Charlie. Not definitely.'

Polly was stirring on the sofa.

'If we leave it and wait for him to slip up, this is going to go on and on. If we bring him in for what we've got so far, it may stop this whole…cycle,' she said.

I had to agree. No more death, no more of any of this.

Dave started tapping into his computer.

'I got his address here. Serafin Heights, Seagate. You need to secure that evidence Charlie. And take these dog tags. Take it to Pensborough and go and arrest him,' Dave said.

'What are the dog tags about?'

'No idea, but bring him in and you can ask him.'

'I need to get home. I've got Maddie coming tomorrow and need some rest. Pol, you want a lift back?'

'Sure,' she said.

We got in the car and headed back towards Dallas Brett. Polly seemed better now, just sad and tired.

'You were brilliant tonight, Pol.'

She just smiled at me and closed her eyes, drifting in and out of sleep. I dropped her at her door and helped her inside.

There was a moment in time when she would have asked me inside for more. But at the door, she gave me a hug and said goodbye. I felt a surge of disappointment that the life we once lived of carefree rebellion and wild abandon was coming to an end. It was replaced by a homely feeling, that I knew Polly was happier without me and I without her.

I wondered how much routine kept happy people in unhappy relationships. In a way I loved Polly with all my heart but although it was tough, I was glad I had let her go.

50

I spent most of Thursday at work building a case against Paul Smith. I needed as much evidence as possible and sifted through the mountain of paperwork we had created since the start of the summer.

No matter how hard I tried, I was not convinced we could try him for murder. There was no feasible way of finding anyone from Smith's organisation. All we had were first names, if anything and there was no guarantee anyone would give evidence against him anyway.

Despite the disappointment of this, Polly was right. On a moral level, we needed to end this now. By putting Smith behind bars, even if not for murder, it would surely stop this sex ring in its tracks.

In addition to this, we could make a case against Anna Gibson, for trafficking.

Late on Thursday I took the completed case file to Pensborough.

'I finished the work on Smith, sir.'

'Leave it on the desk,' Pensborough focused on a document on his desk. As I went to leave, he spoke.

'Charlie, sit down.'

I paused before pulling out the old chair, scraping the wood against the cold, hard stone underneath.

'I was right about you. Maverick, difficult, belligerent. I told you not to meddle in this case and what did you do? You carried on behind your colleagues back and delved deeper.'

'Come on, you knew I would. It was the right thing to do. Two local girls have been killed. Girls were being raped. This file can stop all of that.'

'I don't think this makes anything 'better.' By going after this guy, it may make things worse, a lot worse.'

'What do you mean?'

'Paul Smith is a powerful man.'

'He is also a rapist and I believe, a murderer.'

'We'll submit this case against him, Charlie. But don't expect there to be no repercussions. Do you understand?'

'Not really? I mean, if we are off-record boss, can I ask you a question?'

'If you must, Charlie,' he said, nervously fingering a white coffee mug on his desk.

'Well, you see, it seems strange that you arrived around the same time as Smith and Tutton; them at the school, you at the police station… '

Pensborough's eyes widened.

'… And when we were undercover at the house, D.C. Ringwald, seemed to think she recognised you at the party.'

'Charlie, for your own sake, I'm going to pretend I didn't hear that. Seriously. Your friend was under the influence from what you tell me, so be careful making accusations like that.' he warned me, pointing his finger.

'I just wondered, boss, whether you might have a vested interest in *not* sending Smith down? Which is why I've already contacted my guy at the Bugle to let him know the story. It needs to be known, it has to come out.'

'Of course it will, I'll submit the report and have Smith arrested tomorrow. How dare you suggest I wouldn't?'

'OK, skip. Whatever you say. Can I bring him in?'

'Let me read the report, speak to the Super and I'll give you the nod sometime tomorrow. OK?'

'Sometime tomorrow?'

'First thing tomorrow! Jesus, Charlie!'

'OK boss,' I said getting up to leave, feeling pretty pleased that finally justice was being served.

51

It was Friday and my long weekend with Maddie was finally here.

Tara and I took the train to pick her up; Tara really was becoming quite beautifully entwined and inter-woven into our lives. She made both Maddie and I very happy. For as much as I doted on Maddie, there was a whole world of princesses, ponies, hair glitter and make up that I just couldn't really deliver; Tara helped fill in those gaps.

Tara made herself scarce when we got to Faversham. She had liaised with Jo when I was poorly but I'm not sure she liked her that much. Tara was quiet, serene and understated; Jo was bullish, belligerent and defiant.

Maddie was overjoyed to take the train home, it was way more exciting than the car. She had her Rubik's cube with her and she was determined to complete it. Tara being a mathematician was only happy to help.

On the train, Polly texted asking if she could pop over in the evening for a catch up about the case.

I asked Tara and she was fine with it, so I organised for her to meet us in an hour, when we were back indoors.

There was a new found revelry and bonhomie in our little trio. Tara brought an equilibrium which had not been there previously, as much as I tried to keep matters simple and fun with Maddie, Tara was the icing on the top.

We walked home laughing and joking, talking about the weekend we would have. Maddie wanted salmon and waffles for dinner which I found a peculiar combination, but was more than happy to make.

We got indoors to the flat and the evening light streamed into the front room.

Tara said she was happy to put Maddie in the bath while I put the dinner on. Not long after, the doorbell rang and it was Polly. She looked far better than the last time I had seen her. She smiled sincerely, as if life was good and she felt pleased with her lot.

'You seem… happy, Pol?' I said, tending to the peas on the hob, while the sound of Maddie's shouts from the bathtub provided an enjoyable, domestic backdrop.

'You know, I am. I feel different after the Manor house. Like something that was missing has been filled. I always thought being an officer would be enough, but what we actually did, it's going to change people's lives – *for good.*'

'I know what you mean. I just feel bad that I put you in danger. It can't have been… nice… '

'Well, you know what? I found it exciting. That's *real* cop work. No-one got hurt and we made a difference. Thanks to you Charlie, I finally feel like I've done something worthwhile,' she smiled put her hand on my hand. She wasn't flirting, she was genuinely happy and I hoped we had become real friends.

Tara came through to say hello and we all went through to the living room and sat down. I had noticed that the low sun was still shining through the sash window and was going to cause bother soon, so I got up to pull the blind.

I was always anxious when Tara and Polly were in the same room, but if Tara could tame Jo, Polly would be a breeze.

I looked down and noticed a black, luxury car over the road, by Brimstone Gardens. I thought immediately to dive down out of the window's gaze, but before I could, I felt a sting in my shoulder and blood began to trickle out. I had been shot. I felt like I was moving in slow motion as commotion rained around me. Further shots flew through the window and Polly grabbed Tara, diving on top of her to protect her.

I fell to the floor and tried to gather my thoughts. I had no gun, only some old blades from when I was a kid and some kitchen knives.

'Maddie! Maddie!!' I screamed.

Two men dressed in black, made their way from the car, around the side of my flat block and towards the main entrance. I heard it open and the rumble of footsteps coming up the communal stairs to my front door.

'Go! Charlie! Take Maddie and get out of the bedroom window. You can get down that way!' Polly said.

Maddie was screaming. She had no idea what was happening but knew something was wrong. She was dressed in her My Little Pony top, her hair still soaking from the bath as the front door was being smashed by the shoulder of a hired gun outside.

I ran into the bedroom, pulling Maddie and Tara with me. Polly remained on the outside.

'Polly, hurry up!'

'Shut up, Charlie! Go! For once, do as you're bloody told!' She ran to the front door and held her body against it, keeping it shut.

I ran to the sash window, opening it fully. We were on the first floor but Maddie couldn't make that jump. I vaulted out of the window and rolled onto the grass of the private garden below.

'Throw her now!' I said. Tara had Maddie in her arms. She was screaming, as I raced to my feet and stood to catch her.

'It's OK, Maddie! Daddy's here,' she looked down as Tara let her go and she fell through the air and safely into my arms.

'Now you!' Tara was clambering out of the window and she took what seemed like an age to eventually jump. She did and landed into my arms too, knocking me over in the process.

We got to our feet and ran to the end of the garden. The wall was low and backed on to someone else's garden. As we ran, I heard the sound of my flat door smashing open and the sound of female cries. There were two gunshots and then silence.

I helped Maddie over the short fence, before vaulting Tara after her. Tara and Maddie ran to the sanctuary of the large, mansion house on Twyford Gardens, banging on the patio doors of the old house.

Luckily, due to the large pine trees, that lay at the back of the property they were out of sight from the gunmen. I wasn't and as I vaulted over the top of the fence, made the fatal mistake of looking back as one of the gunman's bullets caught me once more.

I slid over to the safety of the large garden and heard the sound of sirens and further gunshots before everything faded to black.

52

I was in a bar, but it was completely white, white tables, chairs and there was no ceiling to it, just fluffy clouds.

I felt like I was new to this bar but knew exactly where to sit. I could see my stool and was slowly drifting towards it. As I got nearer, I noticed two people sitting on the stools to the left. One of them turned around.

'Hey son,' the voice said.

'Hi Dad,' I returned. Mum was right, there was a heaven.

'You shouldn't be here yet,' he continued. I wasn't having it and pulled up a stool. The bartender was wearing white and he came over and asked me what I wanted.

I noticed my godfather, Mike Teefy, dad's best friend at the bar too.

'Wait one moment,' he instructed the bartender, who took a step back.

'I'm glad to see you boy, but you shouldn't be here now, it's not the right time,' he said. I wanted to point out the irony of him dying at sixty-two, not being the right time for me either, but I left it alone.

'I was tired son, I over-complicated my life. Too many women, too much lying. It took its toll on me. I know it's taken its toll on you. I'm sorry.'

'It's OK. You're my Dad.'

'I made a mess son. But you can put things right. You've got a good girl there and Maddie is going to need you,' he continued.

'Jo doesn't think so.'

'It doesn't matter what she thinks.'

'I thought you liked her?'

'I did. So did you. It doesn't matter now, does it? You've got two good girls. Go back. Look after them. We'll see you soon.'

Can you come back too?' I asked. 'I miss you.'

Dad laughed, 'get going son, I'll see you when I see you.'

I looked at the bartender who nodded in agreement. I shook Mike's hand. He always brought me Dairy Milk chocolate when I was a kid, I liked him.

'Son?' Dad called after me.

'Yes?'

'Thanks for looking after Mum. I never stopped loving her.'

I smiled and turned from the bar.

The lights were bright on my opening eyes. I was at the Walter Tull again, in a different room this time.

I looked around to see who was here. Same as last time, except one person was missing.

'How're you feeling, Charlie?' Tara asked. She was perched on the side of the bed.

'Been better. How's Maddie?'

'She's fine. She's with Jo,' I exhaled deeply with relief.

I looked at my strappings and injuries. My shoulder ached when I moved and my leg was strapped and elevated.

'Polly?' I asked. Tara looked down to the floor and Dave just shook his head.

I knew what that meant.

'She died happy, Charlie. She came to see me before she went to yours…'

'…I should have protected her!' I said. Tara was crying.

'You did the right thing. Maddie wouldn't have got out, if she hadn't… ' Dave added.

I felt tears of rage fall down my face.

'Why did they have to kill *her* though?' I asked.

'It's all messages, Charlie. Coded messages and warnings. Trying to scare people off. She wanted you and Maddie to live, so she got in their way.'

'What about Smith?' I asked. Dave looked to the floor.

'We can't find him,' I jerked my arm in rage, forgetting the gunshot and winced in pain.

'Pensborough. I bet he's let him go,' I said, cursing my luck.

'He has asked me to help find him, in like an advisory role,' Dave said softly.

I looked up at him. 'Every cloud, I suppose.'

We both smiled.

'I bet you're glad you met me, huh?' I directed my attentions to Tara.

'Of course I am, you're a good man, Charlie. Everyone knows it except you,' she held my hand.

'Is Maddie really OK?'

'She's fine, no injuries. Just shaken up. She understands though. We told Jo it was a household burglary. Nothing could be done about it.'

I felt terrible that I had put her in such danger. I felt awful for Tara. I couldn't even begin to comprehend my feelings for Polly.

I asked the guys to leave me alone. Tara said she would stay in the café if I needed her. Dave told me Polly's funeral was in two day's time at the Appleton Road Cemetery. I'd see him there.

For now, I needed to rest. My injuries were worse than last time.

A long time ago, I took Polly to Los Amigos on Seagate Road. It was kind of a first date. We had slept together and there was some chemistry for sure. We flirted on the phone and knew something was brewing.

It was one of those peculiar situations our hearts wanted it to happen our heads did not. It did though and things had been confusing since.

We sat opposite one another; I got out my debit card to pay for the meal.

'Charlie, I like you, but let's give it six weeks. Yeah?'

'Six weeks? Why?'

'I just want to be sure this is what we both want. We can get swept up in the excitement. You're my boss, I'm in your department, and this is a really bad idea!'

'Yeah, but don't you want it?'

'I do, but… we need to wait,' she said looking out of the window.

I didn't know what she wanted. I was separating from my wife and wanted her, or at least I thought I did.

She kept her cards very close to her chest.

'Wait, six weeks. Then we'll see,' she reiterated.

I agreed, paid and went to my hotel room, on my own.

I was angry, frustrated and wouldn't wait.

So I went back to my wife and never found out what might have been, what our life could've been like.

We had a bond and I smashed it to pieces out of churlish, arrogant pride.

I watched Polly, like a ghost in my department. Dealing with pain and embarrassment as I swanned in and out, like the cat that got the cream. I let her go. My vulnerable friend.

I tried to talk to her and she said she wasn't bothered, but I knew her better than that. So I spoke to Dave and got moved into homicide. Then we ignored each other for a number of years. Like people do.

I'm sorry, Polly. I'm sorry you ever met me.

53

I woke and found that my arm felt slightly better and my leg was lying vertically on the bed.

My bandages had been changed and the bedding was fresh and clean. The TV was on in the corner of the room and I could hear people talking out in the corridor.

'Hello?' I croaked, trying to get someone's attention from outside.

A head poked around the corner.

'Hello, stranger,' Tara said, coming into the room. She was wearing her knee-high grey boots and skin-tight jeans. She looked utterly ravishing.

'What day is it?' I asked.

'Tuesday. Polly's funeral is in an hour,' she put her hand to my head and checked my temperature, before kissing me softly on the lips.

'How do you feel?'

'I feel better, thanks, help me get ready will you?'

'Charlie, I don't think they want you to leave.'

'They never do. Grab my jeans from that chair would you and help me get out of here.'

Once I was ready, we went downstairs under the premise that I needed to stretch my legs, which was ironic as I needed crutches to get anywhere. The nurses frowned at me.

Once outside, we navigated the extensive car park and found Tara's car. She helped me in and we made a hasty exit, back to Folkestone.

There was a large crowd at Polly's funeral, many of them coppers from the nick. I smiled and made small talk as I hadn't seen a number of them properly for a while. I had spent more time in hospital than at work in recent weeks.

Despite catching up with the guys, I actually wanted some peace to say goodbye to my old friend.

I stood with Dave and Tara, waiting for the service to begin, the cool breeze on my face helped me with the waves of nausea rising in my stomach.

I hadn't been asked to talk which was merciful, I was free to stare at the wooden box and wonder what might've been, if I hadn't told Polly to come around that fateful night.

It may have been me in that box instead, which would have been fair. But there may well have been two other boxes also.

I looked at the perimeter of the cemetery and there was a heavy police presence. This was rare, but a police funeral was often televised and photographed, so I guess the Superintendent was not keen on any further danger or incident.

I kept my head bowed while the Priest spoke; his hypnotic tone helped me grieve. I opened my eyes and noticed something shining in the distance, through the hazy moistness.

It happened again and I tried to refocus. I nudged Dave, who put on his glasses and looked where I was intimating.

Within moments, he had moved to the back of the mourners and was speaking with Pensborough. He moved with precision, his radio to his lips in an instant. Suddenly four PCs jumped in two squad cars and pulled away. The priest's eyes darted around at the sudden, slick movements of the on-looking policemen.

I looked at Dave, who was itching to follow.

I turned to Tara, who had read the situation and nodded her approval for us to go. She could clearly see the anxiety rise in me, as any path that lead to Smith's arrest, was one I had to follow. I nodded back to her and then hobbled across the cracked concrete and over to Dave's Honda.

'Who was it?' I asked Dave as he revved the engine and pulled away.

'Can't be totally sure, but looked like Smith to me. As soon as I raised the binoculars, he drove away,' Dave said, racing through the gears.

'Why would he come here?'

Dave paused, 'maybe he wanted to finish off the job he started.'

His GPS system had picked up the two squad cars which were now racing along Seagate Road following another car that was about a mile ahead. The radio was calling more squad cars to the scene. There were two in Hythe, which maybe, just maybe if they got this right, could box in the car we were tailing.

The suspect's car took a sharp left onto Royal Military Road and made its way down the beachfront. The squad cars needed to take a swift detour from the main road out of Hythe but managed to create a roadblock further down the long road, just in time.

The sea crashed against the shore to our left as we also took the turning; we were about twelve seconds now behind the squad cars and thirty from the suspect's car.

Dave floored it along the straight. We were now up to eighty miles per hour and it wouldn't be long until we all reached the roadblock.

The suspect's car suddenly ground to a halt, the end was in sight. The golf course one way or the sea the other. There was nowhere left to run.

The squad cars and Dave's old Honda came to rest behind them. Dave left the engine running.

The car was a grey BMW with a two thousand and fifteen number plate. At the wheel was the unmistakable figure of Paul Smith. He sat back in the driver's seat and awaited instruction. There seemed to be a momentary pause, like in a Western before the shootout would start.

With calm assertion, Pensborough stepped out of one of the squad cars and read Smith his rights. He asked him to slowly get out of the car and placed him in handcuffs. Smith looked at Pensborough in disbelief as he was led away.

After all the pain and suffering this man had caused, part of me wanted him to die in a hail of bullets, sprawled on the floor in a heap. But here he was, being taken calmly and quietly to the station, my station, where I had spent many happy days of my life.

Eventually Smith's lithe, languid frame was pushed into a squad car.

There was a wry smile on his face, as I watched the door slam firmly behind him.

54

'Mr Smith, as you have been made aware, you are under arrest for the rape, sexual assault and murder of Amy Green,' I said to him as we sat across the table in Folkestone Police Station.

Dave was outside watching through the glass and Pensborough stood next to me in the interview room, leaning against the wall.

Smith's hot-shot London lawyer sat next to him, scribbling notes.

'You do not have to say anything but anything you do say may be taken down as evidence and used in a court of law.'

Smith sat staring at me. His deep blue eyes seemed glazed and unfazed by what was happening around him. He was wearing a blue suit, top button undone; the complete opposite to his lawyer, who wore a fitted black suit with a waistcoat underneath. Smith looked stern, fierce and steeling for a fight.

'Mr Smith, we have reason to believe that you were in charge of an underage sex ring, which you ran out of the town of Folkestone,' I said.

Smith briefly conferred with his lawyer.

'Let me clarify,' Smith said, turning back to me. 'These women that you refer to were not underage, they were all eighteen. We're not perverts or paedophiles as you seem so keen to suggest, Mr Stone.'

'Well, if you think what you have been doing is either gentlemanly or lawful, you are wrong.'

Smith sat staring.

'So you confirm you were in charge of this… organisation?' I demanded.

'I wasn't necessarily in charge, but some of my friends and business associates did engage in activities while I was present, yes.'

I looked at the tape whirring around in its spools, silence filled the room as I waited for him to elaborate. He didn't.

'It seems peculiar that a majority of the girls who were part of your sex ring were from HG Wells Grammar School. They were targeted from school, groomed, if you like?' I asked.

'Not at all. Purely coincidental. I add once more for the record, we're not perverts, sergeant.'

'Well, it seems *extremely* 'coincidental' that you happen to take up a position in charge of the school at the time this all seemed to begin… '

Smith laughed, 'yes, it is. As far as I am aware, there is no evidence to suggest that I was in charge of getting the girls… recruited, if you like.' Smith smiled to himself.

'You did rape Amy Green, though, didn't you, Paul?' I said, leaning forward, looking deep into his eyes.

Smith, who was equal to the challenge, leaned forward and stared back.

'No, I did not.'

I thumbed through the file of evidence to find the plastic bag housing Amy Green's diary. Underneath it was the missing pages.

'This is an extract from Amy Green's diary… ' I said fumbling with the pages.

'Is it? It looks like something you made earlier sergeant,' Smith said, his lawyer tapped his arm and shot him a cursory glance.

'Well, I guess it's for the judge to decide when you go to trial.'

'Touché.'

'As I was saying, these are the missing pages from her diary. They graphically depict what you did to her. She was an innocent girl. You lured her into a life of debauchery and then raped her. Do you not feel any remorse?'

'It's just not true. The girls we met with were consenting adult females. There was no rape or anything non-consensual.'

'"*He turned me over hit me and raped me… It was agony…* " that's you Paul. She's referring to *you.*'

Smith conferred briefly with his lawyer and nodded silently.

'No comment.'

'So explain to me, about this… organisation you were privy to, if you can.'

'There is nothing to explain,' Smith said curtly.

'Well I think there is Paul. This isn't normal, you know. Coercing, grooming, drugging teenagers, having sex with them?' I was beginning to grow irate, I was determined to bring this guy down a few pegs. Let him rot in prison, let the freaks in Broadmoor have their way with him.

'Goodness me, how dramatic! Honestly, I don't know what you mean. Prostitution, sex trafficking, that's what you mean, I think? I've already said, I had nothing to do with that. If you want to charge me for having sex with consensual young women, go ahead.'

I had to raise it up a notch.

'I understand you, Paul Smith. You're not clever or different; you're just like every other perv on the dark web looking at pictures, aren't you? You want the forbidden fruit, the girls who aren't quite women, something somewhat… '

'… English,' Smith said calmly.

'Come again?'

'It's fine, Stone, I'll do your job for you. It's an English thing. Every massage parlour and brothel all over this nation, is filled with Thai's, Slovaks, Eritreans. It's an English thing, you bloody cretin!'

'I need five minutes with my client. Can we step out?' the lawyer said.

'No, no. Don't mind us, you stay here.' I got to my feet and headed for the door, grateful for the fresh air and to be away from Paul Smith's arrogant aura for a moment.

I walked to the water cooler and grabbed a cup. My eyes were wired as I downed the icy liquid and reached for another. I slammed the cup in the bin and turned back for the interview room, opened the door and sat back down.

'Right, you two, play nicely,' Pensborough chimed in. I had forgotten he was even there to be perfectly honest.

'Glenn Tutton worked for you?' I continued, changing topic.

'At school and in some other business matters, yes.'

'I watched him murder an eighteen-year-old girl. I suppose in your world, because she's of legal age, that's OK, right? Here, let me show you some of the pictures.'

I thumbed the evidence folder once more and pulled out several photos of Mina Burrows' corpse.

Smith eyed the photos, his lawyer looked away.

'Hmm, he always was a sick bastard.'

'Do you not remember Paul? I was there. You were there! And you ordered this murder. I watched you do it!' I said.

'Sergeant, as far as I'm aware, this is not a murder you are charging my client for. Am I wrong?' the lawyer said.

'Leave this Charlie. In fact go and get a coffee, we'll resume this at another time,' Pensborough said softly.

I looked at him exasperated, but his look told me he wasn't kidding. I slowly rose to my feet and exited the cold interview room, hitting stop on the tape as I made my way outside.

When the warm air of the nick hit me, I realised how immersed in the moment I was. Dave emerged from an adjacent room and we went up to the canteen.

'He's going to get away with it, Dave. He's going to get off these charges.'

'You've got him on the rape, Charlie. Trafficking also, but the murder… I can't see it,' Dave replied.

'But he's guilty, Dave!'

'Calm down, we made a decision to get him. It was your decision and Polly's, as well as mine!'

'We can't let him get away with this. He will get a reduced sentence for good behaviour and then be out doing it again! There must be something we can do!'

Dave paused and placed a brown paper cup into the coffee machine. He paused, then pressed the green button for black, sweet coffee. This was why I respected Dave so much. While I was irate, he was calmly gestating, mulling over the options.

'Did you ever speak to Glenn Tutton?'

I paused, 'No, but I was supposed to wasn't I? After I got reinstated. Where is he?'

'I don't know. Might be worth asking your friend Ron,' Dave picked up the warm cup and took a sip.

'Dave, you're a genius,' I said and ran down to the holding cells below.

I found Ron, he was perusing an auto trader magazine and playing with some chewing gum he had, masticating slowly, while pulling the gum out of his mouth and twirling it around his finger.

'Ron. Ron!'

Startled, he turned and a slow grin spread across his face.

'All right, Charlie! How're you doing?'

'Not bad mate, but I need your help,' I said a bit too quickly for Ron.

'As long as it's not too hard. Out and about last night was I, at the Prizz was this guy, met a blonde girl called Kelly, found out she was a little bit… '

'… Tell me all about it later, mate. I need you to tell me where Glenn Tutton is.'

He lurched up from the desk and went to his big blue folder.

Hmmm… On remand in Sheppey, Swaleside. What you want him for Charlie?'

'Just need to say hello.'
'Good luck. He never said a bloody word to me!'
'Indeed. Hey, listen Ron. You never saw me, right?'
Ron tapped his nose with his finger, '*Mi casa, su casa,* Charlie.'
I didn't bother correcting him; I had a road trip to go on.

55

I jumped straight in the car and headed for the M20 at breakneck speed. I didn't want to raise any interest, so didn't inform Pensborough of my plans.

Bugger him, I thought. I know he was crooked but he would have to wait. For now, I needed something on Smith, and Glenn Tutton was the only man I knew who was alive, and could help me.

I ran through the many options I had to glean information from this man. I weighed up and balanced his nature and history, I used my professional judgment to ascertain the best course of action; the best I could come up with was to rough him up a little.

The phone rang and Dave's name came up on the screen.

'Hi Dave,' I said, hoping he wasn't going to call me back, I had flown past Ashford and was heading towards Maidstone now.

'I ran a background search. Can you believe Glenn Tutton has a grandmother who lives in Belham? Lives on her own. Ethel Tutton, 44 Grand Canal Street. Looking at the Land Registry details, Glenn bought the house for her. They must be close you'd have thought?'

Leverage. The best cop I knew.

'Great work Dave.'

'Good luck, Charlie.'

The drive took less time than I thought. The sat nav took me right onto Sheppey, a place I knew surprisingly little about. Our criminals rarely came out here. They usually went to Maidstone or Banstead after the holding cells.

Tutton was quite a character though, so I guess they decided on a little extra security for him.

The prison building was surprisingly modern but large and imposing, dominating the barren landscape. The grey walls that came off the main entrance seemed to extend eternally into the distance, like an ethereal ghostly photo of the death camps in the war.

I sped up to the front of the building and went through the main entrance. There was a plump, male receptionist in a blue uniform, behind a large grey desk. He rose to his feet at my arrival.

'Can I help you, sir?'

'Good afternoon. I need to speak with Glenn Tutton, in relation to an ongoing homicide case,' I pulled out my badge and showed him.

'Charlie Stone! Congratulations on solving the case, I have been reading all about it. Nasty stuff… '

'… Thank you, but I really need to speak to Tutton as soon as possible if it can be arranged?'

'I understand completely. Let me see,' he tapped some keys on the keyboard.

'He's in Cell Block C. I'll get you through.'

'Thanks, Officer…Woodward,' I memorised his name in case it came in handy later on.

He pressed the buzzer and the steel door clanked open. I walked briskly through, following the signs for Cell Block C.

The prison seemed like an endless maze of corridors. Everything looked the same. Grey, soulless and never-ending. After what seemed like an eternity, Cell Block C finally appeared on my left.

'Sergeant Stone?' the D.C. behind the desk asked.

'Yes hi, I've been… '

'No, need sir. Officer Woodward on reception has phoned down. He's in cell seven. Just this way, follow me.'

That was much easier than I expected. No wonder prisoners seemed to have access to more illicit material than the outside world if this was the level of security that was operated. Still, I couldn't complain.

'Strange bloke, this one. He hasn't said a word,' the DC informed me.

'That certainly seems to be the pattern. Let's see if I can get him to sing for us.'

'Good luck!' he said while turning the key in the lock of Tutton's cell.

'Lock it behind me. I will knock when I need you,' I asked.

The D.C. looked concerned.

'It's OK. I'll be fine.'

He nodded in accordance and left me in the cell with Tutton. The door closed behind us.

56

Tutton's eyes lifted from the floor. He exhibited a look of shock as his eyes met mine.

'Surprised to see me? Thought I was dead? Not so lucky, Glenn,' I smiled at him, as he hung his head and leaned back against the wall.

The rage I had been internalising for Amy, Mina and Polly suddenly surged through my veins. I ran at him, grabbing him by the head and flinging his body to the floor. I watched him tense and eager to rise from the cool stone floor, but before he had, I kicked him in his gut.

I picked up his body and punched him three times as hard as I could, watching the breath leave him momentarily, before throwing him back on the wooden ledge.

'Smith's your boss isn't he, Glenn? He told you to kill those girls didn't he? He told you to kill Amy and Mina, right?' Tutton just looked at me, empty-eyed and limp.

'You need to tell the truth here Glenn. You need to atone. Be honest! Otherwise you will burn alone, just you.'

I held him by the throat, lifting him from the bench.

'Come on Glenn, we all know it, just admit it! You work for Smith, right? He raped Amy and then had you kill her, to send the message to the rest of the girls, not to snitch, not to grass? Right?'

There was still nothing, yet his eyes were engaged now and I could sense something rising in him, a feeling, a desire. I threw his body like a rag doll against the cold, white wall. Blood appeared from his mouth.

'The thing is Glenn, there is no loyalty in this game, for you or for me. You think you're protecting your master, like a lap dog and that's fine, but he's already sold you out. He told us he had cars watching your Grandmother's house in Belham.'

Tutton looked confused.

'That's right. He said he would cut off Ethel's fingers if you didn't do the job properly or if you snitched on him.'

'You're lying,' he said.

'I'm just telling you what he told us. Ethel Tutton, Forty-four Canal Street. Luckily for you I sent a squad car to pick her up earlier today. She's in police custody. In a holding room no doubt though. Gone are the days of nice, cosy hotel rooms for police protection. In fact, in modern Britain, you're lucky to have any policemen to protect her at all. She'll be cold, hungry, and unhappy. But I'm sure nothing will happen to her. Fingers crossed, she'll be OK, no pun intended.'

'But...'

'But there's nothing to protect her from, *right?* Or is there, Glenn?'

He paused and thought about his situation. His breathing was rapid and for the first time since I had met him, he was agitated.

'I was ordered by Paul to kill Mina and Amy,' Tutton confessed.

'Tell me more.'

'That's it!'

'One phone call Glenn and Granny goes back home to whatever fate belies her. It's your choice.'

I waited while Glenn pondered.

'Tell me what happened the night Amy died!'

'I never wanted any of this. I never wanted to get caught up so… it just became so wrong,' Tutton confessed.

'What do you mean?' I said softly, putting my hand into my right hand trouser pocket.

'The girls they wanted got younger and younger. The men whom we worked for, were all businessmen – rich, corporate. They could have anything they wanted. If they wanted a high-class escort for the night, they had her. If they wanted three grams of coke and a bottle of Cristal, they had it. They had the world. When you've had the world, what else can you possibly want?'

Then it dawned on me. 'What's not allowed… ?'

'Exactly. Folkestone's off the grid, away from London, but connected. High Speed Trains, the motorway. Folkestone's half asleep. This has been happening for years.'

I cringed at the thought.

'These men are bored with Eastern European sluts for a hundred quid a go. They want English girls, middle-class, innocent, suburban white girls. That was their thing, the forbidden fruit.'

'Virgins, like Amy Green?'

'They were paid more... '

'But are harder to persuade. That's why you use the MDMA?'

He nodded.

'Tell me what happened to Amy, Glenn. Listen, I can make this easier for you, get the judge to see you in a different way… '

He laughed. 'I'm a dead man, either way. The judge is frankly irrelevant,' he mused.

'Tell me about the night Amy Green died,' I asserted, trying to retain his focus.

'After her first time at the house, she was angry, *really* angry. The whole experience had changed her. She was a kid in a world of adults, really horrible adults. Anyway, she came into school to find Paul. She burst into his office, red-faced and crying. She slapped him across the face, shouting about how she was going to the police and was going to lift the lid on everything.'

'It seems like a reasonable response, if you ask me Glenn… '

'Maybe, but no-one talks to him that way, let alone hit him! It just doesn't happen. Anyway he went mad, flew into a rage and ordered me to follow her. That night she had work at the garden centre, she stayed until about ten-thirty as she was running the café and they had a delivery come in late. Then she left and went to Troy Wood's flat.'

'Troy, really?'

'She needed a consoling voice I guess, but Mina would have warned her to keep her mouth shut. I think Troy was a friend to her, he supported her, but he was out of the situation.'

'He wasn't part of all of this?'

'Troy? No! He's too cocky for his own good. Anyway, Smith phoned to find out where she was. He told me to get her and bring her to the Manor House. So I waited for her to leave and then as she walked home, I bundled her in the car and drove her to Godalming.'

Tutton breathed a sigh of desperation. He realised the gravity of his confession, torn between two worlds.

'Come on Glenn, get it off your chest, imagine how good it's going to feel,' I urged. Tutton looked at me, defeated, before continuing.

'Paul was there, beyond angry. What I didn't know was that he had called four of his friends beforehand.'

'Right... '

'They're really nasty guys. Part of Paul's organisation, but into really kinky and weird stuff. He took her upstairs for half hour as we waited for them to arrive. When they did, Paul brought her down for them. They made me undress her and tie her arms behind her back. Paul muzzled her mouth with a strap. She was forced to… completely naked and… '

Tutton's flow of words began to falter.

'Yes, Glenn?'

'She was passed around, beaten…they did things to her. She cried and cried, but Paul didn't care, he wanted the rest of the girls to know what happens to people who threaten him. I hear her crying in my sleep, it's wherever I go, wailing like an animal. Trapped and lost.'

His tears fell on the dark, stone floor as he spoke.

'When all the men were finished, he brought the girls down who were there and made them watch.

'He had a dirty, old thick rag and pushed it into her throat. We all watched as she suffocated and died.'

I took a breath and tried to remain composed.

'Then you dumped the body in the sea?'

He nodded. 'One of the men has a speedboat and I took the body out. The next day it washed up.'

'And Wood took the fall for everything, right?'

'After the body was dumped, Smith had me go to Wood's ex-wife's house… '

I took a deep breath. 'Go on, Glenn.'

'I tied up his ex-wife and woke their daughter. She's only nine. He made me cut her hair off, all of it. He told me to tell them if they said anything then the daughter would disappear. I took pictures then went to see Troy. I showed him the pictures of his girl tied up and her hair all gone. I told him that she'd be killed if he didn't do as we said. He knew about the organisation; I think Amy had told him what they were capable of… what happened to her... he didn't have an option.'

It was a lot to digest. I took a deep breath, got to my feet and made my way slowly to the locked cell door.

'You did the right thing, Glenn, by telling me this. I hope that comforts you.'

I meant that. Glenn Tutton would spend the rest of his life in a cell, for what he had done, but I hoped his confession made him sleep a little better. I had seen a different side to this silent assassin.

'It will make no difference, Charlie. He'll get off. He's got judges and lawyers. They're all part of it. I won't give evidence in court,' he said, staring at me.

'But, I thought you were a dead man anyway?'

'Yes, but there's ways and means. I'd take prison over being let out now anyway.'

'Do you know what they do to men like you in prison? You're a child killer and a rapist in their eyes, Glenn.'

He laughed, 'Oh, I know what they'll do to me. Rather that than *him*.'

I made my way to the door.

'Don't worry about giving evidence either, Glenn. You won't need to,' I said, reaching into my trouser pocket and retrieving my Dictaphone, which had recorded the whole conversation.

I knocked rapidly on the door.

'No, don't… don't use that… you don't know what he'll do to me!' Tutton moved nearer to me and I heard the keys jangle on the other side of the door.

'Sit down, Glenn, it's done,' he came closer and closer, a look of maniacal fear burned behind his eyes.

'Glenn, sit down!' I roared at him. Once again he was the lapdog, frozen in my gaze and cowering back to the sanctuary of the bench, weeping into his shirt.

The door opened and the D.C. looked Tutton and I over. He passed me a disapproving look, but nothing more than that.

'Sort him out for me, please. Tidy him up.'

The D.C. nodded. 'No problem, Sergeant Stone.'

'I was never here, OK?'

'Right you are, sergeant.'

I made my way through the maze of corridors and back to the car. I couldn't wait to get back to Folkestone; the end was finally in sight.

57

On the way back, I got caught in the afternoon traffic. It was heavy through Maidstone and Ashford, so I got the opportunity to back up Tutton's evidence to my cloud as well as send it to Dave. I had lost so much to bring these people down, it had to remain safe.

I eventually pulled into the station at around seven pm and ran straight in to play the evidence to Pensborough. He was not as happy as I thought he would be.

'Y'know, one of the things D.I. Marsh said to me is that you always create a mess. What is it this time?'

'The job's done, skip. The mess is minimal.'

'It's great work Charlie, but you're reckless. Utterly reckless!'

'Can I charge Paul Smith now, please?'

Pensborough sighed. 'You're like a force of nature, do you know that?' He waved his hand, signalling for me to go.

'Yes, I've heard that before, boss.'

It hurt my feelings that Dave would say that about me, but in the cold light of day, he was probably right.

I walked down to Smith's cell and asked Ron to open it up.

Ron looked even worse now, he could barely open his eyes, and I don't really know how he did it. I think my days of drinking myself into oblivion are firmly over.

He opened the door and ushered me in. Smith was lying down, staring up at the ceiling.

'Sit up, Paul.'

'I'm not saying anything, without my lawyer he… '

'… Sit up now!' I bellowed.

He looked at me and slowly rose to a vertical position. It was a shame aggression and violence seemed to be the only way to communicate with these people.

'Paul Smith, you're under arrest for the rape and murder of Amy Green and Mina Burrows.'

He looked at me shocked. He couldn't comprehend how this had been allowed to happen. How could enough evidence be found? I watched his face change, bemused.

'I hope you know what you're doing, Charlie Stone, I really do,' he said, growing increasingly irate.

'Oh yes, Paul. I most certainly do. I'm doing what's right and I'm going to watch you get life,' I turned on my heel and walked out, hopeful that the next time I'd see Paul Smith's face, was in the dock or behind bars.

The Crown Prosecution Service believed we had a strong enough case to charge Smith for the murder and rape of both girls. I collated everything together and handed it over, with a final exhalation, a relief that I could finally put this to bed.

I was travelling to meet Jo in Faversham. I felt aglow as the train rattled along the tracks, looking out of the window at the green fields and the blue sky resting lazily above them.

The fights, the bitterness, the nasty texts, the lengthy emails, the arguments with partners, the history, the back-biting and the horror had all become too much. As soon as I handed the folder over to the CPS, I felt different, all of my problems seemed smaller, and I wanted to resolve things, for Maddie.

Break-ups are tough when one of you wants to go and the other doesn't. We were lucky, we both wanted to end it. My subconscious had been telling me for months previously that things were wrong, that I was unhappy. Jo's pride eventually gave way and she agreed. She felt like she ended it, but I'd left months before. It was just my ghost wandering the halls and rooms of our old home and Jo was too proud to try and pull me back.

Despite the relief we both felt, there was a dull ache. Pain. That pain turned to blame, that we had never worked through, until now.

We were meeting at the White Willow pub in the centre of Faversham village. It was one of my favourites, with hops adorning the walls and peculiar ales sitting in barrels, old men sat with their beer in jugs reading the paper as the autumn evening candlelight glow gently illuminated the rooms.

Jo was already sitting down at a table in the corner. She saw me but couldn't raise a smile. She had a glass of water in front of her.

'Would you like a drink?' I asked.

'I've got one thanks.'

'I mean a proper one!'

'I'm driving, Charlie,' she said dryly.

'Hm.' I went to the bar and ordered an ale before sitting down nervously.

'Charlie, I think this has gone too far. All the arguing and so on.'

'I agree; I want it to stop. We're foolish to think Maddie is not picking up on it.'

'She is, she's unhappy,' Jo said. This was strange for Jo to admit, a weakness on her watch.

'What do you mean?'

'She doesn't like the bad feeling. She may only be five but she can sense things.'

'Well, she tells me that you are not always nice about me. You put me down. Her words, not mine,' I responded a little churlishly.

'And you believe that?'

'I don't believe she's lying, Jo. You probably don't even realise you're doing it.'

She took a deep breath and a sip of water.

'When we Skype, why do you always stand over her? Why do you make her put the phone on loudspeaker so you can listen in? It's not right.'

'She wants it on loudspeaker, Charlie!'

'But why?'

'I don't know, she's just a kid. Anyway, that's not the point.'

'I think it is. You don't see me as an equal to you. You see yourself on some sort of higher plane. One day, she'll realise it and she'll be cross. I don't want that for you, I don't want it for her. I want everything to be fair and right.'

'And that's your problem isn't it, Charlie? It's the world according to Charlie bloody Stone, everything has to be just and moral and sometimes it just doesn't work like that!'

'I don't see why it can't be like that!'

'Because I'm her mother, Charlie! Do you not *get* that?'

I sat in silence. Of course I got it, but I wanted to be part of her life equally too.

'It will never be equal. *Never*. I'm sorry, Charlie. It's the way it is.'

'Then society is wrong,' I said rather foolishly.

Jo looked on, cooling the fire that had risen in her.

'I want to see her more,' I continued.

'It's not going to happen.'

'Why?'

'Because it's not realistic. Your life's all over the place, Charlie. Do you realise how much risk you put her in with your job?'

'Look that's over now. Those people are behind bars.'

'But we all know, 'Charlie Stone' will be at it again next time, trying to change the world, piece by piece. It will never end.'

'I love her and she loves me, I want to see her more.'

'Then you'll need to speak to the court, Charlie.'

She finished her drink and put the glass on the table.

'I have to go.'

'When am I next seeing her? Friday week as per usual? It's too far away, Jo. I miss her. You don't understand how hard it is! I don't want to become a bit-part in her life!'

'Speak to the court. I'm done.'

With that, Jo got up from the table and walked out.

I knew if I applied to the court I wouldn't get anywhere. Fathers just aren't seen as equal to Mothers at all. I thought about the emotional pressure that Jo put on Maddie, she probably didn't even realise she was doing it, but it wouldn't make a blind bit of difference, I would still be ignored.

Maddie was loved and wanted by her mother. She endured a suffocating, subjective love, but she was loved. Because of that I was a ghost. I barely existed to my daughter anymore.

These were the ups and downs of separated parenting. I became angry, mulled, drank, sat depressed and then had to get on with things. You couldn't google the solution to people's feelings, so I had to keep working away with Jo and taking what I could get with Maddie.

One day, I hoped things would change.

58

I went home on the train. I bought a bottle of vodka and two bottles of diet coke from Sainsbury's for the journey. When I woke in the morning, all of it was empty.

My next stop was Troy Wood, currently being held in High Down Prison in Banstead, Surrey.

I went back to Folkestone and picked up the car before making my way down the M26. Often in this line of work, I had to deliver bad news. Soul-destroying, spirit-crushing news at times, but not today. I was looking forward to seeing him.

Banstead is an affluent commuter town in the suburbs of Greater London in North Surrey. Trendy coffee shops, chain restaurants and affluent middle classes.

It felt peculiar to have one of Britain's high-security prisons here, but that said, the locals could be entertained by the occasional inmate escaping, the ensuing panic and helicopter intervention, before ultimately everything returning to sterilized, middle-class normality.

I knew very little about Troy Wood, except that he was a teacher. I have nothing but respect for teachers, it is a difficult job in my opinion. Having to hold the engagement of thirty children who would rather be anywhere but in the classroom, for seven hours a day, does not sound enjoyable to me.

I admired his swagger when I met him and to watch someone be destroyed like that, to become a shell of a man was despicable, so I couldn't wait to grant this innocent man the freedom he deserved.

He was in a cell at the back of the prison, I bounded up to the controller and told him who I was.

'Wood, you have a visitor,' the prison guard announced with a gruff, South London accent.

Troy seemed genuinely surprised, putting down the book that he was reading and sitting up on his bed.

'Good afternoon, Troy. How're you doing?'

'Oh, hi officer. Not bad thanks,' he said.

'Troy, I'm going to ask you a question and I need you to answer it honestly and truthfully, OK?'

'Sure.'

'You can call me Charlie. You didn't kill Amy Green did you?' I sat next to him and put my arm on his shoulder. He flinched at the tactility, but then accepted the contact, like an old friend.

'We've been through this… '

'… I *know* you didn't kill her. I've found her murderers. Paul Smith and Glenn Tutton.'

A brightness behind his eyes flickered. Kindness; I think he had forgotten what it felt like.

'I know they threatened you. I know they threatened your daughter, they made you take the rap for her murder. You're innocent. Say it, Troy.'

As I spoke the words, he melted into tears, a soggy, wailing mess that I heaped into my arms and hugged.

'I didn't kill her. I didn't hurt her; I wouldn't ever do that!' the words poured from his mouth. 'They took my daughter. They manhandled her Charlie, they showed me the pictures, she was… she… '

'… I know, Troy. But she is safe now and they are locked away, awaiting trial. It's over. You can go home.'

Tears flooded his eyes once more. A joy he never thought he would feel. Salvation.

'One more question Troy. And at this point, it doesn't really matter what the answer is, but I want you to be honest. Did you have sex with Amy?'

He looked at me with wet, bleary eyes. There was a long, difficult pause.

'No.' He took a deep inwards breath before continuing.

'I didn't. I loved her, she was beautiful and young and wonderful and I wanted to, but not until she left school. I cared for her and I supported her when she needed me, but we never did anything, I promise you Charlie.'

For what it was worth, I believed him. Even if he had, Troy Wood had paid a heavy price for his transgression.

I waited as he slowly pulled himself back together, the weight of his lie, easing from his shoulders.

'I'm going to go and get a bite to eat and a coffee. When I come back, I'll take you home to see your daughter. You're free, Troy.'

'What? Free… ?'

'Obviously the paper work needs to be done but in a fortnight or so, you're out of here.'

'Oh my… thanks Officer Stone… I don't know what to say…'

I put my hand on his shoulder, 'Call me Charlie from now on.'

59

Troy saw his daughter for the first time in months. He wept when I helped him reunite with her and with his ex-wife. They were taking things slowly, but there was a chance that maybe they could reconnect.

By the time I got home, it was eight-thirty in the evening. I texted Tara and she came over for an early night. We were both tired and she had to work in the morning. I had a day off and it felt strange. No Maddie, no Tara, no work.

When I woke, Tara had left. I thought I should probably grab a Bugle and have a flick through, so I headed to Morrison's for a bite to eat and a coffee.

I had been avoiding a lot of the news output recently. I didn't like reading about my cases as most were misrepresented in some way.

Morrison's cafe was always busy, filled with all kinds of people. The well to do, the elderly, the white van man. It was a real mix.

I placed my order, a vegetarian breakfast - no mushrooms and double hash browns with hot black coffee. I wondered how many vegetarians didn't like mushrooms? There couldn't be many.

I sat in the plastic chair and perused the local paper. Nothing much to report on a personal level, mercifully. I flicked to page three and the smaller articles appeared, one that piqued my interest.

It was Anna Gibson, the front from the garden centre and the woman who took Polly to the manor house.

She was found dead at her home in what police are regarding as unsuspicious - the likelihood seemed to be an overdose of painkillers. Another dead body chalked up, thanks to this torrid affair.

I had my last mouthful of soggy hash brown and took my plate up to the counter, smiling at the lady as I did. I wasn't sure she was used to people returning their plates but I'd figured enough mess had been left around my table and chair, so really my act of kindness was nothing more than an act of guilt.

I walked along Appleton Road, the morning air feeling cooler as summer slowly faded. I noticed white air from my mouth as I exhaled and forced my hands into my pockets. Normally, I would feel disappointment at the end of summer, but I was quite glad for it to take its leave this time around.

I took the bicycle alley south off the main road and walked under the graffiti'd train bridge, past the college.

I liked this walk and was beginning to know it well – the overhanging trees providing solace from the outside world, while the chickens in East Kent College next door, cried their wake up call.

It was left past the college and then right onto Edgar Road, past the grand houses of the west and one final turn into the garden centre. The place was a graveyard, locked with a large silver padlock on the front door. The entrance around the back of the building had also been boarded up.

I had only popped out for breakfast, so had with me just my wallet, keys and phone but I wanted to explore the old place further. I wasn't sure how to get in, so I left the site and walked to the old trading park a few doors up.

Nowadays, it was a grassy wasteland, with a cottage and a few old garages. Probably due to the crash in Folkestone when the Rotunda and shipping went.

I went around the residential cottage and saw a fence to the rear. I vaulted it quietly and was onto the garden centre site.

There were a number of old crates and bags of compost. I walked through a covered area that smelt of damp and moist soil, which eventually came out into the courtyard of the tea room.

I went around the side of a brick wall and up the ramp to the locked doors of the tea room entrance. I had a brief look in and around - deserted.

I barged the doors, getting my body low so I could put pressure on the metal Yale lock. After the third push, the wood cracked and I was able to reach through and open the door from the inside.

The old tea room was still and quiet. Sugar bowls and tea cups still adorned the tables as if the place was ready to open. It should be really; it was peculiar seeing it as a graveyard, covered in dust.

I went around the back of the counter into a kitchen and walked through. There was an electric blue light over the sink that gave the room an eerie glow. The next room was a stock cupboard. A broom stood against the wall and an old paint bucket sat on the floor.

Two doors lay ahead. Both black, both locked. I stayed silent for a moment to see if I could hear any noise from where I came. Then I listened through the doors. Again, silence. There was nobody here.

I kicked in the first door and opened it. I was through into another room – warmer, with a metallic feel. I took a look in and noticed some safety goggles and suits hanging up against the wall. Towards the end of the small metal corridor was another door. I wanted to go in, but felt it was best to check what was behind the other black door first.

I went back and tried the handle, to no avail. Once again my trusty right trainer came into use and the door eventually gave way. As the door opened, I gasped for breath, shocked at what I saw.

It was an old brick garage. In it were four black Mercedes, with blacked out windows, just like Tutton's. How many people were working for Smith's crew? How deep did the rabbit hole go?

I needed to see what was in the other room next door and went back, suddenly sensing danger ahead of me. I went through the corridor and into dark gloom. There was plastic tubing across the floor, old metal canisters and round-bottomed glass flasks sitting on the table.

The bottles to my right were filled with hydrochloric acid, calcium chloride and there were two gas cans – a drugs lab. This must be where they made the drugs for the party! It was all connected and Anna Gibson was the link.

Perhaps this is where Alex had been out all night and the girls worked late shifts, to protect this lab.

I needed evidence, but noticed a beeping getting louder from the corner of the room.

I followed the noise to see what it was, probably an old timer for the mixtures. I looked down into a cobwebbed corner. It was a rigged device, a bomb. One minute and seventeen seconds left, typical.

I turned and ran back through the kitchen and out through the front of the café. I made it over the fence and ducked back behind the old cottage, and waited for the explosion.

It wasn't a large blast, but enough to destroy the lab and the drugs paraphernalia. People came running and I made it my business to get out of the area as quickly as possible. Despite being unable to collect any evidence I'd seen all I needed to see.

Now that Anna Gibson was dead, I had no real way of knowing why she killed herself, if she even did. I ran searches on her and her family – there was no-one left to talk to. Her parents had both passed away and she never married. I was left to pick up the pieces with pure guesswork.

It looked like the garden centre was a front, a place to launder money and to make the drugs. The girls were placed in the café to be vetted and groomed by Gibson. The girls were perfect, pretty young things to keep prying eyes away from the boffins in lab coats out the back, cooking up.

I imagined the late nights they worked in the garden centre were to mask deliveries of illegal substances, pharmaceuticals and drug paraphernalia. The workers probably didn't know what they were unloading in big brown boxes and large black plastic bags. They probably didn't even care as long as they were getting paid.

I went straight home, far later in the day than I'd wanted. I was going to cook a healthy dinner for Tara before she came home from work as I had an evening invitation from Troy Wood.

It pleased me to get this, I knew he must've been grateful for what we'd done for him. His life was back on track and the last I heard he had big plans for his future and was leaving teaching.

He had a speech at one of the local union meetings, so after I cooked a vegetable stir fry and left it on a plate for Tara, I walked to the Turlinton Hotel, where Troy was speaking. Tara stayed in and watched her soaps as she was tired. In all honesty, I didn't really have the energy but felt it was the right thing to do, given all Troy had been through.

60

Troy Wood was released eight days after I went to see him. Those last few nights must have been eventful for him. He had quit his job as an English teacher and decided to move into writing and freelancing.

Troy made his way to the front of the stage to begin his speech.

'So, as you probably know, a week ago, I was in prison serving life for the murder of Amy Green. Firstly, I want to say, Amy was a wonderful student. Kind, caring and hard-working. I cared deeply for her and am devastated that she is no longer here.

Secondly, I need to thank a friend. Without him and his relentless, tireless search for the truth, I wouldn't be here in front of you. The case was closed, I was forced against my will to confess to a horrid murder I hadn't committed. But Detective Sergeant Charlie Stone knew better. He caught the guys who had cast a spell of fear and hate in our local community. He brought these evil men to justice. Thank you Charlie.'

The crowd then erupted in applause as Troy intimated to me from the stage. I refused to join him, but humbly accepted the vociferous applause and the pats on the back that I received.

I indicated for Troy to continue his speech. He nodded, respecting my decision to remain as out of the spotlight as possible.

'The problem with full-time work in education is that it's crippling - creatively crippling. Teaching is a debilitating force, you become completely absorbed and involved in it. Every worthwhile energy is spent marching to the beat of someone else's drum. You sleep well at night through exhaustion and a feeling of peace because you know you are helping - but even that feeling ended up leaving for me.

'Why?

'Because I didn't feel I was helping. Not because I'd become a bad teacher, in fact I felt I'd become better.

'The other staff valued me, the students valued me but ultimately it was not enough. It wasn't enough because I was not being me. I have one life which I'm half way through. I'm tired of telling myself that it's cool because I get good paid holidays. You spend the first part of the holiday getting over the term, often sick, and the final part dreading going back. It's no life.

'I try to drag students through exams they don't want to do, hanging my hat on the fact that I am a positive male force in their lives, knowing they have no chance of 'passing.'

'It's a joke. A sick one.

'Poetry as an exam topic is like studying haberdashery. It's niche and ultimately for the academic elite. I like poetry but I'm sure a lot of people like haberdashery, it doesn't mean that sixteen-year olds need to be examined on it, in an examination that determines the fortunes of the rest of their lives.

'In addition, you must care deeply about your students, but not too deeply. You must care within the carefully defined parameters that don't truly meet their needs.

That's education.'

There was rapturous applause as Troy Wood left the stage. He shook hands with a number of suited individuals and made small talk with the union members who lapped up his words.

I had to agree with him too. I had no desire to teach or be in education.

He was most certainly a different man from the one I once knew. He was humble in person, but his experiences had given him the confidence and freedom to speak his true mind. He had turned from having his wings clipped in a profession he found false and will fly away to something of which, I'm not sure. That uncertainty can't be easy.

I heard he was writing a book on his experiences over the past few months. I hoped for his sake he could make it work.

Troy saw me, nodded and made his way over.

'Hi, Charlie. What did you think?'

'Almost Churchillian, Troy. You mean all that, do you?'

'Every word. I might become a road sweeper or something. Teaching is difficult work these days.'

'And the book?'

'Oh you heard about that did you?' Troy laughed. 'Anything to get me out of education! I wondered whether you wanted to contribute? You did catch the killer after all.'

'No, Troy. You're the wordsmith. I'll leave it to you.' The last thing I wanted was more press coverage.

'How's everything else? Since you got out?' I asked. I did a bit of searching around and I know it wasn't plain sailing for him in prison. It rarely was for suspected paedophiles and rapists. Not that he was either, but most inmates aren't too bothered about the details.

He shuddered. 'Getting better. They've given me a shrink to talk too. It makes things easier.'

'Good. I'm pleased. And your daughter?'

'She's good. Still gets comments in the playground. "Your dad's a paedo" and so on. Once you're accused you can never be innocent again,' he mused.

'It'll get better,' I lied.

'Well at least the National Front lot have stopped sending me hate mail. I guess that's something.'

A young man with a side parting wearing a suit jacket with skin-tight jeans stepped in and whispered something in Troy's ear.

'I have to go Charlie. Meeting with the union bods. But it's good to talk to you.'

I shook Troy's hand and left him to it.

I returned to the flat and Tara was watching Friends on TV. I gave her a kiss and grabbed my laptop, before settling down next to her.

The case had drawn to a tidy conclusion, there was not a lot else I could do to find out further information. Smith and Tutton were awaiting trial.

Gibson was dead, Amy Green and Mina Burrows were dead. Jennifer was a husk of her former self, crippled with self-loathing and doubt over the death of her child. The only person left was Alex and the mystery of Amy's diary pages.

I made it a priority to talk to him tomorrow. I had some paperwork at the station to complete in the morning, but when my shift finished, I would put the final piece in the puzzle.

61

Work dragged, as it tends to do when you have more pressing matters to deal with. Eventually five o' clock rolled around and I made my way into town.

I went to the Old High Street for a coffee. There were now three coffee outlets in the Creative Quarter, all with varying attributes, but today I went to Bongo.

It was a small independent shop in the middle of the cobbled road, cosy and sparse at the same time. The coffee was of very good quality, imported from Croatia and you always received a warm welcome from the owners.

I took the time to think of what I wanted to say to Alex. After an Americano and a Double Espresso, I was certainly energised but not entirely sure.

I paid the bill, tipped and headed towards the Harbour. I walked the full length of the Leas and filled my lungs with the early evening fresh air.

I walked up to the Commemorative arch in memory of the World War One soldiers who gave their lives, children were playing football underneath it as the sun glinted gently of its curved beams.

Some of the locals were up in arms about the arch being used as a playground. I couldn't really see the problem. I enjoyed the Leas being used by youngsters. As I made my way towards the Cliff Hall, revellers were out in force. Dog walkers, afternoon drinkers, couples out for a stroll.

'Hey-hey!' I heard a youthful voice shout from behind me.

I turned to see the frame of Harry Wise, holding hands with a beautiful, blonde girl of a similar age. She smiled at me, it was a different girl to the one he was with the last time I saw him.

'Hello Harry, how are you?' I asked.

He had a beaming grin and his complexion was far ruddier than I remember.

'Good, officer. And you?'

'Call me Charlie. Yes, fine, I think we caught the guys who-'

'Yes, I know.' Harry looked to the ground. 'Thanks Charlie, she didn't deserve what happened to her.'

'Well, I think that's the last we'll be hearing from them for a while.

I glanced at the girl Harry was with.

'Good afternoon,' I said with a friendly smile.

She sprang into life with a big smile and looked at Harry for the introduction.

'Hi there!' she said back.

'Oh, sorry, this is Evie. Evie, this is Officer Charlie... '

' ...Stone,' I finished the sentence for him.

'Oh, hi,' said Evie. 'You're a policeman?' she gave Harry a sudden quizzical glance and I wondered whether she felt uncomfortable talking to a cop.

My suspicions in this respect were confirmed by the next thing Harry said, which was: 'No, no. He's all right. He's *safe,*' Harry confirmed to her. I wasn't fully sure what he meant, but it sounded good, so I left it.

'Harry, what's the plan for you, now that the summer's nearly over?' I asked, changing subject.

'Well, I got a place at Brighton Uni.'

'Oh, congratulations! That's great!'

'Well, it's not Durham, where my Dad wanted, but hey, it's better than not going, right?'

'Exactly. You can't have everything in life, sadly,' I uttered, almost embarrassed by my own pop psychology.

'And you Evie? You off to uni?'

'Oh, I'm in the year below. Going into my second year in the sixth form at the HG Wells school.'

I tried not to wince at the thought of Tutton and Smith stealing innocence from the girls at the grammar school, and I thought that this relationship between Harry and Evie was somehow an antidote to all of that perversity. Harry and Evie seemed genuinely in love with one another.

I was glad Tutton and Smith were soon to be behind bars.

'Great, well, all the best, I'd better be off.'

'See you later, Charlie!' Harry said as he smiled and walked off into the late evening sunshine.

Alex sat in his leather arm chair behind the desk in his study. His demeanour had changed somewhat. He lacked that air of confidence he had previously. I was surprised he even let me through the front door. His usual tone of disdain had been swapped for one of quiet hostility, but he clearly wanted to speak with me too.

'My Abloy key is back where it should be now,' he flashed a cursory glance my way and indicated for me to sit down.

'Well I needed to solve Amy's murder. I didn't have much choice I'm afraid,' I wasn't going to apologise to him for doing my job.

'I had no idea what was in there. Paul asked to use it, I didn't have much choice but to oblige,' he added.

'I can imagine; he seems like a very persuasive character...'

'You have no idea. What was in there?' he asked, a little twitchy at the thought.

'Come on, I know Smith is a powerful man, but you can't convince me you had no idea what was there?'

'I swear to you, he came in and used the study often, sometimes when I was at work. Jenny would let him in if I was tied up.'

‘Or at the garden centre drugs lab?’ I searched for a sign that he knew what I was talking about.

‘I wouldn’t know about that.’ His eyes didn’t leave the floor.

I wondered if I should tell him the truth about what was in the safe. I came to the conclusion that if it was my daughter, I would want to know it all.

‘The main thing was the missing pages to Amy’s diary. There were also some military-style dog tags.’

Alex looked into the distance. His skin turned pale, he looked as if he was going to be sick.

‘The pages... what did they say?’

‘Alex, I don’t think this is a good time to discuss this. Paul Smith is going to trial and Amy’s diary entries are pivotal to the prosecution. If you don’t wish to wait until then, we can organise a time for you to come to the station.’

Alex nodded serenely.

‘What I don’t understand is how the pages made their way from Amy’s bedroom to the safe,’ I said, letting the comment sit in the air. Alex was staring into thin air before registering my words and focusing his gaze squarely at me.

‘You think *I* took the pages?’

I remained silent.

‘You think I gave my daughter’s diary pages to Paul? You think I had something to do with it?’

‘I didn’t say that, Alex.’

‘I can’t believe you would think that!’

He paused, exasperated. The truth is there was no other real explanation. This was a masterclass in the dark arts by Alex.

‘OK. What about the dog tags? They had a name and a date.’ I quickly checked my notebook, ‘Millie, 17/1/00... ’

He looked at me blankly.

‘I’ve no idea.’

His eyes met mine and then filled with water and turned red. He looked away, wet with tears. I saw him for what he was; another puppet in the Smith regime.

He was the epitome of the middle class dream. I looked at his navy cardigan and tie as he broke down in tears. What a performance!

He was the serpent underneath the flower. I reminded myself of Dave's old advice. If it seemed true and evidence pointed to something, in most cases it was true. I just couldn't believe that this man was oblivious to the dark world that surrounded him. Either way, I decided to change subject.

'There was an explosion at the garden centre. It seems a lot of evidence went up in smoke.'

I paused but there was no response. 'I only bring it up because I know you spent a lot of time there, as did Amy in her final weeks. Do you know anyone who might benefit from losing some of the stock on Edgar Road at the moment?'

He took a deep breath, bringing himself back from tears once more. 'What do you want to know, Charlie? Don't play games,' he was beginning to feign composure and was talking audibly louder than before. I saw a chance.

'Well, as I said, drugs were being made there. The coffee shop thing was a front. Right?'

A further pause.

'Yes you're right Charlie!' he was nearly shouting, eyes wild with the delirium of confession.

'We vetted the girls through the coffee shop. Anna prepared them for working with Smith as if you could ever be prepared for *that...* '

'Why did you get Amy involved?'

'Not Amy. I tried to keep her out of it. It was Mina, she knew that boy Harry and he worked for us. He was selling our stuff and going out with Mina. He would drop her off and pick her up and get the drugs as he did so. Then it got complicated.'

'Go on.'

'Mina was wild and Harry got bored of her. She was too much, too crazy. He met Amy, she was quiet, different and they started seeing each other. Once that happened, Amy would just turn up for shifts unannounced.'

'So she never knew about the drugs?'

Alex shook his head slowly, his glassy eyes looked straight through me.

'You're just a pawn in this. Who else is in on it? It can't be just Smith and Tutton? There's got to be more.'

Alex laughed.

'Well that's easy, the ones left standing at the end of all of this. Anyway it's good to see you and thanks for stopping by, but I think you need to go now,' he said emptily.

'We can help Alex, with the grief if you need,' I had to offer him the help even if I knew he was just a great actor.

'Thanks, that won't be necessary. I'll see you out.' Alex got up and opened his study door.

As I walked through the hall and said goodbye, I shook his hand for what would be the final time, Alex looked at me a broken man and one who knew that his time had come.

62

Three weeks passed in a glorious autumnal haze of relaxation, fun and sunshine. It really was true what they said about Folkestone, it seemed to have its own micro-climate. It may not get as warm as the thick London weather, but boy did the sun shine in late August and early September.

I laid to rest the ghost of Polly Ringwald, my good friend. In truth, she will never leave me, but I could rest a little easier knowing that she died happy, knowing that she made a difference to the world. She died to give my daughter and me a chance to live.

I vowed that I would visit her as often as I could, at least once a month. She had a rose bush and a plaque at Appleton Cemetery. The roses were in bloom at the moment and the plaque read 'In the line of duty, for love.'

Tara had moved in to the flat, not officially of course, but most of her clothes and belongings were there. In fact, since she'd first stayed, it felt like she had always been there. It made Maddie and me very happy.

Tara fits in like the missing piece to a complicated, beautiful jigsaw. Dave loves her, Maddie loves her and I know my father would've too and that meant a lot to me. So much so that after a few weeks, we were getting on so well we decided to buy our own flat.

It raised a few eyebrows and I knew it was fast but I didn't really care. After the case, I just wanted to be happy. There were too many demons, ghosts of the past that haunted me in the night. I saw the face of Mina Burrows night after night as the breath left her body, her vibrancy evaporated and death took her.

Also Maddie. I wanted her to have normality, a happy home. She deserved it. She had begun to question things in life; why her Mummy and Daddy stopped loving each other for instance. It was hard to explain to a five-year-old. I think secretly she worried that we might stop loving her and the last thing I wanted was for her to grow up insecure like me. It never truly leaves you. Tara will help with that.

Finally, for me. I loved her and I wanted to have her with me. More importantly, she had witnessed the 'Charlie Stone' whirlwind first hand and wanted to be with me. That meant a lot after the divorce.

So we found a little two bed place on Appleton Road. It needed a lot of work, but the second bedroom was already pink so Maddie could move straight in, much to her delight.

It had a forty-foot garden, overgrown and untidy but I was looking forward to the project of making it liveable for my ladies. I could see Maddie next summer jumping on a trampoline, while I tended to the tomatoes and Tara relaxed with an icy drink.

Hope prevails.

The new flat was vacant and we had handed in our notice on Brimstone Avenue, so we had a little bit of time to pack and tie up all the loose ends. We were experiencing a marvellous, 'Indian summer' or so they called it. The sun was weak but it was out, so we decided to make a final visit to the beach.

It was the last official day the Folkestone Harbour was open. This was a new idea, where local bands were playing and there were food outlets and funfair rides for the kids.

At three o'clock they would be unveiling the official Folkestone Harbour sign. Due to its success this summer, it was going to become an annual event. Folkestone was on the up.

Tara, Maddie and I popped in to see Dave before we headed to the beach. Maddie rang the doorbell, a little too long to be polite, but she didn't mean it.

The door to the garage clanked open and Dave's smiling face appeared from behind it.

'Hi, Dave! How are you?' Maddie asked.

'Good, thanks angel. Lovely to see you,' he said, thrusting a sherbet dib-dab into her hand.

I gave Dave a hug and we chatted over coffee about his new consultancy role with the Dover Police force. Reading between the lines there seemed to be a case Dave wanted me to work on over there. At the moment, it could wait.

Tara told him about how the new term had started well and Mrs Jones was back in charge of HG Wells Grammar School, much to the relief of the incumbent staff and student population.

I was taking a brief sabbatical. Dave was not surprised, given the intensity of the case and so on. The truth was I felt happier, but I was a little disillusioned and if I'm being totally honest, my shoulder had not fully healed after the gunshot I took in the flat.

We finished our coffees and started to say goodbye when Dave threw a set of keys at Tara. We perused them together, they looked like car keys, but ones from a bygone era.

'What are these for?'

'They're for the Mustang,' he said.

'OK… why have I got them?'

'Because I want you to have it.'

'You mean, drive it?'

'No, I mean *have* it.'

'Dave, what're you doing? Stop pulling her leg!' I said.

He looked at me, 'look, you don't really like driving right?' I thought about how much I did like his Mustang, but eventually nodded. I don't really like driving that much. It was a means to an end for me.

‘And every time *I* drive it, I’m always listening for something to go wrong, I can’t enjoy it! It was great doing it up, but it’s not the same driving it now. It needs a new owner.’

Tara was shell shocked.

‘How… much… do you want for it?’ she asked.

‘I’ll pretend I didn’t hear that, young lady,’ he said in return, collecting our mugs and walking towards the kitchen.

‘Anyway you deserve it for putting up with him!’ he said nodding in my direction. He gave me a friendly wink.

We said our goodbyes and got into the metallic blue muscle car, not really believing we were going to be driving it away. I looked at the immaculate cream and wood dashboard and the chrome gearstick in amazement. Perhaps I could get into cars after all, I thought to myself.

Tara turned the key in the ignition and the car growled itself from slumber, while I swapped the child seat from her old Peugeot into the Mustang. We looked at each other and smiled.

Maddie squealed with delight as we reversed off the drive and Dave waved us off, smiling as we went.

We drove the short distance to Sunny Sands and parked up just off Sea View, near the beach. We walked down, Maddie running with the football at her feet, dribbling in fact! Once we got down to the sand, she insisted on a match. She wanted to score as many goals as she could.

The gulls swooped and glided against the bright blue backdrop and the tide sat way out in the distance, lazily lapping the sand.

The beach was not as busy as at the height of summer, there were perhaps twenty people spread out in entirety. It was lovely not needing to think about anything. The people I cared about were here and we were all happy, so I could just relax, in-between letting in a few of Maddie’s shots.

We finished playing and it was nearly time for the sign to be unveiled. It was an important event for Folkestonians, so Tara was keen to stroll up to the Harbour and see it take place.

I put on Maddie's flip-flops for her, while Tara grabbed the beach bag and we walked to where the crowds were gathering.

The mayor of Folkestone was standing up on a ledge about fifteen metres into the air. She was joined by the head of the Creative Foundation and two other people I didn't recognise.

They smiled and joked, before the Mayor took up a megaphone and began speaking.

'Ladies and gentlemen, thank you all for attending this marvellous event. The summer may nearly be over, but fear not. Next year Folkestone's Harbour Arm will open on twenty-sixth March, *bigger and better than before!*'

There were cheers and whoops from the crowd.

'Next year, we will be inviting more of the local pubs and restaurants to get involved, as well as ensuring we are much more child-friendly, with face painters, bouncy castles every weekend for our children to enjoy.'

There was a growing murmur from the people around me and I listened to their conversations, '*typical Folkestone, someone's always playing a joke, probably one of the Zombie Walk lot having a laugh.*'

I wasn't entirely sure what they were talking about so I focused back in on the presentation. The mayor had handed over to the Creative Quarter representative, who stood in an open white shirt and tight jeans.

'Folkestone has come on leaps and bounds in the past few years…'

I watched people around me begin to squint into the sun, further down the beach.

'The work that the local community have done to make this town somewhere we are proud of has been unprecedented… '

Fingers pointed towards the old iron bell that hung high up in the blue sky.

'The work of Unusual Fare and its affiliates proves that *everywhere means something to someone* and the only way is up for Folkestone, so after three, let's reveal our new sign! Three… '

I couldn't quite see what the hubbub was about, as the sunlight which came from directly in front of us was being blocked by the bell. I wish I had brought my sunglasses as the bell seemed misshapen in the brightness.

'Two… '

I heard a scream, followed by two more as mothers grabbed their children to their breasts and hid their faces.

'One… '

There was commotion on the presentation stand as a cloud floated across the sun's beaming rays, bringing Alex's lifeless body hanging from a rope, in full view of the waiting crowds.

'Wait here!' I said to Tara as she held Maddie close and led her away from this gruesome scene. The masses were running and spreading in different directions, confused and disgusted.

'Please,' the mayor said, 'what's going on…' and he tried to quell the throng of people now rushing back towards the town and away from the horror.

I sprinted as fast as I could towards the old bell and Alex's body. He was hanging from a rope twenty metres into the sky, the breeze swaying his half-naked body.

His trousers and shirt were ripped, revealing cuts and abrasions on his arms and the top of his legs. His eyes were wide open, intense, like a frightened animal.

Jesus. A sign hung from his neck that read, 'This one's for you.'

My heart raced and I felt sick. Crowds were beginning to develop underneath the body, staring up. Teenage boys were pointing, shocked yet drawn like moths to the horror.

'Get back! This is now a crime scene, get away!' I said, but no-one listened.

I went to my pocket to get out my phone, but before I could dial a number, I was greeted by the sounds of a fire engine, the cavalry for once arriving in good time.

I scanned the scene for any immediate clues or pointers. None to be seen, so I headed back towards the Harbour to try and find Maddie and Tara. I presumed they would head to the Royal Windsor pub, a safe place in the Harbour area, but I wasn't sure.

I immediately felt a wave of panic, as if they were in immediate danger.

My phone buzzed in my pocket. I took it out without checking who was calling.

'Charlie, Charlie! What the *hell* is going on?' It was Jo. She was crying, panicky.

'What? What do you mean?' I slowed my pace to a fast jog as I came around the back of the Grand Dolphin Hotel.

'I've been sent some photos… weird photos, Charlie, they're really freaking me out... !'

'What photos, tell me!' My walk became a run towards the Harbour. It was busy, angry voices wondering what on earth they had just witnessed. Children crying, unable to understand why a dead body hung high in the Folkestone sky.

Jo was apoplectic now with panic, 'Photos of Maddie *sleeping!* Some of her at school in the playground with her friends. Charlie whoever took them has been in her bedroom! They've been here in *my* house!' she shrieked.

'Have you locked all the doors and windows?'

'Yes, I'm safe, but I'm scared. Who are these people, what's happening?'

'Where's your boyfriend?'

'He's due home any minute.'

'OK. Call 999, report the photos. Make copies and email them straight to me. Copy the backs of them too, so I can check for any clues. Then call the police. Don't panic, Jo. It's not you or Maddie they want. They want me.'

'You'd better make sure you protect her, Charlie! I'm warning you! Don't let anybody hurt her!' she said screeching at me now, before I put the phone down.

I looked up the hill towards Sea View and in the distance, I thought I saw two figures I recognised, dressed in black. I had no time for police work now. I had to find Tara and Maddie.

I ran back to The George but there was no sign of them. I sprinted around to the Fisherman's Inn, a place we sometimes went, but again they weren't there.

I was panicking, a sickening feeling of dread rose from my stomach and up to my throat. I checked the Ice Cream Parlour and even upstairs at Culpepper.

I stood under the bridge at the harbour, racking my mind as to where they could have gone.

'Daddy! Daddy! What're you doing?'

My head swung to my right and there my girls stood, Tara smiling, Maddie holding a rapidly melting ice cream. I breathed again.

'Maddie, fancy a piggy back? Pass Tara that ice cream,' I said.

Maddie jumped on, giggling and bouncing up and down as I made my way across the cobbles. Now I knew they were safe, I had to follow the two strange figures.

Tara stood forlornly. 'Come with me, I need to check something.'

I didn't want to let either of them out of my sight.

Maddie clung like a monkey to my back as Tara grumpily headed away from us. I caught sight of the two figures once more. They were both wearing black - one female, one male. I recognised the man's gait and his haircut. It was Pensborough.

He kept his head bowed, as if he didn't want to be seen and held his hand over his mouth when he spoke, like the gangsters in the movies, protecting themselves from lip readers.

They picked up their pace past the Fisherman's Inn and the Chip besides the cobbled street.

Flip flops were not the best form of attire for brisk walking on the hard stone, but I managed to keep them in view.

They turned right onto Harbour Way where Pensborough's Volkswagen Passat sat by the side of the road. I stayed just out of sight around the corner as the woman who he was with turned to face him.

She kissed him twice, both cheeks, before he got into his vehicle. It was Jennifer Green. She looked different, I hardly recognised her dressed in a business suit and with heavy make-up.

She was standing outside a black Mercedes, with tinted windows. The same black Mercedes that I had followed. Glenn Tutton's Mercedes.

Jennifer Green checked her hair and adjusted her suit, as Anna Gibson rushed out of the driver's seat and went to open the passenger door for her. I couldn't believe what I was seeing. Anna Gibson? She was dead! Her photo was in the paper!

Jennifer stepped into the car and pulled her door gently closed. The black Mercedes purred off slowly, covertly, like a cat in the wild stalking its next innocent prey as the fire services slowly lowered Alex Green's lifeless body to the ground.

THE END

ACKNOWLEDGEMENTS

Firstly, I would like to thank my mum who has helped and supported me every step of the way. I would also like to thank James Essinger, my agent and publisher whose keen eye, kind words and good advice have been integral to this process, and Annelisa Christensen for extremely helpful guidance with part of an early draft of this novel. Finally, to Tnaesha and Skyla for caring enough about me to let me follow my dreams.

For more information about the writer please visit
www.trevortwohig.com